LOSING ARTHUR

Paul A. Mendelson

The Book Guild Ltd

First published in Great Britain in 2017 by
The Book Guild Ltd
9 Priory Business Park
Wistow Road, Kibworth
Leicestershire, LE8 0RX
Freephone: 0800 999 2982
www.bookguild.co.uk
Email: info@bookguild.co.uk
Twitter: @bookguild

This work is entirely fictitious and bears no resemblance to any persons living or dead.

Map illustration by Haleema Karim

Typeset in Garamond

Printed and bound in Great Britain by CPI Group (UK) Ltd, Croydon, CR0 4YY

ISBN 978 1912083 961

British Library Cataloguing in Publication Data.
A catalogue record for this book is available from the British Library.

For Noah, Woody, Nancy and Arlo

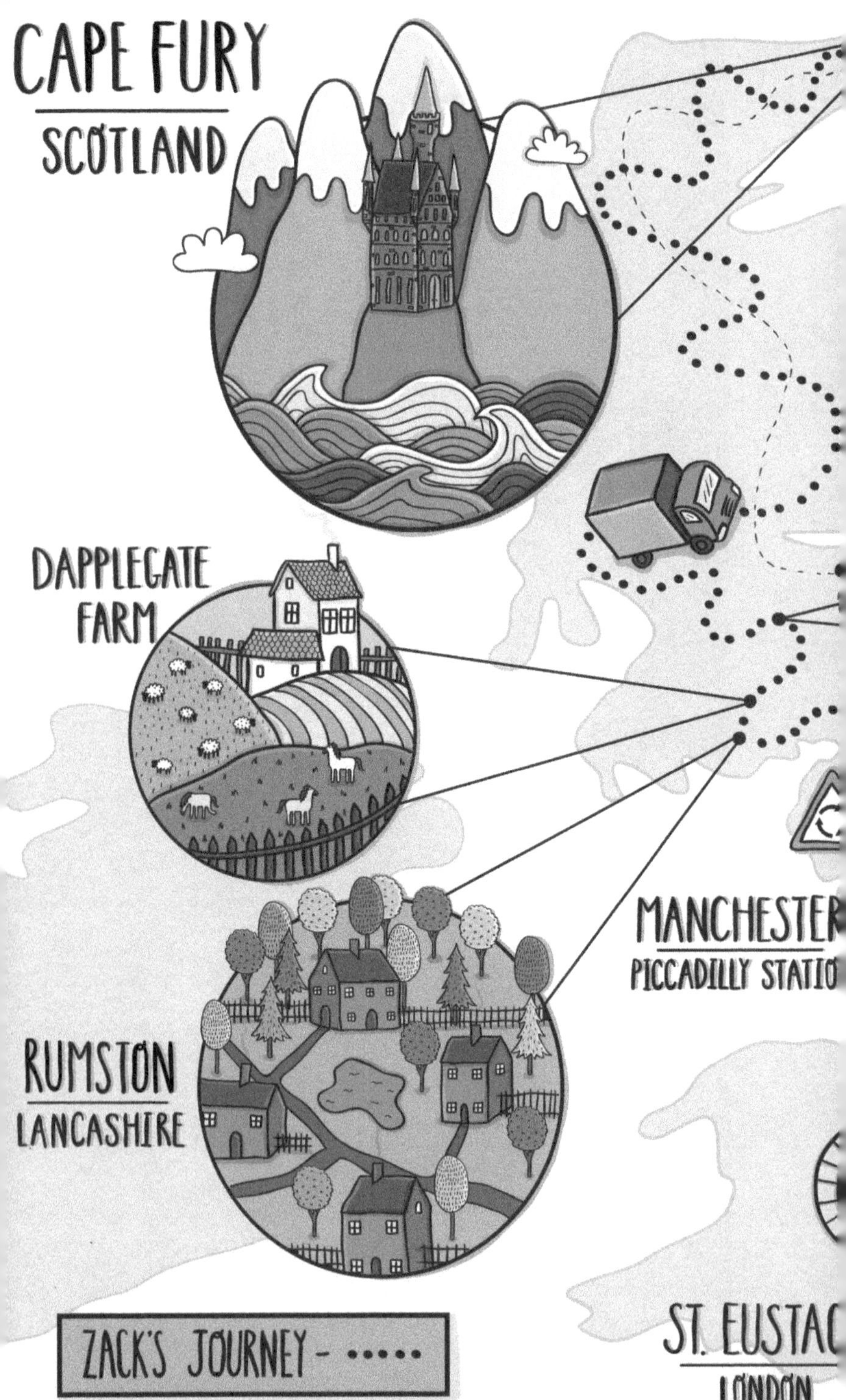

CAPE FURY
SCOTLAND
DAPPLEGATE FARM
RUMSTON
LANCASHIRE
MANCHESTER
PICCADILLY STATION
ST. EUSTAC
LONDON
ZACK'S JOURNEY — ......

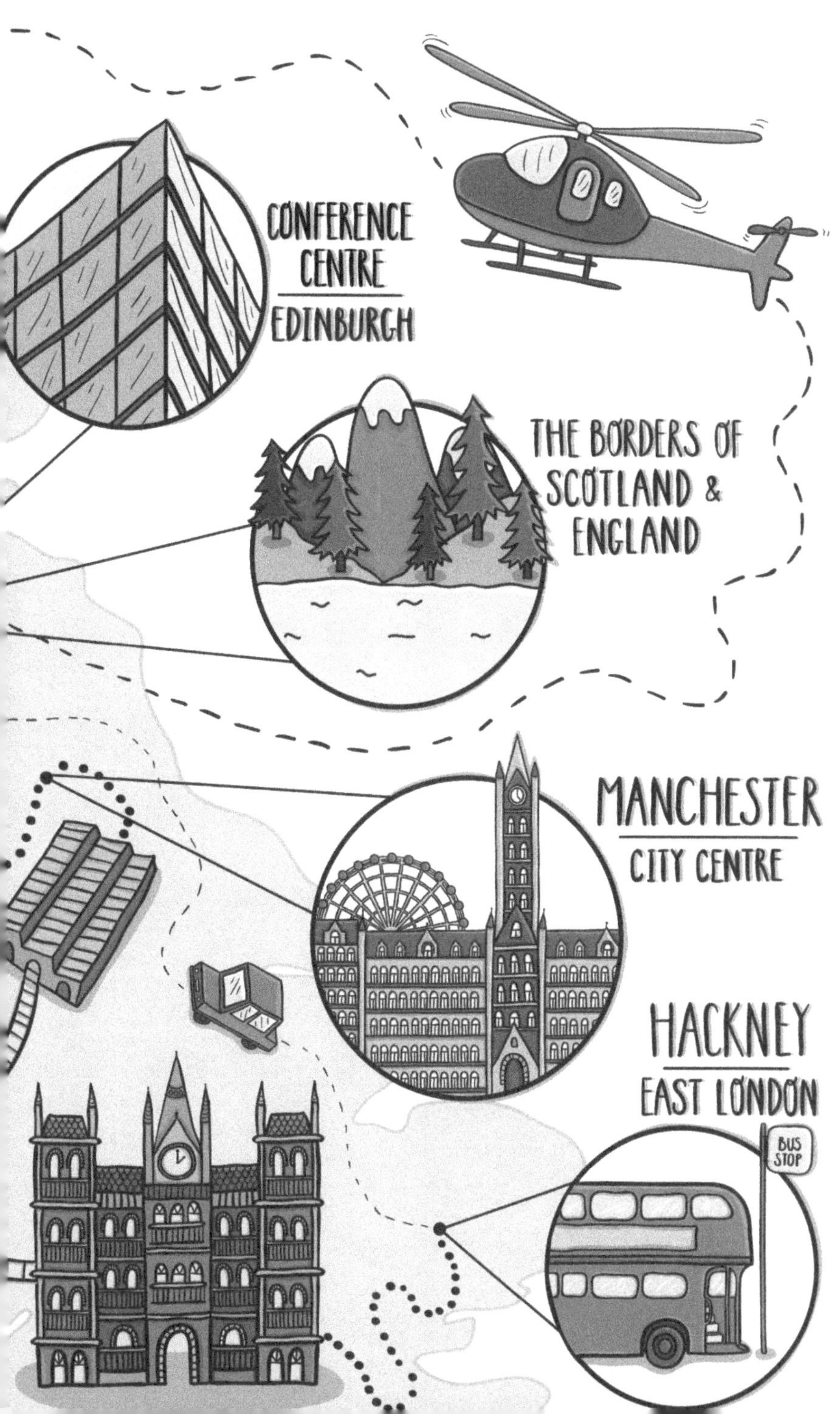

CONFERENCE
CENTRE
EDINBURGH
THE BORDERS OF
SCOTLAND &
ENGLAND
MANCHESTER
CITY CENTRE
HACKNEY
EAST LONDON
BUS
STOP

Weekend: Friday evening, Saturday and Sunday, usually regarded as a time of relaxation.

Zack Farmer's Dictionary

You think?
Zack Farmer

1

'YOUR LITTLE FRIEND
WON'T SAVE YOU NOW, ZACK!'

3.35pm: *Friday February 15th. Hackney, East London.*

"I've no idea why the boys are chasing me, Arthur!"
yells Zack Farmer.

He knows this is not strictly true. Zack has a pretty
good idea – it just doesn't seem like a very good reason. Of
course, he's not stopping to ask them. Not when they're
bigger than him and on skateboards.

Not when they're catching up fast.

It's probably lucky that his school is near a market.
This is Hackney, in the east end of London, where you
can't move for markets. Clothes markets. Flower markets.
Food markets. The last ones are the messiest.

"Ahhh! Nearly lost it that time, Arthur!" he cries, as
he slips on some discarded cabbage leaves and slides on a
rotten tomato. Food market – just my luck.

The stallholders know Zack now – they know to step
aside, when he's running through. They know he talks all

the time to no-one. And that the no-one he talks to all the time is called Arthur.

His pursuers are just one stall behind him now.

It's a sweet-stall, with everything Zack would love to stop and eat. But, of course, he can't. Not even if the bullies were chasing someone else – not that they ever do.

He can't stop and eat, because the Sugar Police are there – in their candy-striped uniforms – as they always are when school comes out.

Why is he worrying about the Sugar Police now?

I wish I didn't think about things so much, thinks Zack Farmer, especially when I'm running. Sometimes he even wishes he didn't have weird conversations when he's running. Because maybe then he wouldn't have any reason to run.

"Can't slow down. We mustn't slow down, Arthur!"

The boys are expecting Zack to fall on his face and let them kick his narrow ribs until he screams. (Which doesn't usually take long.) They're expecting him to beg them to stop.

They're not expecting him to sing.

"*'There was a soldier… (pause), Who wandered far away… (big pause), There was none bolder… (bigger pause)'*"

Zack knows that anyone listening would wonder 'What sort of weird song is this?' Pause, pause, pause. It's like every other line is missing. But they aren't missing to Zack – he can hear someone else singing them. Okay, not very tunefully and not very well – the guy wouldn't win any talent contests. But it gives Zack a kind of courage, as if he's part of a team. Which, in a way, he is.

Now he's off again.

Away from the rainbow market, through the dappled, afternoon streets, panting like a dog out too long in the sun.

Faster – faster!

He can feel the sweat leaving his armpits like an orange being squeezed, hear his feet in their worn-out trainers pounding out their rhythm on the pavements. As if someone has sampled his fear and made a dance-track out of it.

He's tearing down roads of once-elegant Victorian houses, pelting across open spaces splattered with sculptures and dog-poo, hurtling through the familiar housing estates with graffiti on the walls.

Yet still he's singing his half-a-song and nodding to the thin air beside him.

"Your little friend won't save you now, Zack Farmer!" cries one of the boys.

They're right, he thinks – he won't. But at least we'll go through whatever happens together. Like we always do.

Zack has reached the alleyway. He thought he could avoid it, go home a safer way, but somehow his feet were ahead of his brain. The alley is narrow, dark, slippery. Deserted. Dirty brick walls high on either side, leading down to the tow-path. And the canal beyond.

Now the skateboards are louder, the noise amplified by the steep alley walls. And he's quite alone – almost. He thinks he can still hear the breath of the two boys behind him, fast, ragged but scarily in control. He can almost smell their excitement, hunters primed for the kill.

He's on the tow-path. Only two ways to go – left or right? Either way, the boys are going to catch him.

There's no escape.

Then a voice right beside him tells him, *"There is a third way, Zack mate."* And, as he always does (even when somewhere deep inside he knows that he shouldn't), Zack stops and listens.

"What – the canal?!" he says. "I can't… Because it's a long way down! And I'm scared… Yes, I know they're coming for me!!!"

Three seconds. Hands stretching out towards him. Two. The breath. One.

No more time. He takes the advice and jumps. Right down towards the water.

How is Zack to know there is a passing barge just down below? A floating-home, out for a leisurely, afternoon sail. And who would expect that the lady of the house (of the boat? The ship?) has chosen just this moment to swab down her dusty decks with a bucket of soapy water?

Which makes them so slippery that Zack doesn't just land, he glides and slides all the way along the soaking floor, feet fighting for footing, banging into wooden crates and coils of rope and the terrified family dog, like a ball in a crazy pinball-machine. Before falling right off the edge of the barge, into the mucky, city water below.

On the tow-path the older boys watch in amazement. They laugh, but they're not quite sure whether they're thrilled that the canal got their quarry or frustrated that they didn't.

"We'll get you next time, Zack Farmer! You *and* your little 'pal'."

But Zack isn't listening. The only thing he can hear in his head is a word, a name, although he can't tell whether he's just thinking it or actually shouting it out loud, because of all the filthy, canal water in his mouth.

"*ARTHURRRRRRRR!!!!!!*"

4.15pm: *Friday February 15th. Hackney Hospital. East London.*

The Accident and Emergency unit of a city hospital is not a fun place to be. Unless maybe you're a zombie, thinks Zack, diving into one of his secret stories again. But Zack isn't a zombie. Right now he's more like a squelching, dripping sea-urchin.

Right now he's squelching and dripping all over the place. But this doesn't stop him from telling a middle-aged lady, who is just about to sit down on the chair next to him (the waiting-room is very crowded), that the seat is taken.

"No, it isn't," she protests, looking at it. "It's empty."

I don't have the energy to argue, thinks Zack, so he just puts his wet hand over the 'empty' seat. About two feet over it. The woman moves off, shaking her head. Whatever the sopping kid fell into has clearly damaged his brain.

Zack looks around the room. There are people in bandages, people with bruises, hands clutching stomachs, stomachs making noises. Little kids crying, drunken men moaning. But he's used to it – he has been here before, rather a lot.

One man has an evening newspaper obscuring his

face. The headline reads: *Exclusive! Parliament Approves Six-Day School Week!'*

"Look at that, Arthur," Zack says to the empty chair. "Six whole days at school!"

The man behind the newspaper peers round and stares at him – Who's he talking to, this scrawny little kid, with the shiny, brown eyes and wet hair? But Zack is thinking about school. Terrific, he thinks – thanks guys, gracias very much, Prime Minister whatsyername. "One more day to be chased," he tells the chair. "One more day to be laughed at."

He senses movement in front of him, at the triage desk where a queue is dispersing. He knows both of the nurses, the tall, friendly Afro-Caribbean lady, whose name is Niomi, and the kind but worn-looking lady of about the same age, with the scowl on her face. He has a strong feeling that he might be the cause of the scowl.

"Oh, not again!" says the lady with the scowl, who has just noticed him and wishes she hadn't. Yup, he was right on that one. A patient at the desk asks her if Zack is a regular.

"Regular as clockwork and a vegan's bowels," she replies. "Regular, flaming nuisance." She turns to Zack. "So, what was it this time?"

"I slid off a barge."

The nurse just stares at him. Both nurses do.

"It was wet!" he protests.

More staring.

So Zack turns, as if for help, to the 'vacant' chair beside him. As the women watch, Zack nods like he's listening to the chair. *Really* listening. He smiles a bit, shakes his head a bit, does something like a high-five, only there's no other five holding anything high, then says the one thing that might just calm the angry nurse down.

"Sorry, Mum."

2

'HE HAS GOT TO GO!'

5.00pm: *Friday February 15th. Hackney, East London. Zack's flat.*

The graffiti on the dingy walls of Zack's block of flats isn't really worth reading.

The spelling is terrible and the colours are rubbish. Which is a shame, Zack reckons, as the block is so bleak, so like all the other blocks on the estate, that it could do with some cheering up. He reckons he could do better himself, especially with all the great words he knows (and not just rude ones). But making clever graffiti would be dangerous these days. Very dangerous. Children's Army-dangerous.

Just as writing stories the way he does is dangerous.

Or – to be honest – reading them.

If there's one thing Zack doesn't look for it's danger – even if it seems to spend most of its day looking for him.

There's a lot more colour inside the neat, little flat, with its primrose-yellow hallway, bright-blue kitchen units and angry-red flush on his mother's face. But luckily the anger has temporarily shifted focus, onto Zack's older sister, Lily. When Mum has a bee in her bonnet, and right now she has a whole hive of them, nobody escapes.

"Where on earth *were* you?" she bellows. "You were meant to be walking Zack home!"

She's actually asking it from inside the hall-cupboard, while she's chucking all kinds of stuff behind her into the hallway. Boxes, vacuum-cleaners, things that need fixing, the family cat. Like she's looking for something important.

Lily Farmer, Zack's only sister (*thank heavens!*) is fifteen. So she can give as good as she gets. Zack often wonders if he'll be able to give as good as he gets when he's fifteen. Whether giving-as-good-as-you're-getting is something that develops as naturally as face-hair (well, if you're boy). Or whether certain people are born to give and others simply to get. He has a feeling it could be the last one and he's pretty sure he's going to get it again, just as soon as Lily stops giving.

"I didn't know Spider-nerd was gonna jump in the canal, did I?"

Spider-nerd, that was a new one.

Zack looks at Arthur, standing right next to him, and wonders if he has heard it before. But the small bloke with the shiny-green skin, bright orange hoody, turned-around baseball cap and skinny legs in chinos that just show the top of his emerald bottom is shaking his head. It doesn't seem like he has heard it before either.

Zack's had far worse from Lily actually, but he's still a bit sorry that she can't stand him. He would have liked at least one friend in the family. Even if that friend does dress like a Goth and do Goth things with her Goth mates whenever she gets a chance, slapping on a white, Goth face and dark lips, with zips and skulls on her gloomy clothing and her hair dyed jet-Goth-black. While listening to Goth music so loud in her room that it makes him want to close his door and his ears and all the electricity in Hackney, London.

Yet it's probably not so surprising that Lily can't stand him, as Zack can't really stand her either. Perhaps that's what being little-brother and big-sister is all about.

"*We jumped on a barge!*" he protests, in italics. "The canal got in our way."

Zack can see – from Mum's backside tightening – that this hasn't cooled the atmosphere. (He knows Mum so well that he can tell she's angry, even when her front-half is deep inside a cupboard.) So he decides to do something to help the situation – he'll set the table. Perhaps he can read one of his secret storybooks at the same time, maybe even out loud, so that Arthur can enjoy it too.

He finds an old book about a time-machine, one that he has hidden away behind the cooker. It was one of those books he discovered in a neighbouring street, on that huge pile left out for burning. Why would any government want to *burn* kids' books? When did all that start? Was it the same time as the Sugar Police and the Children's Army?

Zack Farmer feels he deserves a good story today – and a time-machine. He knows the time he'd go back to. But he also knows that in life, sadly, there's no going back.

"Half our hospital files are on you, Zack Farmer," comes the voice from the cupboard. "One day you'll really hurt yourself. And will you put that book *down*, please? You know you're not meant to be reading stories!"

How does she *do* that? Zack wonders. Has she got eyes in her backside? But, suddenly, she sounds a bit more concerned. "Is everything okay in school?"

Zack just nods. Let her bottom work that one out.

He doesn't want to bother Mum about what's really going on in school. The chases, the isolation, the way the other kids taunt and tease him. The teachers too, especially that big one with the moustache – Mrs Grindling. *'Grow up, Zack Farmer!'* The line that has almost become like the school song – everyone sings it now.

'Grow up, Zack Farmer!'

Like it's that easy!

He knows Mum has enough on her plate these days. Mostly because she tells him and Lily how much she's got on her plate these days. Enough is how much she's got.

"CAN I SMELL SMOKE?" That was loud. Even for Mum.

Yes, of course she can smell smoke. Zack's been smelling it on Lily since she came home from school. But the one thing Zack knows Lily really is brilliant at – and it certainly isn't her school-work – is changing the subject.

"What are you doing in that cupboard, Mum?" she asks.

'Way to go, Lily!' That's what he thinks – it's what they say in those American movies he and Mum watch, when Mum has one of her 'rare moments' off. Well, the movies he used to watch with Mum, before the government went and banned films for kids. But now, unusually, he can see an opportunity to get one over on Lily.

"You're looking for a suitcase, aren't you, Mum?"

The bottom nods. Excellent. Now for the killer blow.

"Have you forgotten, Lily?" says her younger brother, 'innocently'. "Niomi's driving them all the way to Edinburgh tonight. Fancy you forgetting that. Mum's giving a really important nurse-talk on Sunday, aren't you, Mum?"

The bottom nods again, this time appreciatively. Score one for Zack, even if that was a bit smug of him. Especially when he says the same thing all over again, twice. Especially the 'fancy you forgetting, Lily' bit. But Lily is appalled.

"*Tomorrow!*" she protests. "Well, I can't look after river-rat. I'm going out tomorrow. Me and Ashleigh've got a big, Goth-girl gig! Last one before the Government stops them for good!"

Now Mum's out of the cupboard and her face is even angrier than her rear-end.

"Once a year I go to a nursing conference. *Once a year, Lily!* Do you know, they probably call it 'annual' for that very reason?"

This is what his mum does so well. Sarcasm. Zack wishes he could do it too – this and giving as good as he gets. And changing the subject. They're probably all connected, actually.

He's so full of admiration, he forgets that he's just put himself in the line of fire. Because Mum has noticed the table and is staring at it. He stares at it along with her.

It is a beautifully-laid table, even if it's a very small one. Well, the kitchen itself is tiny and they never have many people around it. Zack has set out clean knives and forks, all sporting the same colour handles and all in their right place, next to the everyday supper-plates. Nobody could fault his table-laying. Except maybe Mum.

"The Queen coming again, is she?"

Hear that? It's the sarcasm thing again, but Zack knows just what she means, because he has set the table for four and the Farmer family consists of only three. It has done for quite some years now.

"O-kay. *Enough!*" says Mum, as she rips one of the place-settings off the table and hurls the cutlery back into the cutlery-drawer with a clatter, slamming it shut. "Time you made some real friends, mister. With sweaty feet and stage-one acne. Are you listening, Zack?"

Of course he's listening. He always listens. "They all call me weird," he says.

He turns to talk to the chair, the one that seconds ago had its own plate and cutlery in front of it. The one that looks empty to everyone but him.

"And Arthur *is* real, aren't you, Arthur?"

"And they call you weird!" This from Lily, who is delighted that the million-watt mum-spotlight is no longer glaring down on her.

"Stay out of this, Lily!" yells Mum.

Zack doesn't exactly help his case by starting a huge tickle-fight with Arthur. One that makes every bone in Zack's skinny body quiver and forces laughter out of his mouth at the same time as rivers of snot decide to stream out of his nose. He knows he's probably a bit old for tickle-fights or streaming snot. To be honest, he knows he's probably a bit old for Arthur and that most children his age have grown out of their Arthurs way before now (and half of him really wishes he *was* most children). But what can he do – Arthur is a member of the family.

Okay, he's a shiny, green member (Zack's favourite

colour), who does really look like a person, except of course most persons Zack knows aren't green *or* shiny and most don't have an extra eye on the back of their heads (which often comes in really handy – who doesn't need eyes in the back of their heads?). Arthur also has a fluorescent-orange hoody that actually glows in the dark and that he never ever takes off, because he wasn't imagined that way.

And he gets Zack into more trouble than Zack would ever like to be in.

But no family is perfect, is it? Zack bets that most families have at least one person in it who other people think is pretty odd. Okay, not invisible-odd, but odd.

So, the guys do a bit more laughing and tickling. And snot. Until Mum steps in-between them.

Mum's face is practically in Zack's face now. He can see the little lines that used to happen only when she smiled, but no way is she smiling today. In fact she hardly ever smiles these days.

"Zack, Arthur is NOT real! Okay?" she moans. "If he was, I'd be charging him rent."

Now this is too much for Zack. It's all well and good for her to be thinking that Arthur has got him into trouble once too often.

But to deny his very existence?

"Who's tickling me then – eh?" he protests. "Who made yellow stuff come out my nose? He's *here* Mum, right next to me! He's little and brightly-green and shiny and he's got an extra eye in… "

He suddenly stops mid-sentence, as if he's listening carefully to the empty chair. "I'll tell her," he says. Then he turns back to Mum. "Arthur hopes your Edinburgh talk goes *really* well."

"Oh, thank you, Arth —"

Oops!

Mum nearly fell for that one, which makes her all the more cross. But then she takes a deep breath and tries to be a bit more reasonable, which is a tone he's heard before. It doesn't usually last long. "Hey kiddo, look at me… *Zack?*"

Zack looks at her, but he knows what's coming.

"Arthur isn't a person, you do know that? You're a very imaginative young man – with all your words and your stories. But we both know, don't we, that he's just someone you made up when you were little. Big things were happening – between your dad and me." She sighs. "And maybe I wasn't always here for you as much as you needed."

Mum stops, looking a bit sad, then tries to make her face smile.

"But we're a family again now, aren't we? The three of us. The Three Musketeers." Zack looks blank. "It's an old book. And, anyway, you're eleven now. *Almost twelve.* So I would really like it if you left Arthur outside somewhere – and forgot all about him."

Zack turns to the chair – and to his little, green friend, who is shaking his oddly-shaped head a bit sadly. And blinking all his eyes.

"She's only kidding, Arthur," says Zack.

He knows he shouldn't have said this. He knows he's talking to the only thirty-six-year-old woman in Britain who can go from zero to ballistic in less than a second. He knows.

"NO! I'M NOT!" she yells. "NOT KIDDING. NO WAY KIDDING. HE HAS GOT TO GO!!"

If he shouldn't have said that, about the kidding, he knows for absolute certain he shouldn't be saying what comes out of his mouth next. But it's like when you need a pee really badly and, if you don't do it, you just explode.

"Is that what you said to my dad?"

3

'THE POST IS REALLY
GOOD THESE DAYS'

5.10pm: *Friday February 15th. Hackney, East London. Zack's flat.*

Mum doesn't say anything for a second.

But it's a really long second – even the clock above the door seems to be thinking twice about moving. Zack can see Lily, in the corridor, stop right in the middle of taking off her smoky-smelling jacket. As if she's been instantly frozen in a block of ice.

Mum begins very quietly. "Right. Where is he?"

"Where's who?" says Zack. But he knows who.

"You know who – *Zacky boy!*"

It's never good news when she calls him that. Zacky boy. He hates that so much. So he just points to the empty chair, the one without the place-setting. But he can see his finger shake, he can feel his whole body quivering. He has no idea what she's going to do.

It doesn't take long to find out.

Mum rushes round the table towards the chair. Zack

tries to block her, but she's quicker than he is and she grabs something with her strong, right hand. Well, if you're looking at it, as a really fascinated Lily is doing from the doorway, Mum actually grabs *nothing* with her strong, right hand. Emptiness. Zero. And she knows this.

But this isn't how it looks to Zack.

"*Arthur!!...* You're hurting him!"

He can see his best friend practically choking. The green eyes bulge, the green tongue is lolling about and that eye on the back of his head is doing him absolutely no good at all.

Now Mum's on the move again, still holding the fistful of nothingness, muttering to herself. "Maybe the Government should just ban *kids* and be done with it."

When did parents start talking like this? How did it happen? Sugar Police. Children's Army. No time to think about that now. Now, it's about saving Arthur.

"*Mum, what are you doing?*"

Mum doesn't answer, she's too busy scrabbling around in all the junk she just chucked out of the hall-cupboard, searching for something. Finally, she finds it.

A white cardboard-box, a big one with a printed label on it, which must have been posted to her, at this flat, sometime in the past. She swiftly picks off some of the label with her short fingernails, opens the box wide and empties her right hand directly into it, as if she's dropping something important inside.

Zack is speechless.

He watches open-mouthed, as his mum strides back into the kitchen with the box. She finds some sticky-brown tape in the small wicker-basket where she keeps things like scissors and sticky-brown tape and those wiry things you twist round plastic bags to keep whatever's inside fresh. Almost quicker than his eye can follow, she pulls the sticky-brown tape around the box really loudly, once, twice, with a horrible stretching sound, like a cat being gutted, sealing it tight. Just like she did when she wrapped toys for presents, in the days when you were allowed to give children toys for presents.

Suddenly he spies an opening, between her arm and the work-surface. "Grab my hand, Arthur!" he yells.

He lunges, almost touching the box, but Mum's quicker and she slides the box onto the table, making a real mess of his cutlery arrangements.

"Pass me that pen, please," she says. She's shielding the box with her body.

It's the 'please' that throws him. He hands her the kitchen ballpoint, before he can even think what she wants it for. She starts to write. It's a name he knows very well, but one that is never mentioned in their house. Hasn't been for a very long time.

STUART FARMER.

Zack's dad. Lily's dad. Their mum's – Ruth Farmer's – husband.

"Your father can have him. It's his turn."

What? thinks Zack. Hang on! "YOU ALWAYS SAID YOU DUNNO WHERE MY DAD IS!"

But Mum's still writing and now Lily is watching too. She sees her Mum's eyes flick up briefly to the yellowing map of Britain on the pin-board by the washing-machine. She's glancing right up to the very top of the map, where there's more water than land, as if searching for inspiration. But Zack is too busy concentrating on the address she's scribbling onto the box. Over the bits of old label.

'STUART FARMER. THE HIGH STREET. CAPE FURY. THE HIGHLANDS. SCOTLAND.'

Cape Fury?

He's never heard of it, he thought his dad came from Dundee. He must have moved.

Mum notices Zack staring at her, his mouth still gaping, and for a moment she seems a bit uneasy. "The post is really good these days," she says. With that she's off again, moving towards the door, the sealed white box in her hands.

"Where are you going?" asks Zack. Not unreasonably, considering he thinks his special friend is about to become a special delivery. "Where are you taking Arthur?"

He doesn't have to wait long for the answer.

Within seconds the front door is swinging open and he's running after Mum through the darkening streets. She is on her bike and pedalling furiously, with Arthur's box bouncing around on the rack above her back wheel.

Zack can hardly breathe – he's already had quite a run this afternoon and a bit of a swim. But the panting this time is as much sheer panic as it is exertion. He knows he has to stop her, before she reaches the Post Office, before she buys all the stamps and puts the big, white box into the system, whatever that system is.

Before Arthur is gone forever.

He would like to think that his imagination – which even his worst enemies know is really vivid – could just *imagine* Arthur out of the box. But right now it doesn't seem to be working, because his brain itself isn't working. It's like it has closed down in shock. And Arthur is getting further and further away.

But he can still just about imagine Arthur inside his cardboard prison, coughing and spluttering as he's bumped around, unable to spread his spindly green arms and legs. And all his bright-green eyes filled with tears, as the dreadful box rattles mindlessly down chutes, along conveyor belts, into dusty vans or thundering trains.

Maybe he's to be thrown idly from one Post Office worker to another, none of them knowing or caring that there's a real, live, fully-imagined Arthur in there, shivering in the sweaty darkness, getting dizzier and lonelier and more scared by the minute.

"He'll suffocate in there!" yells Zack. "*You're a murderer!*"

But the suffocater isn't listening, the murderer is getting farther and farther away. Very soon he can hardly see them, they're just a tiny, bobbing blob, lost in the Friday-night rush, at the bottom of a busy Hackney street.

And Zack knows that the further away Arthur gets from him, the less he's a part of him. And the less he's a part of Zack, the less Arthur can do anything, be anything. The less he *is* anything. Which goes pretty much the same for Zack too. (Apart isn't 'a part', he thinks.)

Yet Zack is sure he can still hear that familiar voice, the one that talks only to him. It's usually so cocky and confident and reassuring, a real Hackney voice. Rich with the sounds of London. Streetwise. Cool. So unlike Zack.

But now it just sounds frightened and confused. Now

it can say only one word, one syllable, one weak, croaky cry. Echoing his real friend's own unbearable pain.

"*Zack…?*"

4

'TOO MUCH IMAGINATION IS LIKE TOO MUCH ICE CREAM.'

8.15pm: *Friday February 15th. Hackney, East London. Zack's Flat.*

Zack's bedroom feels quieter than it has ever felt in his life.

He's lying on his unmade bed, just staring up at the ceiling, which is painted a very dark blue with stars, so that he can imagine it's the night-time sky, and not simply the underside of old Mrs Riordan's living-room.

Zack spends a lot of hours imagining.

Imagination is like a muscle he feels he needs to work and build or it will just go flabby. He doesn't know why he does it, but perhaps living in his head makes more sense and is a lot more fun than living in the outside world. Especially when he has Arthur for company.

Because Arthur had – *has* – quite an imagination himself. Zack remembers how they used to 'work-out' together, just lying there, side by side, on the bed. Flexing their imaginations – creating way-out stories.

25

Making stuff up. About sea-monsters and alien invasions and dungeons and heroes.

All around him are his important pictures. On the walls, propped up on his second-hand desk and even as the screen-saver on that old computer his dad left behind so many years ago. But these are pictures that only Zack can see, or at least that only Zack can see in their entirety.

Pictures of him and Arthur, together. Having fun. At the park, in their favourite café, in that very bedroom.

Zack stares at the pictures of his little green friend, with the backwards-facing baseball cap that seems like it is attached to his skull and the back eye just peering under the upturned peak. He knows that anyone else looking at the pictures wouldn't see Arthur. They'd look like pictures of Zack on his own. Which is the way most people see Zack.

On his own.

He's certainly never felt more on his own right now.

Who wouldn't, he thinks, if their mum had posted their only friend in the world to some man this poor friend has never met, living in some place no-one's ever heard of? Which might as well be the other side of the world. (Zack has searched for Cape Fury on the internet. It's a long way from Hackney. Practically as far as you can get without falling into the sea. Maybe that's what people do there.)

Zack sometimes wonders whether he has Arthur because he's on his own or he is on his own because he has Arthur. These are the sort of things he tries to work out in his head, when he's on his own. But his memory of all those years ago is really fuzzy and he can't recall exactly when Arthur turned up. It feels like Arthur has always been here, which is the exact opposite of how it feels now.

He knows that Mum thinks he has far too much imagination for his own good. But why is imagination such a terrible thing these days? That's one thing he just can't imagine.

He can still hear the 'murderer' now, in the hallway, giving Lily final instructions before she drives off to her stupid conference. Something about looking after her little brother, because he clearly needs looking after, and not getting a tattoo. If Zack could predict something, it's that the first won't happen but the second just might.

Now his door is opening. *Oh, go away!*

"I'm going now, Zack," says Mum.

Fine, so go, thinks Zack. Drive carefully. Missing you already. Blah de blah.

"O-kay," says Ruth Farmer, her thick, brown hair looking quite shiny now that she has given it a good shower and a brush. Zack knows that, even with all the weariness, she's still really quite pretty, and kind-looking, but he's certainly not going to tell her that.

"Hey, maybe you can go see a friend tomorrow," she says. "A human one, preferably."

Oh ha ha.

She's coming over to the bed, to comfort him. More like comforting herself, because she's done something so rotten that it might just win her the Worst Mother of the Year Award. Even if the competition was really fierce and she'd already won it twice.

"I did it for *you*, love," she says, gently. No, you didn't, Mum. And here it comes. "Imagination's great, but you know what they say, Zack. Too much imagination these days, it's dangerous." Same old. "That new Children's Army is full of kids who…" She daren't even finish. "It's for the best, love."

Zack isn't replying – he makes a point of never replying to suffocaters. Or he won't, from now on. But he can see out of the corner of his eye that Mum looks just a little bit sad as she strokes his spiky hair. She tries to kiss him but Zack isn't in a kissing mood. She even tries to make it up to him, in a way.

"And because Arthur came out of that great imagination of yours, hey – you can just conjure him up again, can't you! So long as he's gone by the time I get back."

Zack doesn't say a thing.

Mum can see that this brilliant suggestion hasn't worked a treat, so she shuffles back out into the hallway to pick up her old suitcase. The one with the broken wheel that makes her back ache. Well, tough, thinks Zack, you ought to be sad. Even if you're sadder than the saddest, sad person in the universe, Planet Saddo included, you'll never be as sad as I am right now.

He stares back up at his ceiling of stars, just thinking. A car horn paps four times outside, which has to be Niomi. He knows it would be polite to go into the hallway, but he just can't move from the bed.

Which, in a strange way, is about to change everything.

Since he's not in the hallway, and has absolutely no intention of waving Mum goodbye, Zack Farmer doesn't spot that there's an odd, disc-like object, bright shiny-green and about the size of a pound coin, just sitting by the welcome-mat on the inside of the flat's front door.

Something that wasn't there earlier on today.

Of course he mightn't notice it even if he was standing right there next to it, it's so small and somehow not quite real. Although he might just catch the faint, green light it is giving out. But it's a light that's far too weak to cast any of its beams as far as his bedroom. Maybe it rolled onto the mat from somewhere else, the kitchen perhaps, but it's certainly not rolling anywhere now.

A few seconds later the front-door closes with a bit of a slam.

And barely a second after that, the loudest music you ever heard begins to blast out from Lily's room. Goth music, obviously.

Welcome to the weekend. Zack can't wait.

But the front-door slamming must have done something else. Because the curious and vaguely unreal, green disc is starting to move from its resting place.

It is setting off slowly down the hall.

Zack is so deep into his own angry thoughts that he doesn't even pick up its glow as it curls round his open doorway and into his bedroom.

He certainly doesn't spot it as it rolls between his slippers and nests on the floor, in a fold of his bedspread. Because right now his eyes are elsewhere. They're looking at the screen-saver with its picture of him and Arthur in happier days and they're staring right into its —

The computer! OMG!

Suddenly an idea occurs to him and even as an idea, not even something he has definitely decided to do (and probably *never* will), it's the scariest thing in Zack Farmer's life.

Ever.

He wishes Arthur was here to share it with him.

He goes over and closes his bedroom door.

5

'RUNNING AWAY FROM HOME, ARE YOU?'

10.00pm: *Friday February 15th. Hackney, East London. Zack's flat.*

Zack's bedroom-door is still closed at ten o'clock in the evening.

This is when Lily and her friends, the ones who turned up just seconds after Mum left, tramp past it on their way to the kitchen. The takeaway-pizzas have arrived and quite a lot of the money that Mum gave Lily for the weekend (and for Zack) has already gone towards supporting the pizza-makers of Hackney and their families.

Lily would have asked Zack if he wanted something to eat, of course she would. But his bedroom-door was closed and it was so quiet in there and she really didn't want to wake him up. And by the time she felt she should check if he was hungry, the pizzas had miraculously disappeared – every last, deep-pan, cheesy crumb.

But if she had ventured into her brother's room

earlier this evening (which is something she very rarely does, unless she wants to take out her anger on somebody smaller and wimpier – or to 'borrow' his pocket-money), she wouldn't have believed what she was seeing.

She would have met with activity such as she's never witnessed in that room. Even in its Arthur days. Zack throwing all sorts of clothes into his school rucksack, not exactly paying attention to the folds or the creases. Forbidden books flying in there too, as well as his treasured, old dictionary and his spare toothbrush.

She would have caught him reaching up for that big, heavy jar on his top-shelf and spilling its contents all over his floor. The contents being all the coins he's saved over the past year, since he discovered that saving is the best way to get the things you want, even though these things are becoming fewer and fewer with all the new laws they keep bringing in.

She might even have heard him grumbling, as he stuffed the money into all his pockets, that every law they bring out these days seems far worse for kids than it is for grown-ups. Maybe because the Government is made up entirely of grown-ups, not kids.

What she certainly wouldn't have noticed (because Zack doesn't either), is that along with all the coins, he scoops up that odd, little green thing. The shiny disc that is there, yet not quite there, and was hiding in his bedspread. The one that seems to grow quite a lot brighter and greener when it makes brief contact with her younger brother's skin.

Zack, of course, is well aware of Lily's friends. He could hear them gobbling up all the pizza practically as soon as it arrived, like pigs around a trough, only noisier and even more pig-like. But he's really glad Lily can't see him right now and that he can't see her, because he knows she would go totally berserk if she knew what he is about to do. Possibly – about to do. He feels like going berserk himself just thinking about it.

AaaaaRRGGHH!!

But then he looks at one of the photos on the wall. That framed one with him and Arthur at the park. The one he took by placing the camera on a wall and setting the delay button (well, who was he going to ask to *please* take a photo of him with his arm around nothing?) and he knows that today's the day he has to do what Mum is always telling him.

'Feel the fear and do it anyway, Zack.'

For the first time since she began to say this, it doesn't sound like the stupidest thing anyone ever said to him. Surely, he used to think, when you feel the fear you do nothing, or you run like the clappers. Actually, he still does mostly think this. It's just lucky he doesn't know how *very* scary things are going to get.

He shoves the framed photo of the two of them into his rucksack and opens the bedroom-door very gently, just poking his head out, as if a poking head can't be seen as clearly as anything else. But, luckily, the Goth girls are all far too busy shouting and smoking and dancing and burping.

They don't even notice when he sneaks right past them and out into the darkest night, closing the front-door really quietly behind him.

They would probably just about notice if he opened the door and ran right back in again, which is exactly what he feels like doing. It is taking every bit of spirit within him

– and a few gallons more – to stop himself from turning around. But instead he takes a few deep, heavily-polluted breaths into his lungs and makes his way through the stark housing-estate towards the nearest bus-stop.

Everything looks so different at this time of night.

It isn't that there's no lighting. It's more that the people standing under the lighting, or just in the shadows, seem to be so much bigger and scarier than they do in the daylight. The fact there are less of them just makes them all the more intimidating.

Zack Farmer loves that word, 'intimidating' (which he knows means scary), even as he is intimidated by it. But words that are scary in the books he isn't supposed to be reading don't even begin to describe the feelings when the situations are real.

Then he sees the boys.

They're the same ones who chased him into the canal this afternoon. Was it only this afternoon – it seems an age ago? They are standing and eating a fish-supper, right by the bus-stop.

His bus-stop.

"Well, look who's come to join us," calls one.

"How's your BFF?" shouts the second, which Zack doesn't understand at all.

"You take one of them, I'll take the other," says the first one. They really laugh at this.

There's no way to avoid them, not if he wants to set off on his journey. All Zack can think of, aside from running back home, is to sing the song, the one he and Arthur used to sing together, even though he knows that this time there'll be no one to fill in the gaps.

"'*There was a soldier...* (pause, then a whole lot more pause)...'"

Oh no, I'm going to cry, he thinks. I've only travelled about fifty yards on my quest and I'm already set to blubber like a baby. *Grow up, Zack Farmer!* To make it worse, a powerful light suddenly begins to shine on his face, highlighting his youth and his shame!

No, hang on, it isn't worse. It's simply headlights – on the front of the bus that's going all the way across the City of London to St. Eustace Station. The proper start to his journey.

"Running away from home, are you?" taunt the boys. "Bet your mummy's glad to be shot of both of you!"

Zack is only half-listening. He's already on the moving bus and mid-way up the stairs, to where it is high and crowded. If anyone is looking at him, wondering where a rather pale and undersized eleven-year-old boy with a thin, worried face, sticky-up brown hair and a bulging rucksack is going at this time of the night, they are being proper Londoners and keeping their concerns to themselves.

As he watches the boys at the bus-stop getting smaller, but still looking far too 'intimidating', he hopes that this is just an early bump in an otherwise smooth road.

With a bit of luck, he tells himself, the rest of my journey towards finding Arthur, and maybe even my long-lost dad, will be plain-sailing.

But he's not sure he believes it.

Saturday.

But not like any Saturday you (or even Zack) could imagine.

6

'CAN ZACK RING YOU BACK LATER, MUM?'

8.30am: *Saturday February 16th. Hackney, East London. Zack's flat.*

It is Mum's Saturday morning phone-call that wakes Lily up.

And Lily begins to realise just what an unholy mess she is in.

Ruth Farmer is calling on her way to the conference centre in Edinburgh (where the Royal College of Nursing is about to commence its annual gathering). She just wants to reassure herself that her kids are alright and that the walls of her dear little flat aren't smeared with takeaway pizza.

Lily Farmer puts on her most reassuring voice. She tells Mum – whilst waving frantically to her friends to *shut up* – that she is fine and rested. She and Zack had a lovely, early night. And of course she's doing her history homework!

Naturally, Mum asks to speak to Zack and here's

where Lily's problems really start. Or rather just a few seconds later, when she's staring at the bed in Zack's room and it's pretty clear that there's no one called Zack inside it.

"Oh, bless," she tells her mum, when the shock dies down just enough to allow some sort of sound to come out of her gaping mouth. "He's asleep, Mum."

Lily pretends to wake Zack noisily, but what she's really doing is searching around the room in a mounting panic. As if her fun-loving little brother might be hiding on one of his shelves or in his wardrobe or under some scrap-paper in his waste-bin. The joker!

Aaaarrghhh!

"Zack, do you want to speak to Mummy? She's phoning all the way from Edinburgh!" She says this in her sweetest voice, doing a great job of not letting it quiver and shake too much. (But somewhere in the back of her mind, she can almost hear a little voice saying, *Who's talking to an invisible person now then?!*)

She does a bit more of this pretend waking-up-my-dozy-brother stuff, then has to tell Mum the truth. "No, it's no use, Mum. He's practically in a coma."

Well, not exactly the truth.

She can tell from Mum's voice that she's disappointed. And Lily really doesn't mean to upset her even more, but on her way out of the bedroom to look for Zack, her hand accidentally bumps against his computer. The screen-saver with that picture of her sad little brother on his own (hand outstretched, arm around absolutely nothing) disappears – to reveal the last website Zack has been looking at.

A train-timetable, showing the times of trains this Saturday morning from St. Eustace Station, London to Inverness, the Highlands, Scotland.

Aaaagghhhh!! (Again)

"Er – Mum? Can Zack ring you back later…? Bye!"

7

'THERE IS NO ARTHUR! DUH?'

9.15am: *Saturday February 16th. St. Eustace Station. London.*

Early Saturday morning in St. Eustace Station isn't like weekdays.

There isn't a rush hour, with everybody scurrying to their offices. The people filling the concourse or lining the platforms or spilling off the trains aren't banging into each other because they might be late for work. But they're still bustling and shoving and pushing, because they might be late for their relaxing city-break or their shopping trip or their big day out or their auntie's funeral.

There's always a reason to bump into someone else in London.

Zack is watching them all collide from a darkened corner of the huge station, beside an unused storage room. He has spent the past few hours avoiding cleaners and station-workers and lavatory-attendants and policemen, hiding under benches, sleeping behind rubbish-skips, waiting for the time when he can get himself onto a train going north. Way north. The time is here and the train that could transport him to the Highlands of Scotland is at the platform, all tidied up and just waiting for him.

He should be exhausted and sore, but instead he feels strangely excited. It's so rare, he thinks, for me to be doing something that someone else isn't telling me to do. *Rare?* Who am I kidding – it's unknown.

Even Arthur isn't telling me what to do right now! If I only had £150 more in his pocket, I would be as good as in Inverness already. Well, even now, he tells himself, I'm just 560 miles and a mere eight and a half-hour rail journey away. And from Inverness the dramatic-sounding Cape Fury is a simple stroll. A simple, 120-mile stroll.

AAAARRRGGGHH!!

Suddenly it all seems totally hopeless. And seriously scary.

"What am I doing here, Arthur?" he moans, before he remembers again that he is here precisely because Arthur isn't.

He picks up his rucksack, which he has been using as a pillow. A very lumpy pillow, mainly because of that big, framed photo with the hard, pointy corners. He takes this keepsake out, to remind himself of why he is there and why he *has* to get onto that train, even though he doesn't have anywhere near enough money.

He remembers when that photo was taken. Arthur had suggested that they climb one of the trees in the park to see where the squirrels hide their nuts. Zack was pretty lucky that there was a gardener cutting branches nearby, who heard his screams. The man came across with his ladder and carried Zack back down again, like a sack of potatoes.

Arthur, of course, managed to jump down entirely on his own.

And *this* is the guy he wants to find again? The guy who was always getting him into trouble? The guy who had him stuck up a tree? Maybe it *is* time to do what everyone at school is telling him.

Grow up, Zack Farmer!

Whoa! Hang on a second – there's something about the photograph that bothers him.

It's nothing he can quite put his finger on, nothing that really glares out. Maybe it's just the station-lighting, but no, Zack can't deny it, Arthur does look a tiny bit fainter. Like someone has diluted his colour, the way Zack recalls paint being diluted with water in school, back in the days when kids were allowed paint-pots and paper and fun.

Zack's heart skips a beat. Forget growing-up – he *has* to get on that train!

But he knows that train companies aren't charities. They don't listen to stories about missing friends and vanishing dads. You have to be way smarter than that.

Zack strolls up to the ticket-collector at the barrier, the person to whom everyone else is showing their tickets. The man is looking very important, with his clipper in his hand, and not particularly friendly. Finally he looks down at the boy with the bulging rucksack and the station-dust all over his clothes.

"Where do you think *you're* going?" says the man.

"My mum's on that train," replies Zack, putting on the face of someone desperate.

"No, she's not," says the ticket collector, putting on the

face of someone who doesn't believe the desperate face he's looking at.

Zack just stares at him – how can he know for sure?

"I saw you when I started in this morning. Sleeping over in that corner."

Oh. That's how he knows.

"I've got to get to Cape Fury!" says Zack, trying again.

"No such place. And if you don't scarper back to where your mum really is, I'll tell that lot you're here."

That lot? What lot?

Zack soon finds out. Marching smartly across the station forecourt, clearing a path through the early-morning travellers, is a small band of smart, young teenagers in their distinctive black, military uniforms. Their sergeant, a slightly older girl, is leading from the rear. Zack knows that beneath their shiny peaked-caps not a single hair sticks out, because it has been sheared too short to peek anywhere. But you don't tease anyone in the Children's Army, or call them baldy, or you might just find yourself their newest recruit.

He looks at the young soldiers, whose eyes hardly move and whose mouths never smile, and wonders what they did to find themselves where they are. Was that young guy with the red hair a storybook-reader? Did the slim girl beside him sneak into the cinema or linger too long at the sweet stall? Did the smaller boy, marching slightly out-of-step, forget to hand in his toys when the toy-crunching vans came round?

As they approach, Zack can hear their heavy boots stomping – it's how they're told to march. Zack thinks that walking in this weird way would give him a headache, but this would probably be the least of his worries.

Suddenly the teenage soldiers turn, as if they're a

single person with a load of heads and twice as many legs, and march towards the ticket-barrier. Just as a large group of people, straight off a train, come walking from the opposite direction in a far less military fashion.

The ticket-collector seems pretty relieved when the young sergeant holds up a single document, which Zack assumes must be a group-ticket for all the child-soldiers heading northwards. Probably to search out and capture some other poor children who have somehow escaped their clutches.

Now's his chance.

He rushes straight at the band of junior warriors, head down, and quickly shoulders his way right in to a secure hiding-place deep within the marching bodies. Of course they notice him, but they know better than to break formation – or even to look. So when he puts an arm around the shoulders of the soldier on either side of him, and lifts his legs up so they're carrying him along, no-one dares to report him. (And, he has the feeling, they might not even *wish* to.)

Through the barrier he goes, straight past the ticket-collector, who is busily clipping tickets. Success! His first so far.

He's just about to slip onto the Inverness train, on this vital stage of his journey, when he hears -

"*Zack!*"

He'd know that voice anywhere.

He stops and turns slowly. It's his sister, shouting at him from the barrier. How did Lily know he was here? And why did she have to alert the ticket-collector, just when he had made it through?

He looks around frantically. A train is about to leave.

It isn't his train, the one going to Inverness. It's the one on the opposite platform, but this is no time to be fussy. Not with his 'baby-sitter' on his tail. He starts to run towards it. He can see Lily out of the corner of his eye, trying to run after him, but the ticket-collector has caught hold of her and is preventing her from going any further. Good man.

"Not so fast, my girl," he says.

Lily looks desperate. She stares at the angry, red-faced man, then swiftly opens her shoulder-bag, the shiny, black one with the skull on it. Out of it she pulls a small, nasty-looking syringe, like the sort you'd find in a hospital or when someone gives you a blood-test. She holds it up to the man.

"He's forgotten this. One peanut and he's history!"

The ticket-collector is so shocked at this that he lets Lily through. You don't argue with a peanut-allergy – he doesn't want someone swelling up like a puffer-fish and blocking his platform.

Lily runs towards Zack and reaches the train, just as her little brother is climbing aboard. She manages to grab his wrist really hard (not that there's much to grab, he's pretty scrawny) and she starts to pull.

It looks to Zack like this is the end of a pretty short road. Lily is a lot stronger than him – she's going to keep her hand, with its peeling, black nail-polish, firmly around his wrist all the way back to Hackney and into his lonely, Arthur-less room.

But fate has a habit of getting things totally wrong.

A passenger, already on the train and seeing the doors

about to close, naturally assumes that a poor little boy is trying to pull his bigger, heavier sister onto a train that she is in serious danger of missing. So he adds his weight to Zack's and heaves with all his grown-up might.

Lily finds herself flying into the train just as the doors finally close.

"You cut that a bit fine, love," says the helpful passenger and goes happily back to his seat.

Lily just glares at the departing man. "Thank you – *not!*" she calls, as the train to heaven-knows-where moves determinedly off. But her real anger is reserved for Zack.

"*Brilliant!*" she moans. "So now where are we going – moron?" She can see from Zack's shocked face that he has absolutely no idea. So she tells him. "Okay, we're getting off next stop, you hear me, and going right back home. Like you have no idea how crucial Saturdays are – when you've got a life!"

She pinches his arm really tight, just to make her point.

Zack is scared of Lily. He has always been scared of Lily. They go through a tunnel and for a brief moment he catches their faces reflected in the darkened window. Hers looks its usual white with anger-trimmings, whilst his seems white too, but not Goth-white. Zack's face is white with fear.

But suddenly he sees Arthur's image right there between them, trying faintly to get a look in. And throwing him that brave, Arthur smile. Zack knows it is just his head playing tricks, there's probably no Arthur within seven-hundred miles, (at least not *his* Arthur), yet for the moment it makes him just that bit more determined."

"NO!" he says. "You're coming with me, Lily." He

thinks hard. "Or… *or* I'll tell Mum you left me home-alone in Hackney. Starving to death. With no pizza!"

Lily looks at him, like she is seriously not getting over-stressed by threats from this friendless, immature, little worm, even if the worm is turning just a tiny bit. Then a roving ticket-inspector approaches, staring right at the two of them, about to demand their tickets.

Thinking fast, Zack does what he does so well – he starts to cry. Proper crying, little boy stuff, really loud. Lily immediately catches on and comforts him by clutching his head to her breast. 'There there, flower.' The ticket-inspector, not wanting to become involved in any emotional stuff, because he can get that at home with his own kids, moves on.

As soon as he has gone, Lily pushes Zack's head away, but he goes straight back into threat-making mode. "And I'll tell Mum that you and Ashleigh drive her car, when she's sleeping off her night shifts."

This really hits home, but Lily tries to shrug it off. "Mum warned you about that imagination of yours."

She doesn't expect what Zack tells her next.

"I took a photo of you," warns Zack, "with my camera. Arthur told me to."

Lily looks white. Okay she's a Goth, but even so. Zack presses on. "Mum'll ground you forever. You'll never see your mates again. And she'll take your precious new phone away."

Lily doesn't say anything, she just grabs Zack's dusty hand and presses that nasty syringe hard into his palm. A tiny, red dot appears and Zack yelps. *Ayyyyy!!!!*

But then she starts to write with the syringe. To Zack's

relief it's just a creepy ballpoint pen, full of blood-red ink, from the old days when you could still buy joke-stuff for Halloween. He looks down at what she is writing.

It reads: '*There is NO Arthur! Duh?*'

Zack closes his eyes to block out his sister's face and the thumping of his heart. He tries really hard to imagine what Cape Fury might look like – so many hundreds of miles to the north.

8

'NO – IT'S A FIGUS BROGIOTTO NERO.'

9.30am: *Saturday, February 16th. Cape Fury. Highlands of Scotland.*

Zack might picture a landscape that's quite different to anything he has ever known. He might even shade in the fine, misty drizzle, the Scotch mist, that can make things really hard to see.

But he certainly won't be imagining the McBride Family.

Yet here they are, with the mist getting into their hair and their clothes and their souls, as they stand by a tiny, newly-dug grave, this damp Saturday morning, in Cape Fury, the Highlands, Scotland.

They're on the village High Street, (which is very nearly the village's only street), in the front garden of a small but pretty, white-walled, stone cottage. The garden could be pretty too, but it looks as if nature, which has nothing to be ashamed of in this part of the world, has at Number 5 been allowed too free a hand.

The big man turning the earth, sweating despite the cold, seems like he is trying to sink all his sadness into the damp ground, but hardly getting rid of any of it.

A little girl, who is his daughter, although with her delicate features she doesn't look much like him, watches as the peaty soil lands softly beside her. But where you might expect tears, there are only gentle drops of rain sheltering on her long eyelashes. The dimmed, sad eyes behind them are totally dry.

The third person, her grandfather, is a stocky, white-bearded Scotsman from Glasgow, with a perpetually mischievous glint. He has been in a different sort of mist himself on many an occasion, due to a drop too much of Scotch whisky, and is trying a wee bit too hard to be solemn as he intones an appropriate prayer.

"Lord, we ask you to take good care of our old friend Nibbles McBride and to see to it that he is really happy up there, with all the other bygone hamsters."

He glances down at his beautiful granddaughter. Just eight-years old but he feels somehow that he has known this familiar face of hers for so much longer. Yet it isn't just this that makes the girl seem older than her years.

"He had a good life, Kirstie," says her grandfather. "Your wee pal didn't suffer."

Even after these few long months, her reply freezes him to his bones.

"Like Mummy," she says.

Grandpa Brodie looks at the man turning the earth, his son-in-law for nine years, a widower the past six months. He's expecting the big man, who married and then sadly lost Brodie's only daughter, to be stopped in his tracks.

He's expecting him to take the little girl into his powerful arms and let her know that he understands her grieving.

But the tall, weather-blown man seems too wrapped up in his own pain, the distance between him and his daughter as great as the valleys just a few miles away beyond the mist, as deep as the roaring sea just below the rear garden. Grandpa Brodie reaches out, cuddles his only grandchild to him, and feels her shift ever so slightly closer to his old, damp coat.

A cheery sound interrupts their separate thoughts.

"Good morning, guys," it greets them. "Oh dear, was it the old cat that died then?'

The postman, wearing his waterproof like a transparent tent, is moving through the mist. In his hands he holds a big, white box, with an address scrawled angrily across it.

"It was Nibbles," explains Grandpa Brodie.

"*The hamster!*" says the postman, running a wet hand through his thinning, grey hair. "How did the poor creature die? Was it a heart attack?"

Grandpa Brodie pauses – he knows, from years of propping up the bar in his favourite Glasgow pub, that timing is everything. "He fell asleep at the wheel."

The postman looks at him, then the two pals wake up the quiet, little street with their full-throated laughter. More laughter than the hamster-wheel joke deserves, but in hard times you take what you can get. The big man, the son-in-law, doesn't join in. He seldom laughs. He just stares down at the white cardboard-box, the drizzle still lingering on it.

"Is that for me, then?" he asks.

"Well," says the postman, looking at the box, "your name's Stuart and you are a farmer. See?"

He points to the scrawl, as he reads it out. "'*Stuart Farmer. High Street. Cape Fury*'. Only one Stuart in this street and just the one farmer, so I'm guessing it must be you, Farmer Stuart. It's really heavy, mind."

The farmer known as Stuart takes the parcel in his huge, earth-encrusted hands, bracing himself for its weight. The total lack of it unsteadies him, as the postman laughs at his astonished face.

"Maybe it's a tiny, wee diamond," suggests Brodie.

"Or a million-pound note," tries the postman.

"Or a hamster that doesn't die on you," says Kirstie, sadly.

"Or nothing," says Stuart, as he rips open the box, to find it totally empty.

He explores it, tips it, shakes it. Definitely empty. As empty as his life right now.

Kirstie looks disappointed. Although she would never admit it, not even to herself, she felt for just one tiny moment that something was about to change. Not in a big way, nothing earth-shattering, but any change, even something as small as a featherweight gift in a big, white box, would be rather welcome right now.

"Who would send someone a big, empty box?" wonders the Postman.

"And did they send it *air*-mail?" asks Grandpa Brodie, making them both collapse again.

Stuart just shrugs and slings the useless box onto a heap of rubbish by the side of the old stone cottage. He'll get round to burning it all, some time. Just behind the heap, and almost obscured by it, is a sad-looking sapling. A tiny, young tree which, even now, is being buffeted by the rough breeze from the sea. Kirstie points to it.

"Daddy, see that wee tree we planted? After we said goodbye to Mummy. Well, I think it's really a beanstalk and one day it'll reach way, way up to the sky. Even to heaven!"

Stuart McBride just shakes his head. "Er no… it's a *ficus brogiotto nero.*"

Stuart the farmer knows his plants, even the ones with funny, Latin names. He went to college. But he hears his father-in-law give a meaningful cough.

"Or – maybe it is a beanstalk," Stuart adds, uneasily. "Aye. Could be. Not quite sure, Kirstie. Now, I need to get on with my work. Load of bills to see to."

He returns to the cottage, his mind already somewhere else.

The postman and Grandpa Brodie give each other a sort of 'Well, what are *we* supposed to do?' look. Grandpa Brodie just smiles to Kirstie, one of his really kind, beardy smiles, and beckons her to come inside out of the rain. But Kirstie shakes her head, so Grandpa starts to go back in alone.

Yet first he looks up at the sky, as he so often does. He smiles sadly at whatever's up there and shrugs his shoulders.

When the Postman has gone and she's quite alone, Kirstie McBride crouches beside the newly-covered grave. She's not sure whether anyone is listening, whether they ever listen, but what else can she do?

"Nibbles, see that you tell my mummy I make my own bed now. *And* my dad's porridge. He has it with salt. Yucch!"

With that she walks away towards the front door,

passing the big pile of rubbish. But because she's starting to feel just a bit shivery out in the February air, even though she should be used to it, she moves fast and doesn't notice what's happening only a few inches away from her.

The big, white, empty box is starting to glow, from its torn-open insides, tinting the misty morning air with just the slightest touch of green.

9

'SAY NO TO STRANGERS!'

Lunchtime: *Saturday February 16th. Manchester. Piccadilly Station.*

I feel no nearer to Arthur than I did this morning, thinks Zack.

He's starting to realise that distance isn't just about miles – it's about something much deeper inside.

Lily just feels truly hacked off. "*Manchester!*" she cries, looking around the huge city station. "OMG! We're in the North!"

She says it like the North is equivalent to prison or the Arctic. Or maybe an Arctic prison. She knows this isn't very complimentary to the good people of Manchester, but Lily isn't in any mood to be complimentary.

As they step down from the crowded train, Zack protests that it wasn't his fault that the train was a non-stop, nor that they had to spend the entire three-hour journey hiding from ticket-inspectors, nor that they don't have anywhere near enough money to get home again (and

Mum will probably kill them both when they do!). But he doesn't protest very forcefully, because he has a feeling that it is pretty much his fault.

The station seems even more bustling than St. Eustace. Who *are* all these people?

Zack – because he loves stories, especially when they're true – wonders where they're all going and whether they're as desperate as he is to find something rewarding at the end of their journey. But he doesn't wonder for long because here's Lily pinching his arm again, her anger made ten times as fierce by those pointless hours on a train. She would have used her brand new phone to pass the time, but she's scared of it running out when Mum calls again.

"Okay, blackmailer, so now we're looking for an invisible friend, who doesn't exist. In totally the wrong place," she moans. "*See him anywhere?*"

Sarcasm again but Zack looks around anyway. All he sees are strangers and all he hears is chaos, except for the strains of a guitar being strummed somewhere nearby. The fear hits him again like a slap.

"Don't you *want* to find our dad, Lily?" he says.

For once Lily doesn't give as good as she gets. In fact she seems, for a moment, a bit lost for words. A tiny flicker of something glances across her face, softening it for a second, before it finally settles back into her more usual, Gothic fury.

"I want that photo gone – the one you took of me and Ashleigh. And a Big Mac or whatever's big up here. I am so starving!"

She spots a food-stall and strides off briskly towards it, leaving Zack just standing there. A chalkboard beside the stall reads 'SWEETS. OVER 18s ONLY'. Beside it two large men in candy-striped uniforms are questioning a child.

"Watch out for the Sugar Police, Lily," yells Zack.

Lily raises a disdainful hand, but doesn't look back. She doesn't need to, she knows he's not going to let her out of his sight. Not here, not timid Zack.

Sure enough Zack follows swiftly, making certain he can spot her black jacket amongst all the other black and grey and slate ones. Why does everyone he knows seem to wear coats that match their sombre surroundings? Maybe, he thinks, they wear more colourful clothes up in Scotland, so that they blend in with all the greens and the browns and the bright blue of the sea.

Will he ever find out?

He's still pondering this when he trips over a bundle on the ground and falls flat onto the cold, grey station-floor. Less than a second later the bundle yelps. Zack turns and sees, to his surprise, that it is human.

"Oh, I'm so sorry," says Zack.

The bundle stares at him. Zack knows enough from wandering around Hackney (and especially around St. Eustace last night) to recognise a homeless person. He's also pretty sure it's not a great idea to trip over one. He should move on and catch Lily, yet he can't stop himself from staring back. Perhaps because it is this particular bundle who has been strumming the guitar so melodically.

Or maybe it's the eyes – light brown, almond-shaped eyes, shining so very brightly from within the dark and very twitchy young face. The boy appears to be of mixed race and is unhealthily skinny. He can only be sixteen or seventeen, but there's a lived-in wisdom here, in these striking features, and a wary alertness, that Zack supposes must come from a life so different and so much harder than his own.

"Can't you look where you're going?" says the homeless boy angrily, in a strong Manchester accent. But when he sees that Zack isn't getting up from the ground, he softens. "Oh. You okay kid? Did you hurt yourself?"

"Eh? Oh. No. I'm fine. Thank you," replies Zack, politely.

Zack gets up, ignoring the pain in his leg, and immediately fishes some of the coins from his pocket. He offers them to the homeless boy.

"Sorry," he says, "I don't have very much."

"Not necessary, no way," the nervy boy protests, shaking his head more than people normally shake their heads. He grabs for the money anyway. "But… yes."

Now a strange thing happens. In fact, probably – no, definitely – the strangest thing that has ever happened to Zack in all the nearly twelve years of his life so far.

As he begins to drop the money into the homeless lad's outstretched and not very clean hand, Zack notices that one of the coins looks more like a green button. Where did *that* come from? Must be one of Mum's. He starts to take it back – a poor, homeless person isn't going to have much use for a button – but the instant that both their hands are touching it, the button suddenly starts to change its shape and glow. Not just glow, but send out tiny, green beams into the dusty air.

They both jolt away, as if the button is on fire. But Zack still holds onto it.

He is totally mesmerised.

His eyes follow the beams of green, as they seem to hit and bounce off something just a few feet away, but not anything he can actually see. Whatever it is, this imperceptible mass, it appears to shatter and scatter the beams, sending green light flying out in all directions, so that soon the whole station is bathed in a rich, emerald glow.

Yet, curiously, nobody other than himself appears to notice. Not the passengers, not the staff, and – fortunately – not the group of Children's Army soldiers (a different group from the St. Eustace ones), who are huddling by one of the platforms, ready to board a train.

No-one in the whole vast, crowded station.

But the beams don't stop moving. They dart around now, almost as if they're sketching something in the air, an outline of some sort, in a firm but invisible, green hand,

Slowly, to Zack's amazement, the outline begins to take on a recognisable form, filling itself in like a child with a box of crayons. He gasps so loudly he thinks the entire population of Manchester must hear him.

It is like nothing he has ever seen before.

Out of this secret, hazy glow is emerging a tall and very beautiful young girl of around seventeen, with long, blonde hair like an avalanche of buttercups, wearing a glitzy, star-spangled, red, white and blue outfit. It's like those costumes he recalls from the American films he used to watch with Mum.

She's a cheerleader!

One of those amazing, precisely-rehearsed troupes of girls, who rally the crowds at American school and college sport events. Or at least they used to.

"Aaaaggghhh!!!" he screams.

The homeless boy stares at this funny, scrawny little kid, who's yelling his head off for no apparent reason. Then he spies the flashing, green button and snatches it from Zack's hand. The cheerleader instantly disappears.

'WHO WAS THAT?' asks Zack, pointing into thin air.

"*Who was what?* Why are you YELLING at me?" shouts the boy. He looks at where Zack is pointing – and instantly he knows.

His eyes go to his own hand, in which the green button sits throbbing with a curious energy. It suddenly seems less flat, less ordinary. Now it is something of incredible and infinite depth.

"Rolling Stone!" cries the young man. Zack just stares at him. The almond eyes are flashing wildly, the dark face twitching even more nervously. "*Where did you get this?*"

Zack shakes his head – he has absolutely no idea – and takes the strange disc back from the young man. It glows even more powerfully at Zack's touch, as if it contains a whole universe within itself, compacted to a coin's size.

Zack looks around him but nothing seems to have changed. People are proceeding happily – or not so happily – to and from their trains. Lily still queues at a sandwich-stall, not giving her little brother a second glance.

But Zack senses something, or someone, behind him.

Turning slowly, he sees her once again, the teenage cheerleader. She's staring with enormous concentration at the green button in this newcomer's hand.

"*Awesome!*" she says, in the strongest American accent Zack has ever heard. "Totally awesome. You know what this is, don't you?"

Zack just shakes his head. This isn't happening.

"You can see her too!" says the twitchy, young man to Zack, totally confusing him. "CAN'T YOU?"

At the sandwich stall Lily finally decides to turn round, just in case her apology for a brother might have been kidnapped by idiots or squashed by a train. (Which she wouldn't *totally* mind right now.) She sees him with a skanky, homeless guy. Typical.

"Zack!" she yells. *"Say NO to strangers!"*

Zack looks at her and instinctively puts the green thing back in his pocket. The cheerleader vanishes, but the 'stranger' immediately grabs Zack's arm.

"'Zack', is it?" he twitches. "Well, Zack, what do you think you just saw?"

Even for Lily this is too much. Nobody in this life grabs her brother's arm. Well, nobody but her. She rushes back from the food queue.

"LET GO OF HIM NOW. OR I WILL HURT YOU!"

The young man instantly releases Zack. Whoever this girl is, with the excessively white but rather pretty face and the disturbingly black lips, he knows at a glance you don't argue with her. There's something else in this glance too, something that neither of them understands, because it isn't there to be understood. Not yet.

"Wh-who are you?" he manages to say, with a slight stutter that Zack notices wasn't there before.

"Your worst enemy," replies Lily.

At this he smiles, a touch wryly. "You haven't met my f-family. Hi – I'm D-Danny."

"You're getting me confused with someone who gives a monkey's," she says, then turns to Zack. "Know what happens to kids who run away from home? *He's* what happens!"

But Zack is still into what happened just seconds ago. He can hardly get the words out. "Lily, I saw this… I saw this… I saw…!

"Doesn't matter," says Lily, cutting him off. "It's the North. We're going home."

With that, Zack feels himself being dragged through the crowds towards the station exit. He's so inside his own muddled head that he doesn't even hear the stamp of feet behind them. So he doesn't notice the small group of Children's Army soldiers marching straight towards the dusty bundle on the ground.

All he knows is that he can't go home. Not now! Not with what has just happened.

Not when the mysterious-sounding Cape Fury is burning a hole in his heart.

10

'ZACK - WHERE ARE YOU, MATE?'

1.15pm: *Saturday, February 16th. Cape Fury. Highlands of Scotland.*

Cape Fury is no mystery to Kirstie McBride. She has lived here all of her life. So she probably doesn't think too often about how beautiful it is.

But if she were to take a photo from her bedroom-window right now (assuming she'd cleared her precious dolls-in-national-costume collection from the windowsill), she would most probably win a prize. At the very least it could be turned into a picture-postcard, like the ones she's seen for sale at Cape Fury's only shop. She wouldn't even have to do much with the lighting – the Highlands does all that for her.

Straight ahead of her would be the mountains. Huge and powerful, looming over the sleepy, coastal village. But with the morning mist on its last lingerings and the sun not yet too sharp, they'd still have a softness to them. Wearing the remaining clouds like an old, fluffy scarf.

Over to her right, beyond the little houses, the local school and the pub, she'd see the coast curl round and into itself, forming an estuary into which the sea pours with colossal force, as if in a mad rush to get into Scotland. And on the wide, grassy cliff-top, just yards from her back door, are scattered massive lumps of grey rock, some as high as the cottages themselves. Grandpa Brodie says it's like some giant has smacked a mountain in the mouth and made it spit out most of its teeth.

And, of course, on the left she'd see the hill.

Big and wide, glowering over the sea, it's not as high as some of the mountains, but curiously far more threatening. Perhaps it is the total lack of colour, of heather or gorse or brush, that offers no softness to the naked rock. Or maybe it's the fact that the great hill is crowned on its wide, flat top with a huge, decaying castle. The grim work of man.

Once it was a fortress, built to keep invaders away, but it looks like the 'keep out' sign is still firmly in place. Although, if you were to look closely, you would see that men are at work up there, busily restoring it for reasons that are none too clear to the villagers of Cape Fury.

But Kirstie isn't noticing any of this today. She's too busy watching her father, as he ducks into his dusty, white van and drives off down the narrow road to the farm he manages, even though it's a Saturday and she would quite like him to stay at home and play with her. Or even just talk to her. Like he used to do when Ma was here.

It's what they call a hydroponic farm. Kirstie never gets that word wrong, but she isn't totally sure what it means. Something to do with vegetables and water and growing things all year round. She waves to her dad but perhaps he doesn't see. He certainly doesn't wave back, like he used to. But, as Grandpa Brodie says, she mustn't get too upset, the big man has a lot on his mind.

When the van finally disappears round the bend into the first of the valleys, she turns away. Yet this time something catches her eye.

She turns back, as if trying to take whatever it is by surprise, and finds herself looking down at that pile of rubbish her dad is always promising to clear. (If Ma were still around, he'd be keeping his promises or she'd be so angry with him.)

To her bewilderment there's the faintest green glow down there.

You could almost miss it, but Kirstie doesn't. She knows at once that it has nothing to do with the sun or reflections. Something peculiar is going on with that curious white box that just arrived out of nowhere – and she needs to be a part of it.

In the cosy living-room, already cluttered with comfy, old furniture and family photos and the sort of books a primary-school headmistress like Ma would collect over the years, Grandpa Brodie is hanging up yet another item. It's a huge fish in a glass case, looking like it has just swum in and decided to stay. Brodie doesn't see Kirstie, as he hammers a 'fish-hook' into the wall. He seems to be talking to himself, which she knows he does quite a lot these days.

"I caught her in a local antique shop. She didn't stand a chance," he tells the air.

Kirstie isn't listening, she's already out the front door and staring at the empty, white box. The green glow has disappeared. Och well, she thinks, as she turns away, perhaps it was never there at all. Perhaps —

"*Not exactly a Lamborghini, is it?*"

Aaaaahh!! Who was that?!

Not someone from around here, obviously, not with that voice, that accent. Kirstie spins round and sees the green glow again. She was right!

But this time it isn't just glowing, it's moving really fast in a dozen different directions at once. Changing, shifting, beads of bright, green light transforming in the dewy, morning air. Re-assembling themselves into a – well, into a what? Certainly nothing she's ever seen before.

"Hooreyoo? Yoo a kelpie?" asks Kirstie, not unreasonably. (She had heard about 'kelpies', spirits of the Scottish lochs, at school – from her own ma.)

But, of course, Arthur, becoming something like himself again, after being boxed-in for so long, has no earthly idea what she is talking about. Not many guys from Hackney, East London would. Especially if they're imaginary.

"*Oh my days!*" he moans. "She don't speak English!" He looks around, at the unfamiliar landscape. "Where on earth am I? France? America? Narnia?!"

"You're in Scotland," explains Kirstie slowly, like it's so obvious to anyone with half a brain. "A kelpie is a – och, never mind… SCOT-LAND!"

It often helps to shout, if someone doesn't understand you the first time. She's seen the locals do it to tourists. But Arthur isn't deaf, just dumbstruck. Then he slaps the baseball-cap that's fixed onto his bright-green head, as it all begins to make sense.

"*Scotland!* Of course!" He looks around. "So, is my Zack's dad here then?"

Kirstie looks totally blank – who's Zack? Arthur shakes his head in frustration, what is it with this little human? Perhaps, if he started to sing…

"'*A Scottish soldier*'… Er, it's you now girl, join in. '… *Who wandered far away…* '"

"I'm Kirstie," says Kirstie, who clearly doesn't want to sing. "Kirstie McBride. If you're not a kelpie, what are you?"

"What am I? I'm a – I'm an Arthur," explains Arthur, as if this settles the matter.

He starts to stretch frenetically, his odd little limbs popping out like the first green shoots of spring.

"Ever been in a cardboard box? It's worse than being locked in the junior toilets by Thomas Mallory and Amit Patel. Not so smelly, mind. Well, not to start with."

Kirstie can't take her eyes off him. Which is hardly surprising, as it's not every day a little, green creature, with a curious accent and an extra eye, emerges from a totally-empty, white box in her front garden. A creature who keeps muttering gibberish to himself, in a really funny voice.

"Did Zack make me up or did I make him up?" he ponders, loudly. "If you can get car-sickness and air-sickness, can you get box-sickness?"

He moves in such a weird way too, as if one of those teenage soldiers she sees marching on the television had been given an electric shock. Except soldiers don't wear their pants hung low, with a tiny bit of their bottoms showing. And they don't really strut to a funky beat that only they can hear in their heads. (They're not usually bright green with orange hoodies either!)

But now the 'thing' has decided to explore. So all she can really do is follow, as it does its 'Hackney-strut' round to the back of the cottage. She doesn't know Arthur nearly well enough to recognise that the confidence he's showing her is hiding a whole barrel-load of fear.

It's also a tiny bit creepy that, even when he's got his back to her, he's still staring at her with his one rear-view eye.

The mist is clearing now, to reveal an overgrown garden that slopes steeply down towards the sea. There are views of breathtaking beauty in every direction. But Arthur scours the rugged terrain like he has just landed on Mars and it's early-closing day.

"Who took all the buildings away?" he asks, in total confusion. "Where's all the buses and the police cars? Why's the world on mute?"

"You talk funny," says Kirstie.

"No, it's you what talks funny, Cur-stee." He starts to sniff. "Why does the air taste new? And what are those big, pointy things?"

He's turning round and around, unable to take in the vastness, coughing at all the fresh air.

"*Pointy things?*" exclaims Kirstie. "Do you not know mountains, when you see them?"

She turns to nod into the distance, at the bleak hill looking out to sea. "And that there, that big, dark, grumpy thing. That's Castle Peak. *Everyone* knows Castle Peak."

Arthur doesn't.

He can't stop whirling – here, there and everywhere – trying to get the measure of the place. Round and round he goes, like a little, emerald spinning-top. Suddenly he stumbles and completely disappears down a slope. Kirstie gasps but he's soon back, shaking his head.

"Oh my days, I feel well funny." Arthur stares at her in confusion. "I want my Zack."

"I want my mummy."

"Well, just don't tell your mummy about me, okay? She'll probably post me to flaming Africa or somewhere!"

Kirstie glares at him, trying to stop her lower-lip from quivering. You're not going to make me cry, she says in her head. Not you, not anyone. So she just turns and stomps her way back into the house.

Arthur watches her go. If he wasn't totally confused before, he certainly is now. He looks around him, into the biggest, widest, emptiest sky he has ever seen.

"Er… Zack? Where are you, mate?" he asks.

11

'YOU'VE GOT A LITTLE GREEN FRIEND. OR YOU HAD!'

1.45pm: *Saturday February 16th The streets of Manchester.*

Zack is still in Manchester. And his arm is really beginning to hurt.

Which is hardly surprising, he thinks, what with all the people who've been pulling it and gripping it today. His leg hurts too, from toppling over the bundle now known as Danny. But right now neither of them hurts as much as the inside of his brain, as it tries to make sense out of what just happened in that very ordinary, yet suddenly extraordinary, station.

But a tiny piece of him is also puzzling over why his sister was so keen to drag him out of there, when just a couple of minutes ago she wanted to use it for their journey straight back to Hackney.

"Where are we going, Lily?" he asks, trying to keep up with her.

"Away from that homeless nutter. He creeps me out,"

she answers. "Anyway, you should be good at this, Zack. You're always running away from someone." He winces, even though it's true. Lily is looking around. "Do you think they've got KFC up here or is it too posh for them?"

He's noticing more people with plastic bags now and less with suitcases. They're approaching what Zack assumes must be the central shopping area of Manchester. He recognises a lot of the shops from home, but rather than making him feel secure, it just makes him feel that he hasn't moved at all.

"Lily, you won't believe who I just saw."

"You got that right," she sighs. "Okay, so we're going to grab something to eat, then we'll have to find a way to get back to London."

"*London!*"

"It's where we're from, Zack. Live with it!"

Zack feels as if forces are pulling him in a load of different directions and it's all starting to get too much for him. He hears words come out of his mouth that should be threatening – intimidating even – but just sound weak and watery.

"I'll show Mum that photo."

"Yes and then I'll kill you," answers Lily. "So we've got a deal. Ooh look, a tattoo place. *Result!* Bet they're cheaper up here too."

The sound of running footsteps, combined with guitar-strings planging, makes them pause. Then that Manchester voice again —

"*ZACK! Stop, pal. Please!*"

They turn to see Danny rushing towards them, the battered guitar bashing rhythmically against his back. He's wearing filthy, flapping trainers, jeans a few sizes too big and held up with a stringy belt (well, a belt made out of string), all topped off with the sort of jacket men wear on building sites, which is probably where he found it.

He keeps looking behind him, as if there's someone there he would really rather not meet, and every so often he'll dodge in and out of a shop-doorway. Zack doesn't want to think that Danny is a nutter, like Lily says, but he has his doubts.

The words shoot out of the older boy like bullets. He knows he doesn't have much time. "Zack, you saw her, didn't you? You saw Holly!"

"*Holly?*" says Zack. "Is that what—?"

"Just ignore him, Zack!" warns Lily, as she turns to the older boy. "We're not talking to you. Go away, go home. Oh I forgot, you don't have one."

Zack sees the look on Danny's shocked face and realises that this isn't far from the truth. The homeless boy seems about to reply, he's looking straight at Lily, but then he turns back to Zack as she starts to pull him away.

"YOU'VE GOT A LITTLE GREEN FRIEND… OR YOU HAD!"

Zack freezes, jerking Lily back. How on earth can this total stranger know about Arthur? He feels in his pocket and takes out the green button-thing that glows.

"Hi again, Zack," says Holly, reappearing like it's the most normal thing in the world – even when shoppers walk straight through her, without a second glance.

"Who *are* you?" asks Zack, almost quivering in wonder.

This seems a reasonable question. It's not every day that he talks to a beautiful, American cheerleader – who

just happens to be weightless and invisible to the world –
in a Manchester shopping street.

Lily just moans. "Here we go again," she mutters,
staring at Danny. Another sad loser who has to invent his
friends. She takes out her cigarettes and leans against a
'Toy-Dumper', one of the brightly-painted skips that have
recently sprung up everywhere, so that parents can dump
the toys their kids aren't allowed to play with any more.
Ready for the nightly Cruncher-trucks to come and chew
them up.

She starts to light the cigarette, ignoring the disapproving
looks the homeless boy with the interesting eyes is shooting
her way. She bets he has done far worse things than smoke
(although to listen to Mum-the-nurse, smoking is pretty
high up on the list of 'worst things'.)

"Don't be scared, hon," says Holly kindly. "Like the
man says, I'm Holly. I'm his IF." Zack looks blank. "That's
'Imaginary Friend'? It is so great to meet you, Zack."

"Are you American?" asks Zack. He knows that she is,
but it's something to say.

"You got that?" she enthuses. "Only as American as
apple pie! And Starbucks. And if Starbucks ever made
apple pie – wow! No, better yet – pecan. Is that sister of
yours for real?" She makes a face. "Eeu-yoo."

Lily notices that Zack is talking and nodding to thin
air. "Doing that weird thing again, Zack. Come on now."

She pulls him away, but not as fast as she would like,
because the pavement traffic has just become heavier.
There's a big shopping-mall up ahead. Zack is still looking
backwards towards Holly, who has begun to do expert
cartwheels right through the shoppers. Every so often she

pops into a shop-window and leans up against the clothes mannequins, making funny faces. Each move she makes is some sort of cheer-lead.

And no-one — well, nearly no-one — can see her!

Zack turns to look at Danny, who is gazing nervously but proudly at his 'creation'. It is so good for once, thinks Zack in surprise, not to feel alone.

"When I was a little girl," chirps Holly, "growing up in the Californian part of Texas, we'd go up the Empire State Building and see Alaska."

Even Zack knows this is rubbish.

"Holly!" laughs Danny, then explains to Zack. "What did I know at six, when I first thought her up? Hey, I used to like American TV shows."

"Not interested," says Lily, although Danny isn't talking to her.

"But she's a grown-up!" points out Zack. "Sort of."

"I grew up with him, Zack," says Holly, jumping right over a passing policeman. "Kinda funny, I know, but you gotta admit it's a lot better than him growing outa me."

This is all too much for Lily, who obviously can't see or hear Holly any more than she could see or hear Arthur. "Anyone like to tell me what is going on?"

Zack gives her the green button. She looks down at her hand. From her point-of-view there's absolutely nothing there at all.

"Yeah?" she says, shaking her head. "And?"

Zack takes back the button and it glows again, but this time more faintly. Suddenly he feels very scared.

"M-maybe you've got to b-believe it to s-see it," says Danny, looking at Lily.

"You r-r-reckon?" responds Lily, a bit rudely. "Bored now. Come on, Zack."

She pulls Zack into the shopping-mall. "They have *got* to do a decent sandwich in here. Say bye-bye to the nut-job. Tramps don't do malls."

Usually Danny would agree, as it's pretty risky going into a shopping-mall looking and smelling the way he does. But he gazes sharply around him and sees smartly-polished, military boots marching ever closer down the street, with just the glint of black, peaked caps.

Suddenly Danny knows that it's pretty unsafe *not* to be in a mall.

12

'THAT IS ONE HUNDRED PER CENT PURE IMAGINATION!'

2.12pm: *Saturday February 16th. Manchester. The shopping-mall.*

People are staring all around.

Not just staring, but sniffing the air.

Why do people do that thing of pretending to wonder where a bad smell is coming from, thinks Zack. They must know that it's emanating from the homeless-looking young man, with the homeless-looking guitar, who just walked into their brightly-lit (and previously unsmelly) mall.

Zack can tell that Danny is seriously ill-at-ease. To be honest, after sleeping rough all night, Zack Farmer reckons that he himself probably doesn't smell all clean and soft, like his mum does when she leaves the house in her morning-fresh nurse's uniform. Why is he thinking about Mum now? Perhaps it's seeing all the kids in the mall, with their mums and dads in tow.

Lily has immediately spotted a food-stall and is onto it,

pulling Zack with her. But Holly suddenly leaps between them and right onto the top of Lily's head. Lily doesn't feel a thing – she certainly doesn't feel like she has a beautiful, six-foot, teenage cheerleader crowning her Goth-black hair-do.

Looking down on Zack way below, the cheerleader starts to explain. She has to shout really loud, above the shoppers, but of course nobody hears her. She could shout 'Marks and Spencer sell children into slavery' and no one would bat an eyelid, not even Marks and Spencer.

"Zack, what you've got there in your hand, that little, green gizmo, it's what we call a Glimmer."

"A Glimmer?" repeats Zack.

"Huh?" says Lily, standing in her food queue. "Is that a type of burger?

"G-L-I-M-E-R!" spells Holly, a bit unsurely. "Or maybe there's another 'M' in there. Anyway, we IFs all have one of these babies way inside of us."

Holly twirls, right there on top of Lily's head. Deep inside her stomach, Zack can see a small disc-shape suddenly flare briefly. This one is red, white and blue – her colours.

"Ever hear of an IF just dumping one, Hol?" asks Danny.

"*Never!*" says Holly, emphatically. "You see Zack, that Glimmer you're holding, *that is one hundred per cent pure imagination.* It's kinda like our – our – help me out here, Danny?"

"Life-force," says Danny. "When you imagine-up a friend, Zack, as I imagined-up Holly, it's the Glimmer inside that keeps your friend alive and ticking." Zack notices that Danny is getting more and more excited as he speaks. "Same way you and I've got a heart – or a car has a battery – IFs, such as Holly and your green pal, they have a Glimmer!"

Then Danny adds a piece of information that sends Zack reeling. "Zack, there's something you should know. I don't just see Holly." He pauses, breathless. "I see *everyone's* imaginary friends."

Zack is lost for words. Lily isn't.

"It's called being bonkers," says Lily, without even turning round. "Ignore him, Zacky boy."

That does it for Zack. He moves away, his face going red.

"DON'T YOU *EVER* CALL ME Zacky boy!"

Zack doesn't realise how loud he is shouting. It must be all the fear and emotion of the day coming out in one enormous rush. But other people notice, including the two huge Security Guards by the door, who suddenly turn in their direction.

Danny sees the burly men and his voice takes on an urgency, like he knows he hasn't much time. If they throw him out onto the pavement, he's pretty sure who'll be outside in their big boots and shiny uniforms, ready to scoop him up.

"Zack, try pointing the Glimmer at that little girl. You see her – the one over there in the blue dress, with her mum? Do it. *NOW!*"

Zack looks at Danny a bit unsurely, then at the little girl, who seems just like any other little girl. But, as he slowly points the Glimmer in her direction, he begins to see something else. Something that drains the strength from his body, yet at the same time sends a surge of almost electric excitement shooting up into his skull.

Right next to the little girl is what can only be described as a fairy. She's just a tiny bit smaller than the girl, dressed in white, with the usual fairy-wings and wand and glitter, but wearing bright-red ballet shoes. She's dancing those little circles, whatever they're called, round and round her 'creator', who's smiling at her with unbounded delight. The girl's mum is smiling too, but clearly she can't see what the little girl is looking at.

"Okay Zack, now move on," urges Danny. "That bigger lad, *quickly*, by the escalator. With the – whatever it is."

What it is, judges Zack, is a sort of robot made entirely out of household objects, with a vacuum-cleaner for a body and a toilet-brush sticking out the top of his head.

Now Zack is really getting into it.

His heart is pounding in his chest and he doesn't need telling any more where next. He's moving his Glimmer all over the place, upwards, downwards, leftwards, rightwards, like a light-sabre from those movies he's not allowed to watch any more. And Danny is providing the commentary.

"See the astronaut? Yeah? And – oh the Bengal tiger. Look look, *there* Zack, the triple-headed alien! And the purple mermaid! Iron Man! Godzilla! Andy Murray!" Zack is spinning around. "Hey – a chubby meerkat! Wow! *See?* See Zack! "

Danny seems to be getting a bit overexcited himself. He's starting to sweat and twitch big-time. Zack notices out of the corner of his eye that Holly is trying desperately to calm her old friend down, but there's no one calming

Zack down. And right now it is he who is shaking the most.

Everything is becoming so much brighter, the mall itself is filled with a dazzling, multi-coloured, almost supernatural light, radiated by so many luminous Manchester IFs. It's like a laser-show, only richer and more joyous, as all the imaginary friends lend their energy to the proceedings. They spot Zack and wave. He waves back. Some of them nudge their IF pals, look who's here. One of them, a miniature policeman, even drops his trousers and moons at him.

It's as if Zack has suddenly, in an ordinary, north of England shopping-mall, discovered an entirely new community. And, equally suddenly, he wants very much to cry.

Grow up, Zack Farmer!

"*I don't believe this!*" says Zack, not wanting to 'grow-up' at all. Ever. "*Wow!!!!!*"

Danny notices what is happening. He also notices that some of the Children's Army have now entered the mall and are looking around.

"You've got the power, Zack," says Danny swiftly, his eyes darting everywhere. "And with your epic imagination and that Glimmer in your hand, *it's like you're being re-charged every second.*" Zack just stares at him. Danny is twitching badly, he looks really concerned. "What worries me is what it cost a certain someone to give it to you."

But Zack Farmer, age eleven years and ten months, formerly of Hackney but now in a different realm, isn't listening. His bright, brown eyes are aflame, his spiky hair seems almost as if it is standing on tiptoe to get a better look.

"I never knew there were so many!" says Zack, gazing around him, wonderstruck.

He notices that one IF, a little football-player in a Manchester United strip, with three legs (which are obviously really useful, in certain circumstances) is holding up a hand towards him. He wants to high-five Zack. Zack follows the IF's lead and high-fives, sparks flying from the contact.

"You can touch them!" says Danny, in amazement.

"It's like electricity!" yells Zack.

Danny takes the guitar from his back and begins to play. He just can't help himself, the occasion demands it. Even if it makes him a sitting target for his enemies.

Pretty soon every IF around is dancing to Danny's rhythm and singing to his tune.

IFs in the shops, IFs on the forecourt, IFs on the escalators, IFs in the gallery. There's an invisible party going on. Ballerinas are boogying with robots, aliens getting it on with star-troopers, turtles going wild with tigers. The sound is deafening. Holly is doing somersaults in a water-fountain – yet staying completely dry.

It's getting really crazy.

Unfortunately the security guards are clearly not invited and obviously not impressed. One of them comes up to Danny, a mean scowl on his face. "Hoy, *you!*" he says crossly. "We don't want your sort here. Clear off and take your pals with you." He turns to Lily, who is almost at the head of the food-queue. "You too, miss."

Lily glares at him. "But I'm one northerner away from a sandwich!"

Danny looks around fearfully – the young soldiers are

going to spot him any minute. So he turns to the security guards and leans right into their faces.

"I've got as much right to be here as you," he yells. "IT'S A FREE COUNTRY!"

Of course it isn't or Danny wouldn't be able to rely on the Security Guards to grab him and throw him out, which they willingly do. As planned, their huge bodies shield him from the gaze of the teenage soldiers, who are just turning around in his direction.

Despite Lily's hungry pleading, the little gang find themselves roughly escorted by the men to the rear entrance of the mall and thrown out into a different, quieter street. As the cold February air hits him once again, Zack considers what Danny just said to him.

How come, he wonders, with all this imagination flooding around and inside of me, and all this so-called 're-charging', I can't even *begin* to imagine what's going on up there in Scotland with Arthur?

13

'GO ON. USE YOUR IMAGINATION.'

2.30pm: *Saturday February 16th. Cape Fury. Highlands. On the Cliff-tops.*

The thing about Grandpa Brodie, as Kirstie well knows, is that he talks even when no one is listening.

"Then, of course, there was Meathead McPhail. I knew him way back… "

Ma used to say it was because her father was getting old, but Kirstie's feeling is that Grandpa has so many stories inside of him, if he doesn't get them all out he'll explode into the salty sea air.

"… Naturally he wasn't *christened* Meathead… " recalls Grandpa Brodie.

In those days he only travelled up from Glasgow for short visits. But once his poor daughter became so unwell, he had been coming up more often. When she finally passed away back in the spring, he decided to stay. You would think that now he's here for good, the stories wouldn't have such an urgent need to pour out. But this doesn't seem to be the case.

"... It was when they chopped his left ear off and you could see all the wee bits of bone and gristle." Brodie thinks for a moment. "Or was it his right ear?"

They're walking along the deserted cliff-top, with the ferocious, slate-grey sea hammering against the rocks below, almost as if it knows it's in Cape Fury and wants to live up to the name. They can feel the fine, Atlantic spray on their faces. Grandpa Brodie still hasn't noticed that Kirstie is lagging some distance behind him.

And talking to someone else.

It's their favourite walk, especially on a Saturday, when there's no school. (At least not yet!) Not that Kirstie goes to school so much these days anyway, what with it being the school where her ma used to be head-teacher. To be honest the other children are almost relieved, as they don't know quite what to say to her, so they find themselves not saying anything. Which is actually fine with Kirstie – she has hardly been able to talk to a soul anyway, not since everything started going so wrong at home.

Nobody thought of little Kirstie McBride, with her sea-blue eyes and hair the colour of gorse in spring, as a quiet, withdrawn child. But they do now and they wish it could be different.

Eventually Grandpa Brodie – his old binoculars bashing against his even older chest – notices that he is probably his own entire audience.

"You used to love my stories, my wee darling," he mutters, as he reaches an old, wooden bench overlooking the sea. He sits down with a sigh. "Ah well. All in good time."

Up ahead of them Castle Peak looks particularly forbidding, shrouded in mist and dubious history.

Kirstie may not be listening to him, thinks Grandpa Brodie, as he turns to look at her, but she certainly seems to be listening to somebody. Or perhaps she has simply learned the family art of talking to yourself.

Kirstie is not, of course, talking to herself. She's talking to Arthur. Although Arthur does most of the talking. He's quite a talker at the best of times. Yatter, yatter, yatter. But when he's as confused as he is now, the words just won't stop at all. It's what Zack's mum would call 'verbal diarrhoea' – and it's Zack that he can't stop yattering about.

"Cur-Stee," says Arthur, "I'm so sorry, y'know, for what I said about your mummy back then. About Africa. I didn't know, did I?" He looks thoughtful. "Funny, my Zack doesn't really have a dad either. The man ran away from 'ackney years ago. Right back up here to Scotland, so they say. And now of course Zack's lost me too, innit?" He talks a bit quieter. "Between you and me, without his mate Arthur beside him, the boy'll be total rubbish."

Kirstie isn't really concerned about Zack's dad. Or 'ackney, wherever that is. Or Zack being total rubbish. Not today. Not any day.

"My daddy doesn't want to play with me anymore," she says.

Arthur looks at this sad, little girl. And right there, despite all that's going on for him, despite even his total fascination with this weird, new, powdery stuff called sand, his heart goes out to her. All his eyes well up.

For the first time since his rough arrival in this most foreign of parts, he offers up a smile. "Hey, don't you worry, Cur-stee. I'm bangin' at playtime. Here. You watch!"

Arthur leaps into all the wild stuff an imaginary, green friend can do.

He begins with street-dancing, something he assumes a little girl in the wilds of Scotland might never have seen before, as it looks like they hardly even have streets. He reckons he's the coolest of the cool, strutting his stuff, jerking and twitching, turning upside-down and twirling on his head, even matching his body-language to the lash of the sea on the rocks. But there's no smile lighting up Kirstie's troubled face. Not yet, not even a hint. Not even when he turns his back on her and winks his third eye.

O-kay.

So he falls right over the cliff edge.

This sort of stunt is always a winner. It never failed to make his Zack laugh, and Arthur is pretty sure he can hear a little gasp from Kirstie, just before he leaps back up onto land again – *see, no harm done* – and launches into what even he considers a display of gymnastics worthy of an Olympic gold. (If IFs had an actual country, that was on a map and not just in people's heads.)

He peeks up at her face. He's not really surprised that she doesn't show quite the joy he was hoping for. But what is truly surprising is that he's starting to feel rather tired and puffed. This certainly hasn't happened before. IFs don't run out of breath, he tells himself, the main reason being that we don't have any. We don't ever feel tired; we just sleep when our humans do.

What's this all about?

And does it mean I can't even *try* to get back to Hackney and Zack, assuming I knew the way?

Never mind that for now. His main task for today, he instructs himself, is to make this sweet but sorrowful little girl smile. So he goes into one of his sure-fire favourites – his banker – his one hundred per cent smile-maker.

He farts.

Loud and long and fruity. One of the great farts of our time.

And now he waits. And waits. And—

Finally, even though she doesn't want them to, the corners of Kirstie's tiny mouth begin a slow, upwards crawl in the direction of her sad, blue eyes, which give just the faintest sparkle.

Result!

Arthur is well-pleased. He looks at her and decides to offer her something he would never have expected to offer anyone other than Zack. But, of course, this is only temporary and right now it's clearly important to the little girl.

"Your turn, Cur-stee. Come on, girl, look at me – and use your imagination."

What he's expecting is that she'll maybe have him try a bit of light skipping. Or perhaps one of those weird Scottish dances he's seen on TV.

What he isn't expecting is that Kirstie will close her eyes really tight, think really hard, and that when she opens them, he'll look down at himself and discover that he has turned bright pink.

Pink?!!

Or, even worse, that he'll reach his hands up to his mouth and feel that sort of sticky stuff that ladies wear on their lips.

Or stretch even higher to find a headful of tight, little girl-curls, exactly where his baseball cap should be.

She's turned him into a – SHE!!

But he hardly has time to think about how wrong this is – because they suddenly hear a voice. A voice that is soon to become a big and rather scary part of their lives. And Zack Farmer's too.

"Is this seat taken?" it asks.

14

'MY ZACK HAD BETTER FIND ME FAST, HADN'T HE?'

2.45pm: *Saturday February 16th. Cape Fury. Scotland. The clifftops.*

If Zack had been there to see the extraordinary person who just spoke, he and Arthur would have happily discussed her for days. This is what Arthur remembers and misses most – their chats.

"I said, 'Is this seat taken?'" repeated the voice.

The lady is talking to Grandpa Brodie. Maybe it's because the grown-ups are pretty old and shouty, or perhaps they're just trying to make themselves heard above the roar of the sea, but Kirstie and Arthur can hear every word.

"Huh?" mutters Grandpa Brodie, who can't always hear every word.

He looks up to where the unfamiliar voice, which is clearly English and pretty 'posh', is coming from. But it's not the accent that makes his eyes and his mouth open wide, like he's just been kicked in the backside.

It's what the woman is wearing.

Tartan is a pattern – or rather loads of different patterns – made of coloured bands criss-crossing at regular intervals. People in Scotland often wear woolly clothes designed with these lovely, traditional patterns. But they don't usually dress themselves from head to toe in the stuff.

This jolly-looking lady, who must be in her mid-sixties, is sporting a tartan cap, a thick tartan suit, tartan shawl and bright tartan tights. Even the laces of her sturdy, leather walking-shoes are tartan. Grandpa Brodie wouldn't be surprised if she was wearing tartan underwear. (Not of course that he would ask her – so he may never know.)

"*Dear Lord, what have you got on?*" he says, as politely as he can. Which isn't very.

Fortunately, the Englishwoman is totally unoffended. "When I come to a place, I like to soak in the culture. I'm even wearing tartan underwear!" *Knew it!* thinks Grandpa Brodie. "The name is Audrey Ames."

"On holiday, are you?" asks Brodie.

"Oh no, not at all," says the tartan lady. She points into the mist, towards the glowering hill. "I bought that dusty, old castle over there. I'm turning it into a retreat."

Grandpa Brodie can't hide his astonishment. *Castle Peak?* A retreat? Even Kirstie, overhearing, finds this news extraordinary. Especially as she has no idea what a retreat is.

"I knew there were men at work on Castle Peak," says Grandpa Brodie, "but it all seemed awfully secret. What gave you the idea to fix up that miserable old place?"

The woman seems surprised by the question. "Well, actually, I heard this little voice in my ear. No idea where it came from, but it said, 'Audrey – go to the very farthest part of the kingdom.' It must have been my subconscious mind talking!"

"Are you sure it wasn't your neighbours?" says Brodie, then worries that this might be one of those things that sound funny, but are actually rude.

He is relieved when Audrey not only laughs, but slaps him so hard on the back that his false teeth nearly shoot out of his mouth.

"We've got the first lot of guests coming to the Castle this week," she tells him. "Big group. Very hush hush. Well, you need hush and quiet in a retreat, don't you?"

Suddenly something causes the woman to turn swiftly away from Grandpa Brodie. It makes her lock her gaze *directly* onto Kirstie, standing some distance away. Even though she has a kindly look to her face, the way Audrey Ames stares, eyes unblinking under their tartan eyeshadow, makes the little girl feel quite uncomfortable.

Kirstie says as much to Arthur, but he's more bothered by how terribly pink he is.

"Is that your 'wee' granddaughter?" asks Audrey Ames. When Grandpa Brodie simply nods, she continues. "Who on earth is she talking to?"

"I have absolutely no idea," says Grandpa Brodie. "But at least she's talking." This makes him smile with pleasure. "I must tell her father. Not that he'd—" He stops, not wanting to give away family secrets. "Oh, maybe you'd like to meet him, Audrey. My son-in-law, Stuart. He runs one of those new-fangled, hydroponic farms – fresh fruit and vegetables all year long. Unless, of course, you're retreating from food too."

Audrey looks thrilled – she takes out her mobile phone, so that she can take Stuart's number, but Grandpa Brodie warns her that the mountains round these parts make mobile phones terribly unreliable. Sometimes they work, but more often than not they're useless.

"Why don't you just pop round to Number 5, The High Street some evening," he suggests. "It's what people do here. Oh – and by the way, my name is Brodie."

"Thanks for the tip – Brodie," she smiles. It's a warm and interested smile, which Grandpa Brodie picks up and returns. "Now, must dash," she says, getting up off the bench and adding 'okk aye the noo', which is something that Scottish people sometimes say, but not often and not in such a truly terrible, Scottish accent.

"Are you going back to see Mister Ames?" asks Brodie.

"I hope not," she laughs. "I buried him last year!"

Kirstie and Arthur watch Mrs Ames stride briskly back to the little, yellow car she has parked some distance away. But what strikes them both as pretty odd, even for this pretty-odd, tartan lady, is that she seems to be *nodding* to herself. It is as if she is listening quite intently to someone or something. She doesn't have an i-Pod in her ear, she isn't on her phone. So what on earth can she be nodding to?

Brodie doesn't notice this at all. He is too busy focusing his binoculars on the old castle. He's surprised to see that all the windows now have thick, iron bars. Retreats are usually places where people go to feel calm and peaceful, to get away from the world for a while. So why the bars, he wonders.

He turns to Kirstie, wanting to share this puzzle with

her, but there she is a few yards away – still listening and talking to the air.

"If my Zack sees me all pink like this, he'll go mental," says Arthur.

"How would he see you?" replies Kirstie.

Which is true and it makes Arthur very sad. Zack probably has no idea where his friend is, and even if he did, he certainly wouldn't have the courage to come looking for him. Not the Zack Farmer that Arthur knows.

Kirstie can see that she might have upset her new pal. So – with a sigh – she closes her eyes once more and concentrates hard. When she opens them, Arthur is green again and the lipstick and curls have gone. Okay, he's a little bit smaller but he can live with that.

But then something quite disturbing happens. Arthur's usual, bright colour slowly begins to fade. It's as if a pulse has begun all over his body, taking it through all the different shades of green from glowing emerald to the very palest, unable to decide which one to stay with.

Arthur doesn't like this at all. "Can't I keep my nice bright-green colour please, Cur-stee?" he begs.

Kirstie looks at him curiously. "That isn't me, Arthur," she says. "It's not me that's wishing your colour away."

Now Arthur is seriously worried.

15

'JUST KEEP THAT GLIMMER SAFE, YOU HEAR ME?'

3.20pm: *Saturday February 16th. Manchester city centre.*

If I could just talk to you, Arthur, thinks Zack – if I could pick up a phone right now and speak to you – I'd tell you not to worry, mate. I'm on my way.

This is what Zack Farmer is saying quietly to himself, in the heart of Manchester. But he knows that Arthur probably wouldn't believe him. Because Arthur knows that Zack Farmer may be a fine sort of friend, but he isn't any sort of a hero.

The trouble is, Lily knows it too.

So she's pretty sure Zack won't put up much of a fight, when she tells him that they're going to hitch-hike straight back to Hackney right now: A) Because it's Saturday; B) Because, unlike Zack, she has a life; and C) Because they don't have anywhere near enough money for the train-fare home.

"If you live to be a hundred, you couldn't pay me back for today!" she tells him crossly.

She's not just talking about being dragged up to the North. She's talking about being followed by a twitchy, smelly, homeless person, who hasn't just got one imaginary friend, he thinks he has a direct line to them all! And why does he keep looking behind him? (Like anyone would be interested in catching-up with *him*!)

What little sun there was is already starting to go down, as the curious group makes its way across Manchester towards the major road most suitable for hitching. Unfortunately, Lily can't really tell Danny to push off, as he's the only one who knows which road this is. But she's not going to talk to him – why should she give him the satisfaction?

"Where's your little green pal now?" Danny asks Zack.

Zack doesn't answer for the moment, he's staring down into the depths of his Glimmer. It's pulsing, but less strongly. And it's worrying him.

They're approaching a small park that is more like a city-square covered in grass. Zack can see a kids' fairground in one corner, which surprises him, as he thought they had all disappeared by now. But then he notices the sign, in huge, red letters: 'LAST RIDES BEFORE THE FAIRGROUND BAN'.

It's not much of a fair, just a few slow roundabouts with the paint peeling off and tinny music blaring out. But the children seem to be enjoying it and the dads are too, taking videos and smiling just a bit sadly, as the joyous, little faces pass them by. Faces not yet understanding that this might be the last time they'll ever take such a ride.

Lily spots a hot-dog stand and makes her way to join yet another food-queue.

"His name's Arthur," Zack tells Danny, when Lily has gone. He's still looking into the unearthly, green disc. "But my mum posted him to Scotland. To my dad's place. So that's where we're going."

"In your dreams!" calls Lily, who has ears like a bat, when she's not wearing her headphones.

Zack almost doesn't hear this as Holly, shocked out of doing her usual cartwheels, is suddenly right beside him, screaming down into his ear.

"YOUR MOM *POSTED* YOUR IF?!"

She's clearly not the only one appalled by this. Zack and Danny can see two other IFs, sitting alongside their young, human friends on a spinning-teacup ride, whose eyes are bugging out in disbelief. It'll be all over town within minutes. (Zack thinks that his mum had better not ever visit Manchester!)

Zack stops beside one of the more colourful attractions, Old MacDonald's Farm, which features the usual farmyard favourites – cows, chickens, pigs, ducks. There are at least two small children packed into each animal-cab, except for the laughing lamb, which is boarded up for repair.

The ride is being operated by a very round, kindly-looking man, wearing a striped T-shirt and red braces, who's humming along with the familiar nursery-rhyme, as it tinkles out happily through the speakers.

Slipping off his rucksack, Zack takes out the framed picture of himself with his arm around Arthur and shows it proudly to Danny and Holly. The two pals exchange glances, each concerned to be looking at someone's missing friend. A friend who is now clearly beginning to fade.

Then the full shock of it all sinks in.

"Oh, hold the phone!" says Holly. "This little guy actually gave _you_, his human-child, his very own Glimmer? His '_life-force_'?" Zack just nods. "This is heavy, Zack!"

Zack is so busy looking at the fading photo that he doesn't notice the smiling ride-operator, who has begun to stare at him with great intensity.

"Hang on," says Zack, working it all out. "If this thing really is Arthur's life-force, and it's sitting here in my hand, hundreds of miles away from Arthur, then —?" He doesn't need to finish the sentence. They all know what he is talking about.

"He can't last long without it, Zack," says Holly, clearly concerned. "Just keep that thing safe – you hear me? You've _got_ to get it back to him."

Zack thrusts the Glimmer deep down into his pocket, amongst his few remaining coins.

The ride-operator hasn't stopped staring at Zack. Not for a second. In fact, his eyes aren't even blinking now. He has also begun to _nod_ his head, in a very strange, mechanical way. Almost as if he is listening to something. Yet the nods are certainly not in time with music anyone else can hear.

The smile is still on his face, but it's not a kind smile anymore, because the eyes that usually complete a smile have gone small and dead. The large, round face, once so friendly, has somehow taken on a look of pure cruelty.

Beside the man, next to the ride's chugging motor, is a thick, metal lever. Still nodding, he starts to pull it down.

Hard.

Zack's mind is miles away, somewhere in the Highlands of Scotland. But suddenly it's brought right back home again, as a piercing noise bursts into his ears and his consciousness. '*Old MacDonald Had a Farm*' has begun to play a lot faster than it should, at an increasingly loud and damagingly high pitch, that pretty soon only dogs will be able to hear.

Zack looks at the ride. It is no longer gentle. It's whirling now, unusually fast, spinning around in time with the screeching music. The kids in the animal-carriages are smiling – they're enjoying it – because they're sure this is what they're meant to be doing. But inside they're feeling just a little bit scared, just a tiny bit sick. Faster and faster it goes, spinning, whirring, twirling.

Now the smiles are fading, now they're starting to get scared. Really scared. So are their parents, but the ride is moving too swiftly for them to leap on and pull their children to safety. The little ones stare around in panic, their faces a teary blur. Round and around. Faster and faster. Higher and higher. Now the children begin to scream – first one, then a few – then all.

The ride-operator is still smiling and nodding and pulling the lever.

And staring at Zack.

Zack isn't looking at the man, he's transfixed by the frenzied ride, the children yelling, that ear-splitting noise. *What is going on?* Even Lily turns from her food-queue and stares. Colours begin to blend and blur, the kids' faces are like one huge, desperate scream. The sound is deafening. One parent can't stop videoing, his eyes and fingers glued to the camera.

And now it happens.

With a loud crack, like a gunshot, the empty laughing-lamb carriage shears away from its moorings and comes flying away from the ride.

Hurtling directly towards Zack.

Zack can't move, he's rooted in terror to his patch of earth. But Danny isn't. Instinctively he leaps at Zack, pushing him firmly out of the path of the lethal lamb, putting himself directly in the line of fire. By some miracle the carriage just whizzes past him, but close enough to rip away part of his jacket (unfortunately, a part that wasn't ripped already).

The lamb lands in a flower-bed just inside the park gates. Still laughing.

Zack and Danny lie on the grass, stunned but unhurt. Parents snatch up their children. The dad with the camera is still filming.

Lily rushes over and gazes down at her brother, her white face even whiter. "OMG! Zack – are you okay? If anything happened to you, Mum would so kill me."

Zack glares at her, shell-shocked. Thanks, Lily.

But Danny isn't looking her way, or even at the dumbstruck Holly. He's watching the ride-operator, who is staring blankly at them, not smiling, not even nodding any more. Just – nothing, like he isn't really there at all.

Zack follows the older boy's curious gaze and sees the man. But it makes no sense to him.

"*We've got to go!*" says Danny, suddenly leaping to his feet, his torn jacket flapping. "NOW, Zack!" He glances over at Lily. "And bring the 'vampire' with you."

"I was this near a hot-dog!" moans Lily.

Danny hurries Zack away, towards the gates, as parents cuddle their quivering children.

Zack has no idea what just happened or what is going on. Yet, somehow, he knows that he has to let the older boy take him where he must. Once again, he thinks – I, Zack Farmer of Hackney, feel like I have very little control over my life. (And I'm scared, he admits, but of course only to himself.)

Grow up, Zack Farmer!

He wishes Arthur was by his side. Arthur would know just what to do.

Is my one true friend *really* in Cape Fury, he wonders, not for the first time.

Then he wonders, with a fear that goes right to the pit of his stomach – does a place named Cape Fury even exist?

16

'YOU'VE BEEN LETTING HER WATCH EASTENDERS!'

7.00pm: *Saturday February 16th. Cape Fury. Highlands. The McBride cottage.*

If Zack could only meet the good people of Cape Fury this cold Saturday evening, he would agree that they – and their village – really do exist.

But they aren't a particularly nosy lot.

They tend to stay at home and keep themselves to themselves. Especially on a wintry night like this. So there's no reason why any of them should be watching the entrance to their pretty little village, as darkness descends.

No reason why they should count the unusually long line of cars passing the 'CAPE FURY WELCOMES CAREFUL DRIVERS' sign on the road, as they make their way along the coast and up the high, winding hill towards the Castle.

No reason either why the villagers should puzzle over

the fact that all the cars' windows are darkened. Or that they are giving off a faint but unmistakeable, scarlet glow.

No reason at all.

***

Kirstie McBride certainly has better things to do. She has a new patient in her bedroom. A patient who clearly knows how patients are supposed to grab the attention of a conscientious, eight-year old nurse.

"Oh Nurse Cur-stee… *NURSE!* Quickly. I think I've got a nasty dose of acute – er – Peruvian Slobilititis," moans Arthur, really going for it. "I'm burning up here!"

"I'm here, dear," says Nurse Kirstie, in her smart, junior-nurse's uniform. "This should help take the dreadful pain away. You're being very brave, darling."

Her words are awfully kind, thinks Arthur, yet sound just a little like something she has heard somewhere before. A real hospital, perhaps? Or a sick person's bedroom.

"I'm well brave, I am, Cur-stee," admits the patient. "It's me does the all brave stuff back home in 'ackney, innit? You see, we've got people there, instead of just sand." A thought strikes him. "Hey, my Zack's mum's a nurse too! Just like you. In an 'ospital. Oh – and you can call me Arthur."

"You *know* you're not Arthur," says Nurse Kirstie.

Uh oh.

"Oh my days!" says Arthur, worriedly. "Who am I, then?"

"You're Princess Annathesia."

Arthur just flops back on the bed with a sigh, next to more foreign dolls in their national dress.

Princess *WHO?!*

He bets that his Zack is getting on just fine back in Hackney (or – as he calls it – 'ackney) without him. Zack Farmer has probably imagined-up someone brand new and twice as cool.

Arthur (or Princess!) feels a long, long way from home.

But at least he's not the only visitor in the house. Grandpa Brodie is an outsider too, a lowland, Glasgow man. Which could be why he's a fair bit nosier than the Cape Fury crowd. As anyone would tell if they saw the old gentleman this very evening on the upstairs landing, with his ear pressed flat against his granddaughter's bedroom door.

Stuart certainly sees him, as he's walking up the stairs.

"Brodie – what are you doing?!"

Grandpa Brodie gets the shock of his life. He wishes people wouldn't come sneaking when he's snooping. "I'm snooping," says Grandpa Brodie. "What does it look like?"

He turns to his son-in-law, with an excitement that finds no mirror in the younger man's tired face. "Something's happening here, Stuart! Your wee girl is talking again!"

"When did talking ever get the 'neeps picked?"

If this is a well-known Highland saying, it's total gibberish to Grandpa Brodie. "Och, I know you're grieving," he says, "but so's your daughter. For pity's sake man, you're all she's got now. And she's all *you've-*"

He doesn't finish the sentence. He doesn't need to. But his voice is loud enough to bring an angry, young nurse to the door.

"Visiting hours are like six to eight gents. Innit? Oh my days!"

Brodie and Stuart look at each other. What's she talking about? *'Innit?' 'Oh my days?'* Who talks like that in Cape Fury? But then the doorbell rings, which also happens very rarely at Number 5, The High Street these days.

"Who the 'ell is that in my ruddy 'ospital?" asks Kirstie.

Stuart glares at his father-in-law, as he goes to answer the door. "Have you been letting her watch Eastenders again?"

Grandpa Brodie is still shaking his head, utterly mystified, when Stuart opens his front-door and Mrs Audrey Ames strolls happily in. She is bright-eyed and totally tartanned. Stuart is so shocked that all he can say to the curiously colourful visitor is hello, with a huge question-mark at the end.

"*Hello?*"

Fortunately Brodie is there to explain to Stuart, under his breath ("Business opportunity. Be polite!"), before welcoming his new friend at the door. Not that Mrs Ames needs much of a welcome. She is inside the house in a second, with a hugely inquisitive smile on her face.

"What a dinky, little cottage," she gushes. "May I just take a wee peek?"

A wee peak?

If Stuart had his wits about him, he would usher this rather strange, bouncy, English lady into the living-room, where she might blend into the tartan sofa and never be seen again. But her appearance has left him speechless.

So she charges right up the stairs.

It is almost as if she knows *exactly* where she is heading, which of course is impossible, as she has never been here before in her life.

Nevertheless, she's acting like she is planning to move in next week. All that the men can see from down below is her ample, swiftly-receding figure, topped by a bluey-grey head. A head that, for reasons known only to herself, is *nodding* vigorously.

"Why's she nodding?" asks Stuart.

Brodie shakes his head. He has absolutely no idea. Maybe it's an English thing.

Within seconds, Mrs Ames is in Kirstie's bedroom. Nurse Kirstie is almost blown away by this nodding, tartan whirlwind,

"Hello dear, don't get a shock. It's just me, Mrs Ames. I saw you on the cliff-top remember?" How could Kirstie forget! The strange woman is already snooping around. "Ooh, do I spy dollies? Let's hope the nasty toy-crunchers haven't found their way up to these Highland climes."

Kirstie watches this odd woman, who turns about in the centre of her little bedroom, almost as if someone is spinning her. It seems like she's searching for something that she just knows is hiding there.

From the bed the girl hears a tiny moan.

Kirstie turns to see that it is coming from Arthur, now huddled tightly under the covers and looking deathly-pale. He shakes from head-to-toe. What is this all about?

The young girl realises that she has seen this look before. It was on her father's face when he came back from the hospital with her mum, after they had seen the important doctors. It's the look of dread and Kirstie had never wanted to see it again.

Her father comes into her room now, still baffled by the tartan woman.

"*Mrs Ames… ?*" he says. The woman turns sharply, as if she has been in a kind of dream and is just waking up. "Would you like a wee drink?" he offers. "*Downstairs.*"

He escorts the woman out of the room, but the damage is done. Kirstie looks at her petrified patient, lying there so weak and quivery. "Have you taken a turn for the worse, Princess?"

Arthur stares at the little girl with an intensity that is like nothing she has ever seen before. His green eyes are burning in his terrified face. His rear-eye too. His voice is hardly above a whisper.

"You have *got* to keep that woman away from me, Cur-stee. Do you hear me? YOU HAVE GOT TO KEEP HER AWAY!"

Kirstie just looks at him. Why on earth is this cool little guy suddenly so scared? To be honest, the cool little guy is wondering the same thing.

Outside, in the blackness, the cars with their darkened windows are still weaving their way up to the castle on the hill.

17

'I HEAR THEY'VE QUITE A CASTLE IN CAPE FURY.'

7.05pm: *Saturday February 16th. The outskirts of Manchester.*

Zack has an image of the North, as a lot of southerners do.

He imagines that it is always cold and rainy. He knows that this probably isn't true, but he also knows that right now he is standing at the exact centre of a slippery, Manchester footbridge, in the cold and in the rain. It's dark, he's freezing wet and below him is the busy main road going south.

Or further north, towards Scotland.

Lily, as usual, is making all the decisions for him. "Okay, we hitch a lift down there and we're back in Hackney by midnight," she announces. "Rock 'n roll. And tomorrow Zack, I lock you in your room till Mum comes home."

Zack looks at Danny, who is still with them, although to Lily's mind there is absolutely no need, now that they've arrived at the road back to London. Thank you creepy guy, bye bye.

"*What about Arthur!*" protests Zack.

"Zack's right, L-Lily," says Danny. "There's no g-going back now."

Lily glares at him, like she has just noticed he's still here. "Listen. Shut up, all right? He's just a kid – and he's already nearly had one accident."

Danny looks straight at her and speaks very calmly. (Even though, as Zack notices, the older boy stutters whenever he talks to her.) "I d-don't think that was an accident, L-Lily."

Lily just groans at this, but even in the dripping dark Zack can read the seriousness in Danny's face and it scares him. "Is there something you're not telling me, Danny?" he says.

"Yeah – 'goodbye'" snorts Lily. "Don't you have a nice bus-shelter to go to, D-D-Danny?"

Their eyes flare at each other. She turns away before he does. "Zack, get that little thumb out and start hitching," she orders. "Not telling you again."

That special word comes zinging back into Zack's brain. 'Intimidated'. He means to use it in one of his secret stories someday. Zack is well intimidated by his sister, but this time he is also torn. He has heard the expression 'you can cross that bridge when you come to it'. Okay, he's come to it, but he's not yet sure exactly which way to cross.

He takes out his Glimmer, as if this could provide the answer. It is still flashing its pale green light. He can only hope this means that Arthur is still around somewhere.

A woman walks past them, holding the hand of her young son. Zack stares at the boy and begins to wonder again – isn't all this imaginary friend stuff more than a bit childish? Something he should have grown out of years ago, like his mum kept saying.

Could this be the perfect time to put it all behind him? To take the road that leads back home *and grow up?*

He turns to the homeless young man, with his weathered, gaunt and right now very serious face. He sees someone who's not childish at all. Not even with his own IF standing there beside him. Because Holly is tall, grown-up and looking deeply concerned. About something he knows he doesn't yet fully understand.

Zack takes a deep breath and walks across the bridge, to the side that's going north.

Towards Cape Fury. Towards Arthur.

Lily watches this and says a word that could get her sent home from school.

7.45pm: *Saturday, February 16th. The outskirts of Manchester.*

Forty minutes later they're still hitching.

The only change is in the amount of rainwater trapped in their soggy clothing. Except for Holly, who is as dry as a bone and in a state of sunny California. Lily has a face like thunder, which is rather appropriate.

Zack now holds a sign, made from a crumpled sheet of paper that he found in his bag. It reads 'CAPE FURY' in huge, scrawled letters, but it might as well read 'THE PLANET GLOMP' for all it means to the cars whizzing by.

Lily's phone rings. She knows who it is straight away. "Hi, Mum."

She can hear noises of a pub in the background, so Mum must be relaxing after her first Conference day. (Lily could do with relaxing in a pub right now.) She just hopes her mother can't recognise the sounds of northern traffic.

"Hi love. Everything okay?" asks Mum. "Is Zack there? What's that noise – traffic?"

Why are mothers' ears always so good, Lily wonders. Is it something that happens in childbirth? She whispers urgently to Zack, as she passes him the phone. "We're just out for chips – okay?"

"Hi, Mum," says Zack, into Lily's new phone. "We're just out for chips – okay?"

"Well, just don't make yourself sick – okay?" says Mum. "Where are you?"

With a dreadful sense of timing, a small car decides to pull up just a few yards from where they're hitching. A passenger-door is flung open and the group instantly pelt through the driving-rain towards it. The driver is a kindly Asian man, in his thirties.

"Hop in guys, before you get soaked," he shouts above the traffic's roar.

Unfortunately Mum hears him too. "WHO WAS THAT?" she yells.

The kids get into the car, including Holly, who – being imaginary – doesn't take up a whole lot of space. The car-radio is blaring out some news, but Zack is only half-listening.

'In an emergency session today, the United Nations resolved to ban pets for kids and Nintendo for the under 18s.'

The driver shakes his head and switches to Bhangra music.

Danny looks around. He's clearly still concerned that they're being followed – or, at least, that *he* is. But then, on the footbridge that they only recently walked across, he notices someone standing very still, just watching them. Someone not from the Children's Army, yet someone he had hoped they'd left far behind.

The smiling operator from the Old MacDonald ride.

The round-faced man is still *nodding*, the way he did earlier this afternoon. Danny is about to point him out to Zack, but then decides against it. Not when the lad is busy on the phone, telling lies to his mum.

"Zack, are you okay, petal?" asks Mum, wondering why they've suddenly stopped talking to her. "Where are you getting these chips? Where are you?"

Zack answers from inside the car. "Sorry, Mum. I'm on – I'm on the 242 bus. Look Lily, there's Hackney Town Hall!"

The driver is totally confused. Unless he's taken a very wrong turn, they're nowhere near Hackney. "Cape Fury, eh?" he says, to clarify things – and because he has read Zack's sign.

Aaaaaggghhh!

Lily quickly turns her phone off, praying that Mum didn't hear that last bit or she might be even more concerned. Bye, Mum!

Danny is sitting next to the driver, with Zack and Lily in the back. They've hardly travelled far outside of the city before the driver begins to sniff the air curiously. Lily is quick to latch onto this.

"Whatever you're sniffing, it's not us in the back." She points at Danny. "It's him who's the whiffy one!"

Danny glares at her. Zack can see that he seems really upset and it makes him think that it can't be that easy keeping yourself clean, when you're homeless and you don't have a bathroom that you can use any time you want. He's never really thought about this sort of stuff before and he feels that perhaps it's time he ought to.

But Zack starts to realise that what the driver is doing now isn't that sort of sniffing. The man isn't even looking in Danny's direction. In fact he seems like he's in a world of his own.

Funny.

The man doesn't say anything for about fifteen minutes. His passengers don't feel it's their job to make conversation, if a driver doesn't want to talk. It's his car. Then, out of the blue, and in a strange, almost robotic voice, he says: "I hear they've got quite a castle in Cape Fury. Oh yes."

How on earth did he know that, wonders Zack. A castle? It wasn't on any of the internet sites he checked out back home. But the man doesn't seem in a mood to explain – and so the miles go by.

8.05pm: *Saturday, February 16th. Somewhere in Cheshire.*

Soon there are less buildings and houses, more open spaces.

The street-lights grow farther apart, until they disappear altogether. The only illumination in the ever-darkening night is from the cars up ahead. As they drive further into the countryside, even these become fewer, the darkness thicker, like a murky soup. The weary hitch-hikers begin to surrender to their sleepiness.

But not for long.

18

'FASTER, KENNY, MAKE THEM CRY!'

8.15pm: *Saturday February 16th. The Cheshire farmlands.*

Suddenly the car makes a sharp, jolting turn into a narrow side-road.

They're wide-awake again.

Zack has absolutely no idea what is going on – but he knows he doesn't like it. Curiously, the driver doesn't go any slower, so the little car with its confused passengers finds itself bouncing and swaying precariously, as it bumps into the low stone ridges at either edge of the road. They're all thrown against the sides of the car, then sharply back into their seats, then forward once again.

Whoaaaaa!!!

Zack is too astonished to make a sound but Lily yelps big-time.

Yet the driver still doesn't reduce his speed, even though the road is tight and slippery and he is clearly going far too fast in the rain. In fact, he's doing quite the reverse, if you can call driving onwards at even greater speed the reverse. The passengers look at each other and it's not one of those 'isn't this fun?' looks.

Danny is the first to speak to the driver. "Hang on, pal, we're not in *that* much of a hurry!"

But as he turns to look at the man, who's driving more dangerously with every second, he notices that the driver doesn't seem quite so friendly now. What's more, he's doing that strange nodding thing, *exactly* like the Old McDonald guy on the bridge.

Zack notices the nodding too. What on earth is the guy nodding about?

The man keeps glancing at Danny as he drives, all the time nodding and sniffing, nodding and sniffing. Danny doesn't find it very attractive and wishes he'd just stop it and keep his eyes on the road.

"You know what they say," grins the driver. "More haste, more speed."

"Who says *that?*" says Lily, a hint of panic colouring her voice. She's regretting even more now that she came along for this particular ride. How did Zack manage to get the better of her? When did Spider-nerd decide to stop doing just what he was told?

They're being tossed from side to side, from front to back, like a helicopter in a hurricane. Even the driver. But he doesn't seem to care.

"Now don't you wish you were all safely home in bed?" he says, with an odd laugh, which Zack thinks is a pretty strange thing to say to people you've only just met. Especially when you're driving them at lunatic speed down a deserted country lane.

If Zack was scared before, it's nothing compared to

what he is feeling now. He takes out the Glimmer, as much for comfort as anything else. And in a lot of ways he really wishes he hadn't.

Because he knows that what he's being forced to look at right this minute, in this crazy, speeding car, is going to change his life forever.

Sitting up front, right between the driver and Danny, is something that seems very real but is clearly not human. Something so unexpectedly sickening that it makes everything in Zack's body instantly stop working. Except for his stomach, of course, which is going straight into overdrive.

From what Zack can remember in the storybooks he used to read, the creature in front of him would be called a water-sprite. Only they were quite cute and cheeky and this one certainly isn't. Not with his eyes a disturbing mixture of red and black. Made all the more disturbing because the colours glare out like torch-beams and he has never seen pure black light before.

If the eyes are scary, the teeth are doubly so. They're the colour of decay and so pointed that he's pretty sure they could pierce hardened steel. Great for opening-up cans. Or people. And, last but not least, there's rancid, foaming slobber coming out the sprite's twisted mouth and dripping down its scaly chin, which really doesn't add to his attraction.

The only good news is that the thing, whatever it is, hasn't seen Zack yet. It is too busy whispering into the driver's ear.

That's why the driver is nodding! thinks Zack.

But what makes it even creepier, he decides, is that the

driver doesn't look like he even knows what's going on or who's doing the whispering. He certainly doesn't seem able to see what's right next to him – *the creature giving him his orders.* It's as if he's nodding to something going on right inside his own head!

Yet, with the Glimmer in his hand, Zack can hear exactly what the 'monster' is saying – in a rasping voice as cruel as the face it comes out of.

"Faster, Kenny. Make our boy cry. And soon another IF will die."

It rhymes but Zack really doesn't have time to appreciate the poetry, or even the fact that the thing probably wants to do something pretty bad to him – and real harm to Arthur by the sound of it – because suddenly 'Mister Ugly-Sprite' is sniffing fit to bust and turning its monstrous head around.

"There's an IF in here too!" the sniffing creature snarls. "My nose never lies."

That's what the sniffing is all about, thinks Zack. Holly must be giving off some sort of special IF scent. So this creature, whatever it is, can *smell* IFs, even if it can't see them!

The Water-Sprite doesn't look straight at Zack. To his relief its eyes go right past him, and Zack suddenly knows why. He can feel his brain moving even faster than the car itself.

It's because the thing believes that no-one in the car can see him! That it is totally invisible to IFs and humans (especially the ones to whom it is giving instructions, like Kenny the driver!)

But Zack's relief doesn't last long, because the Water-Sprite's eyes suddenly focus on his own, which are, of course, following the frightful creature's every move.

And in that instant the thing *does* know.

"You *see* me?" says the Water-Sprite, clearly amazed and extremely angry. *"You can SEE me!"*

Zack shakes his head, which, when he thinks about it, isn't really the smartest answer. But he can probably forgive himself, because the terror he's feeling right now is like nothing he has ever felt before.

The Water-Sprite's eyes go from Zack to the Glimmer in his shaking hand. And Zack suddenly knows that things just got a hundred times scarier.

Because another weird look is smearing itself across the Water-Sprite's ugly face, as it stares right into the heart of the shiny, green disc. A look of total puzzlement – combined with a confused squeal that all-too-swiftly turns into a threatening growl.

Zack drops the Glimmer in fear and the Water-Sprite instantly disappears from his view.

Meanwhile the little car is racing out of control.

Zack glances at a petrified Lily. She is gripping the door-handle, pulling it backwards as if her puny strength could slow the engine down.

"STOP!" she begs the driver. "*Please*, stop."

"Why?" he replies, laughing. "This is epic. Brmmmm!"

Zack gropes for the fallen Glimmer with his trembling fingers and finally finds it. He catches another nasty glimpse of Water-Sprite, before he thrusts the disc at Danny. The older boy takes it, but it might as well be one of those now-banned M&M sweets, for all the good it does him.

"Zack, I don't know what it is you're seeing, but I can't help you, pal. I don't have the power." He looks into Zack's face. "You've got to do something!"

Me?!

Danny returns the Glimmer to Zack, then looks to Lily and tries to be reassuring. "It'll be fine, Lily. H-hang on."

Which is exactly what she is doing – hanging on for dear life.

There are cars coming from the other direction now.

Their lights flash in the driver's face, warning him to slow down, as they veer away from him in desperation, scraping the sides of the road. Zack can see that the Water-Sprite is still leering and sniffing wildly.

What sort of crazy business have I got myself into! thinks Zack Farmer.

He soon realises that Holly can no more see the Water-Sprite than it can see her. It's like they're from two different worlds. Yet Zack is sure she senses that something cruel is here in the car with them. He can see the panic on the IF's face as she looks to Danny for help. But Danny just shakes his head – nothing he can do. There's no way this reckless little car isn't going to smash right into one of the solid, dry-stone walls coming up on either side of the road.

Yes, there is.

A huge farm-vehicle is coming out of a driveway. This is what the little car is going to smash into. And it's going to be a hundred times worse.

I may have the Glimmer, thinks Zack, but what earthly use is it right now?

Danny looks at the others, reads the terror on their faces and does the only thing he can. He lunges towards the wheel, gripping it with one hand and sending the car even more out of control.

"*Danny!*" cries Lily, using his name for the very first time. "Are you trying to kill us too!"

They're getting closer and closer to the farm-vehicle now, a huge tractor made from thick, unyielding metal. Amidst the screaming and the screeching, Zack knows with a deadly certainty that they're going to crush themselves to pieces. There's no other —

"STOP!!"

It's Water-Sprite, suddenly yelling new orders into the driver's ear.

The smaller car is almost on top of the tractor. Neither can avoid each other – collision seems inevitable. Yet, at the final moment, with barely inches to spare, the newly-instructed driver veers around it at ferocious speed and careers safely away. He finally begins to slow down a hundred yards further along. With an eerie, drawn-out screech.

Water-Sprite is still shouting. "There's been a change of plan, Kenny. This is no ordinary human-child we can just scare off back to his mummy. *We need this boy!*" It stares straight at Zack, but seems curiously preoccupied. Almost – thinks Zack – as if it is picking up new orders from thin-air. "We have to hold him. Here. In this car. NOW!"

What? *Hold* me, not smash me to pieces or scare me off? thinks Zack. Why have the instructions altered so suddenly? Whose instructions? How did the Water-Sprite get them?

And why do they *need* me?

Did everything change when this creature discovered that I could actually see him for what he is? Or was it when it caught sight of the Glimmer?

No time to puzzle it out. He watches Kenny the driver as he nods obediently and reaches beside him to central-lock his car. But Danny is onto it. They hear a twang as the old guitar smashes down hard on the man's wrist. The driver gives a shrill, agonised scream.

"Out of tune, mate," says Danny. "ZACK – OPEN THE DOOR!"

Zack looks at Danny and for a moment he can't move. Until his brain's frantic message finally reaches his arm and he wrenches open the rear-door beside him. Danny does the same with his own door and in a single movement rolls out of the car, which is still moving quite fast.

Zack comes tumbling after, followed by a reluctant Lily. Out of the car and onto the soft and soaking grass. Rolling, scrambling, yelling their terrified heads off.

Holly glides out too, a bit shakily, to join them on the verge.

Zack notices, through the wet mud and weeds, that the car is driving off. He can see, glaring back through the darkness, the Water-Sprite's horrible red and black eyes. In a face that's a mask of pure loathing.

The eyes stay watching Zack, until the car disappears out of sight.

19

'YOU DON'T THINK –
THE OLD LEGEND...?'

8.32pm: *Saturday February 16th. The middle of (English) nowhere.*

Zack's words spill out of his mouth as quickly as his body just spilled out of the car.

"*There was a – a THING!* In the front seat. And it saw me and the Glimmer! It had big pointy teeth and red and black…"

"Yeah, right," says Lily, lying shaken and stunned on the grass, panting along with the others. "Anyone notice a northerner just tried to kill us? What is *with* these people?"

Zack nurses his bruises, wincing as the shock recedes and the pain comes barrelling in. He's never rolled out of a moving car before and he's decided not to make a habit of it.

"When I was scared," he recalls, "my dad used to sing me this song." He starts to sing it. "'*There was a soldier, a Scottish…*'" But he doesn't get very far.

"SHUT UP, ZACK!" cries Lily, who seems unusually upset by this memory. Zack shuts up.

He doesn't see his sister's face, her sudden sadness, because he's too busy gripping the Glimmer and looking at Holly. Naturally, the cheerleader isn't hurt. When there's no substance to your body, thinks Zack, you can't very well harm yourself. But he can see that she's looking pretty shaken-up all the same.

"Danny, we gotta go," she urges. "Shape up, team. Gimme a T, gimme an E, gimme a T-E-E-M!"

Even in his shocked condition, Zack knows she hasn't spelled that one exactly right. Danny tries to help Lily up, but she shrugs him off, so he gives Zack a hand instead.

"Gotta learn to make the darkness your friend, Zack," he tells him.

Zack nods, although he has no idea what the older boy is talking about. How can darkness be a friend? He doubts he'll have Danny's wisdom even when he has Danny's years behind him, but perhaps you need Danny's hard life for that and the pain could be too much to bear.

Holly tries to talk to Zack. There's clearly something on her mind. "Er Zack, honey – that 'thing' you saw. It didn't see me, did it?"

"No, Holly. It couldn't see you." She sighs in relief. "But it knew you were there."

She stares at him. He *sniffs* hard, just the way Water-Sprite did, and she nearly collapses in panic. Zack notices that she and Danny exchange a worried look.

"Hol," says Danny, moving closer to her. "You don't think – the old legend…?"

Lily snorts at this and goes into the worst Scottish

accent ever. (Except maybe for old Mrs Ames, way up in Cape Fury.) "Ooh, the old legend. '*When Great Birnham Wood shall come to High Dunsinane.*' That's Macbeth, by the way. It's a play. By William Shakespeare."

"Didn't he play k-keyboard with the White Stripes?" says Danny.

Lily just glares at him and stomps off down the road, in the direction the car took. Zack grabs hold of Danny's arm.

"Danny," he asks. "Why do they want to hurt us?"

"Not us, Zack," he replies. "*You.* I think they want to do something bad to you."

Nobody says a word.

I wish I knew who *'they'* were, thinks Zack.

But I also hope I never find out.

20

'GET ME ZACK FARMER!'

8.45pm: *Saturday February 16ᵗʰ. Cape Fury. The Highlands. on Castle Peak.*

A few hundred miles away to the north, in a dark, dank, high-ceilinged room in the castle on grim Castle Peak, a meeting is taking place.

It's a large room, because it's a big and very important meeting. But it's not the sort of meeting where everybody is free to put forward an idea and where others listen respectfully, as they await their turn to speak.

Not that sort of meeting at all.

It's the sort of meeting where there are a lot of listeners, but just one voice doing the talking. The voice isn't asking or suggesting. The voice is telling.

There isn't even a body to go with the voice. Just a light – a searing, red light, that bounces off the dripping stone walls and would burst your eyeballs if you stared at it too long.

A light that seems to vibrate according to the words

that come out of it, like a walking, moving, pulsating sound-wave. Only sound-waves don't actually make the sounds, yet this very strange light clearly does.

"Gentleman and ladies," says the voice, which doesn't sound human at all, because it's not. "The greatest opportunity of our wicked lives has suddenly presented itself."

The voice pauses, which is almost more scary than when it talks. Certainly no-one rushes to fill the gap in the conversation.

"We didn't seek this. It came out of the blue. Or should I say – green?" continues the voice, verging on excitement. "Thanks to, of all people, a *mother!*"

You can almost hear the silence in the room. After all, you don't hear stuff like this every day.

"Yes, a mother who *posted* her own son's IF!" the voice explains, in amazement. Gasps from whoever is listening. "But now that it is here, this opportunity – and on such a special occasion for us all – let us be 'imaginative' enough to take the fullest advantage of it."

The voice laughs. It is a laugh without kindness or warmth. But the laughter doesn't endure, because the cruel voice is too eager to get on with the order of the day.

"*Get him,*" it says. "*Get me Zack Farmer!*"

That's the sort of meeting it is.

21

'THEY JUST WANT TO MAKE THE WORLD UNHAPPY.'

9.01pm: *Saturday February 16ᵗʰ. England. The Lancashire countryside.*

I don't think I've ever seen a sky so starry, thinks Zack Farmer, as he gazes upwards.

If his hands weren't shaking so much, he might even write about it, this star-spangled sky above the fine northern county of Lancashire. As he secretly sometimes does, when something worth writing about presents itself.

Lily couldn't care less.

She hates scenery. She's far more interested in the electric lights flickering less than a mile away, down the country road. In what she hopes is a village big enough to have a pub and a pub big enough to have a pie.

"We eat, then we get ourselves home – somehow," she announces. "Cool with that, are we, Zack?"

Zack realises that this isn't a question, or if it is, then it's like one of those ones his mum asks, that don't really expect an answer. He forgets the name of them. All the wonderful words he prides himself on knowing seem to be dissolving in his overheated brain, like ice-cream in a chip pan. But he still has some resistance left.

"Not until I know what's going on, Lily."

Lily stares at her brother. He stares right back at her, which he doesn't often do – he usually gives in within seconds. He's really annoying her now.

Danny watches this and gestures for them all to sit down. He needs to talk to them.

Lily stands her ground for a few seconds, but then sighs noisily and slumps onto a cold, grassy mound, like it was her idea to stay there in the first place. She takes out a lighter from her bag – the flame whooshes as she begins to light a cigarette. For a moment they see the tall trees lit-up behind them. Danny throws her a disapproving look and she bats it right back at him. Whatever.

"I was hoping it wasn't true," says Danny, a bit sadly. "What I'm going to tell you."

He can hardly see their faces now, just the glow from Lily's cigarette. The rain drying on their skin and clothes is making them shiver. Except for Holly, who has other reasons for shivering.

"Nothing else has been true," snorts Lily, "so it's not looking hopeful."

"Ghost-girl is straining my inner sweetness," grumbles Holly and then turns to Zack. He's holding up the Glimmer, so that he can see her. "Zack honey, till now I thought it was just something spooky that we IFs told stories about – on Halloween." She seems very thoughtful. "Till now."

"I don't like scary stories," says Zack.

"Still sleeps with the light on," adds Lily, a bit unnecessarily in Zack's opinion.

"*I do it for Arthur!*" he protests.

"Well, you can stop now then, can't you?"

Danny sighs. He seems truly upset by the way Lily talks to her little brother. "Are you done?" he asks her. She just shrugs, so he carries on.

"Zack, lots of children have imaginary friends. Loads of them. Millions. All over the world. Not just little kids." He looks at Lily. "Bigger kids too. Rich kids, poor kids, kids with snow on their boots, kids with the sun in their eyes. Happy kids, clever kids, lonely kids —"

"Nerdy kids," interrupts Lily, who doesn't care for the way Danny is lecturing. "Saddos."

"No, L-Lily. Not at all. Listen. There's one dreamed up every single second. And I tell you this." He stares into her eyes. "Nothing in this world is as p-powerful as a child's imagination."

Zack looks up once more at the host of stars in the blue-black sky and just for a moment he can see – well, he can imagine – thin, shimmery lines being drawn between them, making all sorts of amazing creatures. Aliens, animals, robots, astronauts – all forming and re-forming with lightning speed. Like a celestial Etch-a-Sketch.

"Well – I didn't have an imaginary friend," snorts Lily.

Danny smiles at her. "Well – j-just imagine that you did."

Lily gives him one of those half-smiles, where you don't really want to, but you can't seem to help it. Holly notices this, and also that Danny has moved closer to the white-faced girl. Like he really wants to kick-start her own imagination.

"You're five years old, Lily. Okay? And really cute." He pauses. "P-possibly. And Tinkerbell is your best buddy." She just glares at him. He has got that so wrong. "Okay, not T-Tinkerbell. Er… ?"

"Little Red Riding Hood!" offers Zack.

"Fine. Thanks, Zack," says Danny, as Lily sighs. "And you and 'the Hood', you go everywhere together."

"Is there a point to this story?" asks Lily, "Because my bum's getting wet and my stomach thinks my throat's cut!"

"Oh, there's a point, honey," says Holly, a bit crossly, but of course Lily doesn't hear.

"Okay," continues Danny. "Now, scroll on. You're nine-years old. You've grown up a bit."

"A lot," says Lily. "I was the youngest Goth in my junior school."

"Fine. Congratulations," says Danny. "Then you wouldn't have needed the Hood any more. So it's 'Thank you, Lily – you've been a good friend to me, but it's time for me to go'."

Yes! I'm beginning to understand, thinks Zack. "*And her Glimmer just fades away!*" he cries. "Her life-force." It's all starting to click. "Hang on – is this what's happening to Arthur? Because we're so far apart – he thinks I don't need him? *He thinks I've grown out of him!*"

Zack looks into the Glimmer, which is still pulsing faintly, as Holly puts her arm around him. He can't really feel this hug, yet somehow he can.

But Danny is looking at him very seriously.

"Looks like it, Zack," he continues. "And, in most cases, that's it. The kid grows up, the IF fades and so the Glimmer fades too. They slip away back to the imaginary nothingness they came from. Game over." He pauses, hardly breathing. "But not in every case."

For a moment there's only silence. Then Zack breaks it. "What do you mean, Danny?"

Danny gets up. He's not sure how to say this. So he takes a long breath. "Sometimes the IF doesn't just fade away, Zack. Even if its Glimmer does."

He pauses. Through the darkness he can still see Zack's bright eyes staring. Taking in every word.

"Sometimes the IF carries on growing," continues Danny. "Not just growing in size, like kids do, but growing bitter and angry and twisted. Fuelled by, well – by bile. By pure hatred." He tries to explain. "Imagine Lily's sweet Little Red Riding Hood as – as an evil old hag. "

"*Like the wicked witch!*" says Zack.

"Something like that. Yeah. Full of resentment and set on revenge. Really furious with the world, because she feels she's been rejected and cast aside by the child who once loved her. Just because that child grew-up."

He pauses and Zack can tell he's coming to the real point of his story.

"So these 'rejects', they want to make the world as unhappy as they are," says Danny. "And *especially* the world of kids."

Lily has stopped listening. Or at least she has stopped showing that she's listening. She is just shaking her head and snorting at the stupidity of it all, but Zack can see by their faces that his two new friends are deadly serious.

"The difference now, Zack, is they can still see all you real guys," says Holly, staring straight at him. He knows that the scariest bit is coming.

"But nobody can see *them* anymore," adds Danny. Yeah, that was the most scary bit. "Not even the kids who created them in the first place. Who've maybe grown up now. Teenagers or even adults, like that driver in the car. These creatures, they live in a – shadowland."

"Works for me," says Lily, which sort of suggests she's been listening to Danny after all – and still thinks it's rubbish. But, of course, she can't hear what Holly says next.

"No-one has any idea, Zack, why some IFs fade away and others don't. But it's said that these others whisper bad things into their humans' ears," says Holly. "Like you saw in the car, right? Telling their guys – the ones who used to be their friends way back – to do all sorts of nasty stuff. And because these guys can't see anything – they don't even *know* they're being whispered to."

Zack's mind is working overtime as he tries to absorb the full horror of this. But, as he looks at Holly, another thought suddenly butts in. "But, hang on – now that I *can* see them… "

Holly doesn't even wait for him to finish. "I'm thinking, honey, that maybe you should just go straight home now. N-O-W-W."

Zack looks at her, then takes out the framed photo from his bag. There's no doubt about it, Arthur has faded even more.

"But that's what they want, isn't it, Holly?" he says. "For me to go H-O-M-E… Er, home." Zack is just beginning to work it all out in his tired, muddled and pretty scared head. "They want to stop me getting to Arthur. That's why the guy was driving so dangerously. To scare me off and keep me from finding my IF, so I won't give him his Glimmer back." He looks pale, even in the darkness. *"They want to make Arthur fade away and die!"*

"Sure they do. Because they hate IF's – and they enjoy making kids unhappy," says Holly.

Zack's mind can't stop whirring, like an overheated engine. "But then why did they suddenly change their plan and want to *kidnap* me?"

Danny and Holly look at him. It's a look that seems to say they know a lot more, but aren't telling. It's a look that sends a chill through his already shivering body.

It's a look that says – you don't want to know.

Lily sees Danny's look and decides it's time for her to move on to the pub. And away from these lunatics.

"I'm not scared," Zack says defiantly. "I'm not scared of anything. I'm well hard, me."

Just then a small, black cat comes out of the long grass and brushes against him.

Zack screams long and loud into the cold, dark night.

22

'PRINCESSES DON'T FART.'

9.10pm: *Saturday February 16th. Cape Fury. Highlands. The McBride cottage.*

Zack isn't the only one screaming this chill Saturday night.

But it takes more imagination than even he's equipped with to hear his old friend crying out to him through the Scottish darkness.

Stuart McBride can't hear Arthur's cries and he's just down below in his back garden, hammering in some new fence-posts by the light of the stars. Wondering whether he should look in on his sad, little daughter upstairs, but knowing somehow that his battered mind and shattered heart aren't going to let him.

PC McKay, the local Cape Fury policeman (in fact, he's the entire Cape Fury police force!) can't hear them either. All he can hear is the sound of his own teeth and gums, as they demolish the huge bag of chips he has just bought. Well, not quite all. He can also hear the squeak of his saddle – more of a groan, actually – as it struggles under the weight of what could be the largest police bottom in the Scottish Highlands.

He tells Mrs McKay that it is his duty to do his rounds at this time every night, just to check that the sleepy village is actually asleep. But Morag McKay knows that it is really to collect his nightly bag of chips, just as the local fish and chip shop is closing up.

In fact PC McKay is so busy enjoying his greasy bedtime-snack that he doesn't bother to look up at the castle on the dark hill above the sea. So he isn't wasting a second in wondering why it is bathed tonight in such a powerful red light.

He doesn't even notice the little yellow car that he's cycling straight past. The one parked directly opposite Number 5, The High Street, Cape Fury. The one with its driver still inside.

Arthur notices, however. Or he soon will, once he stops screaming in his bed.

"Princess Annathesia?" says Kirstie, worriedly. "Did you have a bad dream?"

"I'll say, Cur-Stee," he shivers. "I dreamed my Zack was brickin' it. Er, that's English for scared." He looks suddenly thoughtful. "Hey, when *isn't* my Zack scared? I suppose it's because he doesn't have a dad."

Arthur gets up and starts pacing the room – and farting. But this time not for the fun of it. "Oh man," he moans. "I should never have left it!"

Kirstie looks confused. "Left what? Your 'ome in 'ackney?"

Arthur shakes his head. But how can he tell her about the Glimmer he left behind? She watches as a tiny, green tear glides down his cheek, and another down the back of his neck, as he turns to the window. Suddenly he starts to shake like he did before, only this time worse. Much worse.

"It's that woman again!" he yelps, as he sees the parked yellow car. "The old one who looks like a bedspread. I don't know what it is, but there's something not right about her. YOU'VE GOT TO KEEP HER AWAY FROM ME!"

Kirstie looks out of the window, clearing away her national dolls. "It's just that Mrs Ames. She's English, they're weird. I'll protect you, princess."

Arthur looks at her, then back at the yellow car. Even in the darkness he can just make out that bluey-grey head. Alone in the night.

Nodding.

Suddenly the door opens and Arthur jolts, like he's been stung. But it's only Grandpa Brodie.

"I thought I heard you get up," he says. "Are you okay, darling?"

"Uh huh," says Kirstie, then adds "Grandpa, I know it's very late but…" She hesitates. "Is Daddy coming to read me a story tonight?"

Grandpa Brodie looks quite sad. This shouldn't be his job. He's too old.

"Er… not tonight, poppet. But soon. You'll see. When the stories in his head are nice ones." He kisses her gently and looks at her beautiful, sleepy face. "You look so like your —"

She knows he was going to say 'mummy'. But he doesn't say it. He smiles instead, a cheeky, knowing smile.

"So, what's your wee friend doing now?"

Kirstie looks up at Grandpa Brodie in astonishment.

But she's not unhappy that he's guessed. After all, it isn't a secret.

"She's farting," explains Kirstie. Then she turns to Arthur. "Princesses don't do that."

"Well, I'm very glad *I'm* not a princess," says Grandpa Brodie.

Then he does something rather odd. He looks up into the sky and just smiles. It's a sweet, loving smile. Kirstie doesn't notice. She has turned back to Arthur, who is still looking out of the window – and still shaking.

"Zack," he mutters into the Highland sky. "I dunno if you're coming for me. Probably not. It's not really your style, innit? But if you are, matey, best not be too long about it, eh?"

And then he farts again.

23

'WAITING FOR YOU ALL THEIR LIVES.'

9.30pm: *Saturday February 16th. Lancashire, England. A country village.*

Zack would love to think that his tired feet are taking him closer to Arthur.

But right now it just seems that his ever-hungry sister is taking him closer to a pub. Or at least Lily is hoping that's what those lights are up ahead, blinking out of the country darkness.

Zack knows she's still not the least bit interested in imaginary friends, not even in those secret, whispery ones who get all bitter and angry. And he can tell she doesn't believe a single word Danny has been saying.

To Lily, what happened in the car back there was just a bad hitch-hike with a mad driver. She's probably thinking, reckons Zack, that even she – under-age, unlicensed Lily – could drive Mum's car better than that idiot drove his. (Zack has seen her drive and he's not so sure.)

They pass a noticeboard with a poster advertising a

movie – an adventure film that looks like something Zack would really like to see. But there's a sticker slapped right across the poster, in bright red, saying 'CANCELLED'. Then, in slightly smaller, but just as depressing, lettering: 'Forever'. It isn't the first time he has seen a poster like this – they're everywhere these days – but it just adds one more item to the list of things he feels that he, and a lot of others like him, are missing out on.

Heaven knows why.

He suddenly senses some movement from Holly, on the dark road beside him. He turns to see that she is twisting her body into what looks very like the shape of a letter. The letter 'R'. Zack realises she's trying to tell him something. Or spell him something. Something really difficult. Especially if you're a rotten speller like Holly.

"We call them…" She stops, clearly scared. Her voice is unusually quiet. "I don't even want to say their name out loud, Zack."

He notices that she is looking to Danny, as if for help. Danny stares at her then closes his eyes tight, his face becoming intensely thoughtful. And suddenly, before Zack can respond, there are six identical Hollies beside him, each imagined by Danny. Each taking on the challenge of a different capital letter.

Zack tries to work it out. He even says it out loud.

" R-O-G-E-U-S. What's Rogeus?"

Two of the contorted Hollies swiftly change places.

"Oh – ROGUES!" shouts Zack, still puzzled. But Lily is there and is impressed.

"Wow Zack, your eyes! You can read pub names from

this far away?" She sighs, "I just hope 'The Rogues' does a serious sandwich."

They're on the edge of the sleepy village now. The first building is a small primary-school, an old, grey-stone, Victorian structure, with its small playground. Obviously it's empty at this time of night, yet the playground feels not just closed but lifeless. There's no equipment, no basketball-hoop or goal-markings. No climbing-frame. No fun.

The six Hollies slip through the railings and instantly perform a cheerleading routine, as if they've been performing it all their lives. One of those half-song, half-poem chants.

"Rogues hate little kids to bits.
Rogues hate IFs double.
Cos we make kids H-A-P-P-I.
We want love, not trouble!"

Not a song people will be rushing to download, thinks Zack, yet he watches in amazement as the Hollies end their routine by forming a perfect pyramid with their bodies.

"But what's all this 'ROGUE' stuff got to do with me and Arthur?" he says.

"Think about it, Zack," explains Danny. "When your Arthur fades away, that Glimmer he left you will just die with him. You won't be able to rely on it any more."

The Holly right on the top calls out to Zack, by way of explanation. "So that's one less IF on the scene – and two less prying-eyes. *Yours.*" She looks hard at Zack. "We said that we IFs can't see who the Rogues are, Zack. Nor can Danny or any other human." She looks down to a fellow Holly to complete the thought.

"But for some reason, Zack," says Holly 2, "as long as you're holding that Glimmer, you *can* see them! You've got the power and they don't like it."

The Hollies all go 'yeah', because this is really impressive stuff.

"O-kay" says Zack. He can understand that the Rogues would really want to stop anyone seeing them. (If you looked that hideous, wouldn't you?) And especially people like Zack, who could catch them whispering orders into grown-ups' ears.

But something is still bothering him, something he can't quite put his finger on. "That 'Rogue' in the car. He stared really hard at me – like I was something he *wanted* – not like something he just wanted to get rid of!" Zack is so puzzled. "It was like I was – something special."

"Special needs," mutters Lily unkindly and looks at Danny. "Like 'Mr Big Issue' here."

Suddenly the Holly pyramid collapses, as if from the weight of all this scary talk, and the cheerleaders end up in a flailing, struggling heap of arms and legs. They look to Danny, but he shakes his head. He can do no more – his imagination is all used up.

Instantly Zack is there, gripping the Glimmer really tightly in his hand and staring intently at the pile of Hollies in the playground. Without even blinking.

Nothing is happening. So he stares even harder, narrowing his eyes, holding his breath.

Using his imagination.

Very slowly a few more Hollies appear from nowhere, out of the darkness. Then even more of them. Soon the others on the ground see them and scramble up to join them.

Confidently, as if they have been doing this all their lives, they climb on each other's multi-coloured legs, arms, backs and heads, until they form a structure more complicated than the most complicated geometry lesson. Like something no one – not even Zack – would ever have seen before.

Like something impossible.

All twenty-six Hollies – that's how many there are now – are staring at him, arms outstretched, legs high, mouths open. *A mountain of Hollies!* The one on the second-from-bottom row, in the very middle, is the first to speak.

"There you go!" she says, full of respect. "See Zack, look what you just went and did. Man, you were born with one awesome imagination!"

"Thank you – er – Holly?" he says, thinking about the fantastical stories he writes and the colourful pictures that go through his mind all the time. Even when he's asleep. And, of course, I mustn't forget my greatest 'creation' of all, he tells himself. *Arthur!* Not that Mum or the sniggering kids in my class would exactly share that view. But Holly Number 14 clearly hasn't finished.

"But thanks to your buddy leaving you his Glimmer," she continues, "that great imagination of yours has just been TURBOCHARGED!" She whoops. "You are cooking, guy!"

Zack smiles but then realises that all the Hollies are looking seriously concerned.

"And that's the problem," says Holly Number 22.

Problem? thinks Zack. How can so much imagination be a problem?

"The Rogues have been waiting for you, kiddo." another Holly tells him. "Or someone like you. We don't know exactly why, but it feels like they've been waiting for you to come along all their rotten lives. That's why they wanted to hold you prisoner in the car."

Zack's stomach feels like it's falling into his boots. And it isn't from hunger.

"The Hollies are right, Zack," says Danny. "You *are* special, pal."

That word again!

Lily turns and wonders why her dozy brother is staring so hard at a totally empty playground. "Praise from a homeless stutterer," she mocks, glancing at Danny. "Life doesn't get much better than that."

"Shut up, Lily," yells Zack. Then adds, with a shout: "I DON'T *WANT* TO BE SPECIAL!"

I just want to be Zack, he thinks. Normal, boring, timid, slightly odd, small-for-his-age, not exactly grown-up Zack.

He stuffs the Glimmer deep down into his pocket and walks quickly away from the school, away from all the Hollies, and towards the cosy pub with its golden light spilling out onto the street.

"I can smell food," cries Lily, rushing past Zack to the door. "*Result!*"

For once, Zack is with his sister. I just want life to be ordinary, he thinks, as it used to be. I'm not one of those schoolboy heroes or junior wizards, like out of the old, banned storybooks.

And what could be more ordinary than an English village pub?

24

'STAY RIGHT WHERE YOU ARE, ZACK FARMER!'

9.45pm: *Saturday February 16th. Lancashire, England. An ordinary village pub.*

The pub does indeed feel warm and snug this damp, Saturday evening.

Zack looks around. It's full of villagers, mostly farmers and country-people, chatting and laughing contentedly beside the open fire. Enjoying their night-out together. He begins to relax as he and his companions receive the first smiles they've had all day, the biggest coming from the stocky, ruddy-faced man behind the bar.

"Ah, strangers," says the landlord, in a deep, welcoming voice. "Welcome to Little Rumston." He glances at Danny, who looks well over eighteen. Sometimes, thinks Zack, the poor guy looks a hundred and eighteen. The man then turns to Lily, who clearly wants a grown-up drink and is clearly not going to get one. "You look pale, love."

"It's make-up!" she moans. "You'd think nobody'd seen a Goth before! Is that last sandwich going spare?"

"What about us?" protests Danny.

"You're homeless," retorts Lily. "Your stomach's probably shrunk."

Zack is starting to calm down. Especially when the man agrees to give them Cokes all round (despite Lily's protests that she's really eighteen, but has a youthful personality). He also offers to make a load more sandwiches, so they can all have supper together.

The gang take the only free table and wait in weary silence, lost in their own thoughts. The events of that unusual day – the crazy roundabout, the hitch-hike from Hell – seem like scenes from a scary movie, the sort of movie kids aren't allowed to watch any more, thinks Zack. Perhaps it's just as well. Being scared isn't as much fun as-

"*Zack*," says Danny, interrupting the younger boy's quiet thoughts. "Keep smiling, but turn around very slowly. And take a good look at that group of people in the corner."

Zack freezes at Danny's words, the smile on his face freezing too.

Slowly, he turns around to see that some of the villagers, guys who had looked so friendly when the group first arrived, are now staring at them in a far from friendly way. They're still smiling but the smiles are just slits in their vacant faces.

Worst of all – they're nodding.

It's that peculiar nod again, thinks Zack, as if each one of them has their own special beat in their head.

Or their own special orders.

Then a few of them begin to sniff.

The fear Zack thought he had left at the door comes thundering back in. It isn't helped by Danny's next, whispered words.

"Now the Glimmer," he says. "Slowly does it." Zack doesn't move. "*Zack!*"

Zack gently removes the flickering, green disc from his pocket and holds it in his shaking hand. What he sees brings whatever little food he's still got in his stomach surging back up into his throat.

Beside each of the nodding customers is a grown up, grown big and grown extremely bad imaginary-friend. These must be what Holly calls 'The Rogues', thinks Zack, with a shudder. At one time they would have been cuddly, little storybook characters or friendly Martians, good-natured heroes or amiable animals. Once. Now they're huge, drooling, slobbery, evil-faced creatures, scaly and lumpy, with vicious, pointy teeth and – most scarily – identical red and black beaming eyes.

Zack understands the nodding. These ordinary countrymen and women, usually so decent, are having bad instructions whispered into their ears by their old childhood friends. *And they have absolutely no idea!* Their former IFs, who once did whatever their young 'creators' asked, are now controlling them.

What makes these Rogues suddenly turn up, Zack wonders – or are they here all the time?

Zack can't take his eyes off them, even though they are the most terrifying creatures he has ever come across in his life. But what is truly scary is the direction they are aiming their malevolent stares. It isn't into his face or his eyes, but straight into the Glimmer itself. His Glimmer –

no, Arthur's Glimmer. Just like that mad Water-Sprite did in the car.

It's like they're trying to suck the special energy out of it, he thinks, and take it into their own, horrible selves.

As if it is the most desirable object they have ever seen.

And now Zack spots that the creatures – these Rogues – have begun to sniff. They must be sensing that there's a real IF around. One they can't see but to whom they'd still like to do some serious harm. He looks at Holly, who, of course, can't see them either, yet is clinging on to Danny and is clearly terrified.

It's the landlord's comforting words that nudge him back to reality. "Is everything alright, son?"

Zack can't seem to draw his gaze away from the 'ropey roomful of rabid Rogues'. (Why is he thinking in stupid 'word-pictures' at a time like this!) But he manages to talk over his shoulder to the kindly man.

"Can you help us, please?" he begs the jovial fellow, as his friends look on in wonder.

"Help you?" the man replies. "Well now. I don't think so."

Huh?

Zack slowly turns. The landlord's gentle smile has vanished. And been replaced with a series of stern, robotic nods.

Now a strange sort of drumming fills the air, as Zack moves his Glimmer round towards the bar.

The noise is coming from right beside the man – and is being made by what has to be the most fearsome Rogue he has seen so far. A very tall and very angry-looking toy soldier. He's banging his tin drum in a loud, demented frenzy, as his once-friendly eyes flash red and black. At the same time he is whispering in the unsuspecting landlord's ear.

The big man is still nodding, as he reaches under the counter. And it isn't for tomato ketchup. What he produces is a large shotgun – and an equally grim warning. "Maybe you should stay right where you are – Zack Farmer."

Zack can't move. How did the man know his name? *What is going on here?*

He suddenly feels himself being grabbed. And screams.

To his relief it's Danny who's pulling him and Lily away from the angry villagers and out of the pub.

Zack has no idea where he's going. But, as they rush out into the darkness, he really wishes he was safely back home in Hackney with his mum.

25

'WE FREAKS HAVE GOT TO STICK TOGETHER.'

10.00pm: *Saturday February 16th. Edinburgh, Scotland. The City Hotel.*

Of course, Mum isn't actually back home in Hackney.

She's sitting up in bed in her neat Edinburgh hotel room, just next to the conference centre. Her sandwich is an inch from her mouth, yet she hasn't taken a single bite. What she is looking at on her TV screen has quite taken her appetite away.

It's a home-video, made in a Manchester fairground by the father of a young child. He must have taken it to the TV news people, who clearly felt it deserved a wider audience. It shows a loose carriage from a children's merry-go-round breaking away from its moorings at ferocious speed. You can see it hurtling towards a small, spikey-haired boy, who's standing beside an older, pale-faced girl.

Mum just stares in horror.

Zack? Lily?

Manchester?!

If Zack and Lily weren't in such a state of terror, they might find it funny that while Mum doesn't know where to find them, a bunch of total strangers does.

Zack can see that the angry villagers aren't far behind, still nodding as they pursue them through the dark and narrow streets. Some carry sticks, some wield home-made clubs – others brandish torches and flames.

"How do these guys always know where we are?" yells Zack. "And what makes *me* so important?"

The words come out ragged. Probably because I'm pelting through the streets of a strange village, he thinks, at a speed I didn't know I could reach. Nought to panic in fifteen seconds.

An expression he once heard comes rushing back into his head. I'm running scared.

Despite his longer legs, Danny lags well behind him. Zack turns round and instantly knows why. You're not at your healthiest when you're homeless. You don't find your five-fruit-'n-veg-a-day so easily, when you're scrabbling around in dustbins for food, alongside the rats. But Danny is making it look like he has slowed down for Lily, so that she doesn't feel so lost and alone. Zack admires how he does that.

Holly, as always, is by Danny's side. But Danny can see that she's frightened, in a way that he has never seen her frightened before. Because he has never imagined her frightened.

"Come on, Hol, it'll be fine," he says, wanting to reassure her.

Danny turns to check on Lily. To his amazement she has her phone out and is trying to tap a number, but her hands are shaking too much. The villagers are getting closer. He sees grown women hurling stones they've picked up from the roadside.

It's like the world has gone mad, he thinks, then ponders that his world always was.

Zack glances back too and his view is far clearer than that of the others. Unfortunately. Still holding the Glimmer, he alone can spot the frenzied Rogues urging their villagers on. The poor humans don't suspect a thing.

But now something quite unexpected happens. Once he sees his sister's fearful yet disbelieving face he senses another feeling uncurl deep inside of him. A feeling he has never experienced before. If it wasn't so unfamiliar, he might even call it bravery. Or its rasher cousin – bravado. He holds up the Glimmer.

"It's this that they want, isn't it?" he shouts.

Lily stares at him. All she can see is her brother's empty hand. "Skin, yeah. That'll keep them sweet."

But now Zack is running even faster, moving even further away from them all.

"*Zack!*" cries Lily, then turns to Danny. "We can't like just leave him." (First time she's ever said that!)

"Yeah," says Danny. "L-like we just can."

He pulls Lily down a tiny alleyway, between two ancient workmen's cottages, with Holly following. At the same time he calls to Zack, who is belting down the main village road. Leading his pursuers away into the night.

"Remember…"

"*Make darkness my friend!*" responds Zack, through

the sweat and the panting. Now I understand, he says to himself. Well, I understand a bit. Sort of. Still scary, though!

Zack is running pretty fast, but he realises there'll come a time very soon when his energies will be all used up. A time when he will have to hide from the crazy mob and just hope that they pass him by. But where?

He scours the landscape, with only the dim moonlight to help him. He's a city boy. He's used to lights and people – and not being out alone in the dark. All he can see here, or sense through the blackness, are fields. There's no cover anywhere, except the skimpy blanket of night.

He feels the ground beneath him change. He's on the edge of a muddy track, leading away from the road and into uninterrupted nothingness. Probably just more fields. Without even thinking, he takes it. There's a pain in his chest he's just beginning to notice – is it the fear shooting back in or the bravado trying to escape?

Should I just give up? How much farther can I —?

A church!

The track has led down to an old Norman structure, cloaked in mist. He rushes towards it, splashing through mud and stone, and bangs on the wooden doors. Nothing. They're clearly locked. No cover here, just a load of gravestones all gnarled and broken. Reminders of death everywhere. He reels backwards and his foot gives way. He's slipping into something, struggling to keep his balance.

It's a newly-dug grave. Not for him he hopes. Not yet.

The pain is getting so much worse. It's in his legs now. He flees round the back of the church, without much hope of salvation.

Before he can see it, he bangs into a post sticking up from the side of the road. Something metal glances his head. It must be an old farm-sign that has slipped down into the mud. Yes, there's a farmyard here, right next to the church. But he can't hear any animals. All he can see, through the slivers of moonlight, is – junk.

Junk?

It's a dumping ground, full of rusty, old farm-equipment, long since out of use.

His breath is coming so fast, and his heart is pumping so fiercely, that he is sure they can hear it in Hackney, let alone in the village streets nearby. All he can do now is hide, which he does, behind an ancient, yellow digger. Knowing that it is only a matter of time before his new enemies find him and drag him out. And then what – kidnap? Worse? Funny, he thinks, the digger reminds me of a toy I had as a little boy. Before all toys were banned. How long ago and far away does that feel?

He hears footsteps – they've guessed where he's hiding, they're getting closer.

Zack peeps out and his face just misses the beam of a villager's torch, as the locals scour the yard. He recalls that he still has the Glimmer in his hand. Trying not to let it send out too much of its powerful, green light, he just manages to glimpse the leader of the Rogue ring. The landlord's vicious toy-soldier.

Zack expects the worst – but not what the drumming Rogue says next.

"Leave him, men!" it calls, in a chillingly high-pitched voice. "Zack Farmer isn't going anywhere."

The other Rogues laugh and begin to walk off, along

with the villagers under their command. Zack watches them in total puzzlement. *Leave me?* Why on earth would they leave me now, just when I'm theirs for the taking?

He's about to get up and move on to safety, when he hears it.

The roar of a mighty engine, making the ground beneath his feet tremble. He jolts in blind panic, as the lights of the rusty, old digger he has been leaning against suddenly flare into life.

Lights?

His panic isn't blind any more, but his eyes are seeing what his mind can't quite believe. The huge scoop of the digger is slowly rising, with an unearthly creak, as it tries to lift him up. With a gasp that's more like a squeak, Zack swiftly backs away. But to his horror he glimpses, inside the lit-up cab, someone he never expected to see again. It's the smiling operator from the Old MacDonald farmyard ride, slowly nodding his head.

Yet this time Zack knows for sure that the man is not alone. Thanks to the Glimmer he can make out that seated right there with him, in the cab, is an over-large Pinocchio. Grinning like a demon, his boyish charm a thing of the past. That long, wooden nose points outwards like a spear.

Zack is just taking in this latest Rogue, when another, different noise bubbles up from somewhere beside him. Something even more chilling.

He tries to run but – blinded by the digger's lights – he bangs hard into a second huge machine. His legs scrape on something sharp. A massive, old combine-harvester, its lethal blades already rotating. Ready to rip him into mulch if he moves any closer.

Zack stops dead, paralysed with fear, as the next shock batters his already fragile frame. There, in the cab of this latest machine, is another recent acquaintance: Kenny, the driver from the motorway. And, of course, he's being secretly urged on by his childhood friend – none other than the grinning, red and black-eyed Water-Sprite.

"Remember me, Zack Farmer?" it leers, cruelly.

No time for a reunion. Any second the harvester will push him towards the final trap and the digger will scoop him up. There's no escape.

With the deafening noise of the engines, and a fearful pounding in his own head, Zack doesn't hear the footsteps that are fast approaching. Or see the shape in the darkness. But he feels someone's skinny arms, as they grab him up.

"*Help!*" he cries.

Then he recognises the voice.

"We freaks have got to stick together," says the homeless boy, as they hurry towards nowhere they know, but away from the machines they fear.

"I'm not a freak," pants Zack. Then he thinks about it. "Am I, Danny?"

No time to answer as they smack right into a wooden fence. There isn't a way that Zack can get over this, it's far too high, but next to him Danny is crouching down and cupping his hands, for reasons Zack can't even guess at. Any climbing he has ever done has been just on his own. Or with Arthur. And he always got stuck somewhere.

Danny just shakes his head, unclasps his hands and lifts Zack around the waist, until Zack can get a purchase on a narrow strut running midway across the fence. Using what little strength he has left, Zack slowly pulls himself up and over. As he falls down with a thud onto the other side, he glimpses Holly beside him, smiling proudly. Despite his fear, Zack smiles back. It seems only polite.

He can still hear the rumble of the farm-machines, still see the beams of their powerful lights as they search for him. I may have escaped them for now, thinks Zack, but how long can I keep on running (and keep on being saved by Danny)?

Why do they want *me* so badly?

And one more tricky thought keeps slithering in – what would Mum think about all this?

26

'WHERE ON EARTH ARE THEY?'

10.15pm: *Saturday February 16th. Edinburgh, Scotland. The City Hotel.*

Mum doesn't know what to think.

She still has no idea where Zack and Lily are – but she has a pretty good idea where they're not.

Just to make sure, before she goes into total panic-mode, she decides to phone old Mrs Riordan.

Mrs Riordan, who lives in the flat above them in Hackney, isn't thrilled about being woken up in the middle of the night. After all, she is eighty-four. But she likes the Farmer kids, especially the boy. (The girl is a bit flighty in her opinion, and what's with all the black clothes and lips?) So she takes the key she hides in an old pickle jar and goes to have a look.

Being an old lady, she doesn't leap down the stairs like an Olympic runner – or an Olympic stair-leaper. Mum even starts to worry that the old lady has fallen back to sleep. The minutes seem like hours, but eventually Mrs Riordan comes back with the news.

"Hello, Ruth?" says the old lady. "Ruth Farmer? Are you there?"

"*Yes!*" says Ruth Farmer.

"Well, your kids aren't," says Mrs Riordan and sets the phone back down on its hook. Her last thought, before she falls back to sleep, is that she really should have taken the pickles out of the jar before she put the key in it.

Mum isn't going to sleep any time soon. She's wide-awake, wondering where her kids are.

She is more worried than she has ever been in her life.

10.20pm: *Saturday February 16th. Cape Fury. Highlands. Castle Peak.*

Mum would be even more worried if she knew who else is asking this very same question, at this very late hour. And her only son would be just as perturbed. Especially if someone were to tell them both that it isn't even being asked by anyone human.

If they knew it is being asked by a pulsating, twisting, blindingly-bright, red light, in the dankest, dampest, darkest room in the whole of Britain, they might go completely out of their minds.

But it certainly wouldn't worry any of those actually there, in that bleak place, listening in awed silence to the voice that isn't a voice. They are relishing it. And there are a lot of them – it is a very big room.

"Please. Do not tell me that you have LOST him!" booms the voice that isn't a voice.

The response is massive and apologetic. "Sorry, Rogue Max."

But Rogue Max, for this is how the energetic presence is known, is in a mood to be forgiving. This weekend is, after all, a very special occasion for the Rogues. And what, by pure good fortune, (or delightfully bad luck) has been happening to a young, innocent boy down at the other end of the country promises to make it even more special.

"Zack Farmer thinks he will escape us by getting to Scotland." The audience can hear a smile, even in this cruellest of sounds. "Do you think perhaps he doesn't know where we are?"

The listeners, despite being so awed, beam at this.

The smiley-sound grows. "Oh and by the way, I gather that little Arthur is losing the battle."

He doesn't need to say what battle little Arthur is losing. The Rogues know only too well. Especially when the room suddenly fills with an unearthly, flashing light.

It is the hideous glow of Rogue Max laughing.

27

'WE CAN'T TRUST A SOUL
FROM NOW ON.'

10.22pm: *Saturday February 16th. Lancashire, England. Dapplegate Farm.*

Zack and Danny have no idea where they are.

They don't even know where Lily is. They just wish Lily could be with them, so that they can all be totally lost together. Holly included.

Zack can just about tell, because they're crawling through it on their bellies, that they're in a field. The grass is scratching his face and stinging his eyes. He can smell the heaps of muck and straw from cattle that must be sleeping soundly indoors. But at least it hasn't rained here. Yet. They're crawling because they can still glimpse, through the darkness, the flash of torches – as their enemies tramp through the forests that border them on every side.

"How are we ever going to find Lily in the dark?" asks Zack.

"I have no—"

But Danny doesn't even finish his sentence, because a whoosh of flame shoots up just feet away. It is followed immediately by an anguished cry, some seriously bad language and the sound of smouldering grass being stamped on hard.

"*Lily!*" says Zack.

Who else?

"P-put that lighter out – now!" whispers Danny, urgently.

Suddenly the flame is gone and Lily's face is almost next to theirs. But not before they catch a glimpse of a large farmhouse just up ahead.

"*Where've you been?*" complains Lily. But she is really so glad to see them.

Zack and Danny don't have the energy to explain. "Doesn't m-matter," says Danny. "We're here now. But we can't w-walk all the way to Scotland!"

Somehow Zack knows what Danny is thinking. Or maybe it's the way the older boy is staring through the darkness towards the house.

"*You're not going to steal a car!*" he gasps.

"No, of course not," says Danny. Zack looks relieved. "We're going to borrow one." Zack looks less relieved. "And remember Zack, we can't trust a soul from now on. It looks like these Rogues can turn up *wherever* they're needed. We're on our own."

"Wish we were," mutters Lily. "Nobody wanted to chase me before I met you." She quickly clarifies this, in case Danny thinks she was totally unchaseable. "With sticks, I mean."

Ignoring this, Danny crawls on ahead, with Zack and the others close behind.

"Danny, I don't care about the Rogues," says Zack. "I just care about Arthur. He's my best friend!"

"Yeah. Check him out on no-facebook," says Lily, which actually makes Danny laugh, to Holly and Zack's surprise. And Lily's.

Her phone suddenly rings.

Not now! She immediately switches it off, but not before she sees Mum's name come up. Sadly she reckons that, if she ever gets back home, she'll probably be grounded for life plus 100 years.

They're almost at the farmhouse. Like the pub, it looks old and warm and welcoming, but unlike the pub they're not going to be fooled again. Yet Zack can see a sadness on Danny's face, as the young man stares at the soft light pouring out from the downstairs window. A sadness that can't simply be due to what's been happening these past few hours.

"Danny," he asks, knowing that he's probably getting into murky waters, "Why don't you have a home?"

Danny is so quiet that for a moment Zack worries he has said totally the wrong thing. But then the homeless young man begins to explain and, to Zack, it's almost like the light in the young man's eyes is going back into itself and the glow that makes him so special is dimming.

"Me mum and me step-dad chucked me out, when I was fourteen. Well, I chucked meself out, more like. After he hit me once too often." His voice sounds even sadder. "See Zack, they thought if they beat me hard enough, I'd grow out of seeing and hearing – stuff. You know, stuff like Holly and all the IFs. But, of course, I couldn't, could I? And I didn't even have their excuse of being drunk all the time!" He pauses, thoughtfully. "They just think I'm mad, Zack."

"Tsk," says Lily. "Parents!"

That sarcasm again. But this time it sounds, Zack thinks, like she's trying just a bit too hard.

Zack is hoping for more history (or '*his* story') from Danny, but it clearly isn't going to happen. Danny has already turned away. He is standing on tiptoe so that he can peer through the farmhouse window, mounted quite high up on the old stone wall.

It's very much the typical living-room of a country-farmhouse, with huge, rustic furniture and huge, rustic men and women sitting on it, watching a huge but not at all rustic, high-definition, plasma TV.

"Oh no!" says Danny, suddenly.

"*What?*" asks Zack, scared again.

Danny lifts Zack up, in order to see the big TV. Lily finds some thick stones and manages to raise herself high enough to share the boys' view – and wishes she hadn't. It's the video from the fairground, with Old MacDonald's laughing-lamb, Zack, Lily and all. On the national news!

"If our mum sees that, we're toast," says Lily.

Fortunately, the news moves swiftly on, to a political conference somewhere in England. The Prime Minister seems to be speaking to a huge crowd. There's one of those meaningless slogans behind him: 'NOW FOR THE FUTURE'.

"Never thought I'd be pleased to see the Prime Minister," says Lily, but Danny has lost interest. He sets Zack back down on the ground.

"We need to find that car," says Danny. "Come on, Hol."

Holly is still watching the TV. She doesn't see it much these days. "Where *is* Scotland by the way? Is it like near Norway?" she asks.

Danny rolls his eyes – Americans! – even though he's the one who created her. But as he looks at his oldest friend, he notices that she has gone totally rigid – or as rigid as a weightless object can go. Despite her bright colours, she now looks blue and icy. He has never seen her like this before – and he knows that he's not 'imagining' it.

"Hol?" he says. "Holly, are you okay, love?"

The cheerleader shakes her head. Zack takes out the Glimmer, so that he can see her too. She certainly doesn't look happy.

"Maybe I've seen too many conspiracy movies," she says, pointing at the TV.

Which is a really odd thing to say. It causes Danny to stop what he is doing and look back through the window. What he sees makes him understand *exactly* why Holly seems so shaken.

He lifts Zack back up to the window once again.

And suddenly Zack knows that things just got a whole lot worse.

28

'THEY'RE KILLING IMAGINATION!'

10.30pm: *Saturday February 16th. Lancashire, England. Dapplegate Farm.*

The Prime Minister has a smug smile on his face.

But that's not the unusual bit, thinks Zack. In his experience, politicians do that all the time. What's unusual is that the man is *nodding* – even as he talks and smiles smugly.

"*He's doing that thing!*" says Zack. "The Prime Minister's doing that nodding thing!"

"Point your Glimmer at the telly," says Danny. "I don't know if it'll work, but – do it!"

Zack is also unsure if the Glimmer will do the trick. But it does work. It works only too well. To his horror Zack sees it, right next to the Prime Minister of the United Kingdom.

A large, floppy rag-doll.

It is at least six-foot tall, with a sewn-on smile that is more of a ghastly, mirthless grimace. A grotesque parody of what must once have been this highly important man's beloved childhood friend. But what really chills Zack the most is that the rag-doll is gleefully whispering into the Prime Minister's unsuspecting ear. As the Prime Minister nods away.

"IT'S A ROGUE! NEXT TO THE PM!" Zack yelps. A bit too loudly, actually.

One of the farmers, in the living-room, suddenly looks up and round to the window. Zack and Danny swiftly duck, pulling Lily down with them.

"Oh no," says Danny. "This is way too heavy."

"Oh, please!" says Lily, who has had more than enough of this nonsense. "Is the farmer eating a ploughman's lunch, maybe? Can you see? Does he have a crusty, farmhouse loaf? A live chicken? I could murder a goat."

"Guys," says Danny, turning to look at them. "Who are the people with real power in this world?"

"Mums?" suggests Zack. "Teachers?" Then, almost to himself, "Bullies?"

"Hungry. Not playing," says Lily.

But Danny is insistent. He's working things out in his head, big things, and if they don't come out of his mouth now, that head may very well explode. Zack is listening with every cell in his tired, cold body. Holly is too – she hasn't done a cartwheel for hours.

"World leaders!" announces Danny, but still in a careful whisper. "That's who has the power. Presidents. Politicians. Army generals. Guerillas."

Zack never realised gorillas were so powerful, but he has a feeling he heard that wrong.

"Think about it!" encourages Danny, which Zack

doesn't need to be told, because he and Holly can think of nothing else. "All these important people – making huge decisions that aren't really theirs at all."

Zack is there now, with Danny. He gets it.

"*It's their Rogues!*" he says. "Whispering in their ears. Telling them what to do!"

"Exactly!" says Danny. There's sweat on his brow, despite the chill night air. "All because of some secret, little voices in their heads! All these big guys, they're taking orders and nodding away, but they don't even know they're doing it. They can't see their Rogues, so they think it's all their own ideas! Starting wars. Spreading evil. Doing bad—"

Holly has to interrupt. She's bursting too. "Oh and Zack, who do they hate most of all? *You kids!* Because you grew up and ditched them." She seemed almost in tears "Can't you see that?"

They look up again into the room.

Almost as if Holly had timed it, the screens behind the Prime Minister's nodding head show footage of the Government's greatest achievements in recent years. The Sugar Police doing their rounds, kids dumping their favourite toys for the Crusher-trucks to collect, fairgrounds being boarded up, storybooks burned, movies banned, video-games and pets restricted to grown-ups .

The Children's Army, with its brainwashed teenagers. On the march.

Zack looks at Danny, as the poor young soldiers stomp across the screen. The homeless lad is pale and shivering. Zack gasps as he suddenly understands what his twitchy new friend has been running away from, probably for years. And why he can never be still.

"You know what they're doing with all these laws, Zack?" says Danny. "*Think* about it, pal. It's all around us. What they're doing to kids everywhere."

Now Zack gets it. Like one of the puzzles he still plays in secret, the pieces are beginning to fit. "No toys, no stories, no movies, no games," he murmurs. "No fun!"

Danny grabs Zack's narrow shoulders with both arms. "Exactly!" He can hardly breathe. "Zack, they're *killing* imagination!"

Zack stares at him. This is too big. How can you kill something that is so much a part of every human being on this planet? Something that's almost as important – as basic – as breathing. But Danny's eyes are on fire, with a fury unlike anything Zack has ever seen before.

"They want to make us a people – a species – who can't think for ourselves," continues Danny, as the shock grows. "And then we'll be easier to manage. Easier to boss around. I mean, how can a person think 'outside the box', when they're locking you in one?" Danny is becoming outraged at the sheer audacity of it. "Zack, without imagination to power our minds, they'll have us under their control. The entire world. THE ROGUES WILL BE ABLE TO MAKE US DO ANYTHING!"

"You two can probably get a group-rate for therapy," says Lily.

Hunger isn't making Lily any more fun, but the guys aren't listening. Zack feels totally out of his depth.

"So what do we do, Danny, *call up the Prime Minister?*" protests Zack. "'Hey, guess what, mate, your old raggy-doll is putting nasty ideas in your head!'"

"You are so right, Zack," agrees Holly, sadly. "Grown-ups *never* believe anything about IFs. And know what — they never will. That's what the Rogues rely on. That's how they keep on winning."

This all feels too overwhelming for Zack, especially when Danny grips his shivering arms even tighter.

"Something is going down, Zack – something massive. I dunno what it is, but looks like you just became a major part of it." Zack stares at him, unblinking. "We have got to work out exactly what these guys want from you," he says. "But you stay cool, Zack. Okay?"

Zack nods. Okay. I'll stay cool. Sure. I can do that. Me – Cool Zack. Nothing to it.

Then he hears a little girl's voice coming from nowhere and cool goes straight out the window.

29

'AND WE DRIVE OFF, HOW?'

10.36pm: *Saturday February 16th. Lancashire, England. Dapplegate Farm.*

"What're you doing?" says the voice, in a chirpy, Lancashire accent.

"*AAAAAAHHHH!!*" yell Zack and the others, each in their own special way.

When they look up to a second-floor window, their hearts pounding, they see a plump, little girl gazing directly down on them.

But the yells have caused the other farmer inside the house to turn round. Danny makes the gang all dive down again, just below the window. This time the burly man comes out anyway and starts to look around. The gang back into the wall and try to pretend that they're fancy brickwork.

Zack looks up, wondering if the little girl will tell on them. Why shouldn't she – they're trespassers.

The farmer gives a rich, country belch, then smiles up

at the girl. "Go to sleep now, love. You've had a busy day," he says.

The little girl just nods sweetly and the farmer goes back inside. Zack and the others heave a sigh of relief and look gratefully up at their protector.

"Now give us some food," says Lily to the girl. "And we promise not to make your life a living Hell."

"*Lily!*" says Zack, then thanks the girl for not telling.

"That's okay," says the girl. "I went to a party today at the ice-rink. I didn't eat all my tea."

"Leftovers'll do," says Lily. "*Give!*"

A massive polystyrene box comes hurtling down towards them. Lily catches it.

"But I did eat Jennifer's tea," admits the girl. "And Kylie's."

Lily is already ripping open the box, as the little girl goes back into her bedroom.

"C'mon, guys," says Danny, in frustration. "We've got to find a—"

"Wait!" says Zack, "I've had an idea." They stare at him, as he looks back up at the window and calls. "Little girl... *hello*... ?"

After a moment the little girl returns. *What?* Zack grabs the Glimmer tight and lets loose his brainwave. "Can we speak to your friend, please?"

The girl just stares blankly down at him and then goes away. Danny shrugs. Ah well, Zack, worth a try. Not everyone has a—

But then, as they turn to go, they hear a huskier voice. "Yeah?" it says, in a throaty, northern accent. "What you after?"

Which sort of surprises the lads, as it comes out of the mouth of another, rather tubby, little girl, dressed in exactly the same, homespun outfit as Dorothy wore in 'The Wizard of Oz'. The girl is even in black and white, not just her dress but face, arms, eyes, everything – along with the scraggly, little Toto-like dog she's holding.

Zack recognises her from days long ago, when he was allowed to watch the film with his mum. The real little girl must have found an old DVD and created her own imaginary, Lancashire version. Zack can tell that Danny recognises it too. It makes them both a little sad, for a moment.

"Hi. Er… Dorothy, isn't it?" says Zack.

"Aye," says the lass, in her local accent. "From Kansas, USA."

"Uh huh," says Zack, not wishing to argue. "Is there any transport round here, Dorothy? Y'know, a bus… a train…?" He catches Danny's eye. "A car?"

Dorothy immediately leaps out of the window and sails down to join them. Lily, of course, can't see any of this and probably wouldn't notice even if she could, because her head is almost buried inside the polystyrene food-box. She certainly wouldn't spot the Toto-like dog falling out the window either. But Zack does. He even catches him in his arms.

"Hey up," says Dorothy, seeing him do this. "That's a fine trick." She gets to the business at hand, speaking rather quietly, as she knows she shouldn't be telling them this. "Right, my girl's uncle is staying with us tonight. Nothing's locked round here. He leaves his keys beside the nodding ferret on his dashboard." She turns to Holly. "Love the outfit, love."

Dorothy flies back up again, with the words "You've got to bring it back, you hear me?"

Holly calls back to her. "IFs' honour. H-O-N-N-E-R… Maybe."

Danny is really impressed with Zack. "Great call, Zack, we've got ourselves a car."

But Dorothy hasn't finished. "Watch out for the Wicked Witch of the West. And speed cameras on the A34."

Toto is still licking Zack's nose, they've really bonded. To Lily it looks like her brother is trying to win an ugly contest, by contorting his face every which way. Or he's desperate for the loo and trying hard to hold it in.

Zack finally drops the dog down and it starts rubbing against his leg, the way dogs can do when they've really taken to you, which Zack doesn't like quite so much. So he sends him flying back upstairs, with a really sad growl. (The dog, not Zack.)

"Okay, so there's a car here," says Lily, although she's not quite sure how they all know this. And she really doesn't want to think too hard about it. "We drive off how, without the world noticing?"

Zack and Holly just look at each other. The girl has a point. But Danny is onto it. "Lily, give me your lighter. Gimme!"

Lily hands over her throwaway cigarette-lighter, a bit reluctantly. Danny grabs the polystyrene food-box from her hand.

"What are you doing?" she screeches in horror, swiftly rescuing a big chunk of burger out of it – which right now is far more important than even her cigarette-lighter.

Danny isn't listening. He deftly flicks the lighter and sets fire to the box. "When you sleep on the streets, you get to know what burns best," he sighs and hurls the burning box onto a huge pile of straw.

"That's the rest of my supper!" shrieks Lily, watching as the fire slowly takes hold.

The others watch too. It's amazing the attraction of flames, provided they're not burning something that belongs to you. This is probably why the farmers aren't quite so attracted. It isn't long before they're outside, shouting and yelling.

"Straw doesn't set fire to itself!" says one. "Check everywhere, see who's hiding."

As women come out the front of the house with hoses and buckets, Zack and the others slip round the back to the yard. To find the car with the nodding ferret.

Instead they find a vicious, snarling Doberman.

This guard-dog isn't Toto, thinks Zack. This guy is real and big and he wants blood. But Danny reckons he'll probably settle for a burger, so he swiftly grabs the meat out of Lily's hand and throws it to him. Job done.

Lily's moans are deafening. But Zack's and Danny's are nearly as loud, when they discover exactly what it is they are expected to 'borrow'.

A huge, red lorry. With a mangy, plastic ferret in the window.

30

'NO WAY THEY'RE MAKING
FOR SCOTLAND!'

10.43pm: *Saturday February 16th. Edinburgh, Scotland. The City Hotel.*

While the huge, red lorry stands perfectly still (even the ferret), Ruth Farmer moves like lightning towards Niomi's bedroom door. She knocks loudly enough to wake the dead.

The moment Niomi opens it, with her bedtime chocolate-bar still in her hand, Mum is inside the room and pacing the floor. Up and down. Up and down. Which she knows from films and TV is what people do when they're really scared and worried, but she never thought she would be doing it herself. Especially not in her dressing-gown.

"It's the kids!" she says, without even saying 'sorry' or 'I hope I'm not disturbing you'. Niomi just looks at her. "I think they've run off to Manchester."

"And this is a bad thing, because…?" says Niomi, which isn't really very helpful.

Niomi only begins to understand how serious it is when her best friend explains about old Mrs Riordan and the spare key and what Mum thinks she saw on the news.

"Oh, Niomi," moans Mum, sounding so different from her usual brisk and competent self – and so much softer. "I don't know where to start. What am I supposed to do?"

"Calm down, Ruthie," says Niomi. "Let me just think."

She thinks. She bites. She chews. Chocolate always helps. She thinks some more. She unwraps another bar, as it's a special occasion and she needs to do a lot more thinking.

"I've thought!" she finally announces. "I met this Edinburgh nurse in the bar and she works with the police up here – you should hear the stories she tells! There was this eighty-six year old – okay, another time. Anyway, she's staying here in the hotel for the conference, to get away from her kids. We'll go wake her right now. Why should I be the only one with my night spoiled?"

As they rush down the corridor, Niomi asks Mum if she can think of any reason why her kids might run away. Mum just shakes her head. Of course not – no idea. It's not like them at all. But then a sudden thought buzzes into her brain. No, that's ridiculous. But she says it anyway.

"I did post Zack's imaginary friend to his dad – at an address in Scotland I just made up."

Niomi stops and looks at her, for rather a long time. Well, it's not every day you hear something like this. Then the big nurse shakes her head.

"There is no way they're making for Scotland!"

"Select your destination," says the sat-nav.

"*Scotland!*" shouts Zack, suddenly quite excited, but in a good way. The sort of excitement that doesn't make you want to cry or say your prayers.

They're sitting in a line, on the big front-seat of the huge, unmoving lorry. Which feels even more huge, now that they're sinking into the soft fake-leather and staring out of the massive front windscreen.

In the background the farmers, who just a few minutes ago were happily watching the Prime Minister nodding to himself on TV, are now rushing around with buckets and hoses, trying to save the flaming straw. Fortunately the rain from Manchester is just arriving.

"At least nobody will be looking for us in one of these, eh Danny?" exults Zack.

Danny isn't saying anything. Zack knows the fellow is slowly thoughtful, but actually he's not usually this slow or this thoughtful. Finally, the older boy speaks.

"There's just one tiny problem, Zack."

Lily looks at him. She knows exactly what it is. "He can't drive. Brilliant!"

"You'd be amazed how m-many homeless people don't have cars, L-Lily," says Danny.

Lily just sighs, but Zack has a great idea. "Lily can drive really well. Me and Arthur took this photo—"

"IT WAS A MINI!" yells Lily. She ponders for a second, as a fond memory kicks in. "Mind you, I did drive Ashleigh's dad's van down the Balls Pond Road last New Year's Eve, for a bet."

Zack is shocked. "*Lily!*"

But Lily is already struggling to swap places with Danny. The hard way, without her having to get out of the van. "I'm not getting my hair wet in the rain. Shift round!"

They seem a bit flustered, as they try to swap seats without making too much contact with each other. Lots of 'sorries' going on. All of which Holly notices, but no one seems to notice her noticing. Which she notices too.

Then the thunder and lightning start.

The thing about thunder and lightning is that for most people they're a nuisance and for some they're even rather scary. But Zack realises that when you're trying to start a really heavy vehicle, that isn't your own, and drive it away without anyone hearing you, the sounds of the heavens opening can be very fine music indeed.

Of course, they don't actually make driving a huge, red, 'borrowed' truck any easier.

Tired and cold, 'intimidated' to his bones (yet also curiously excited), Zack Farmer begins to shiver. He will be shivering a whole lot more before the weekend is done.

31

"ARE YOU ANOTHER IF?"

10.48pm: *Saturday February 16th. Cape Fury. Scotland. The McBride cottage.*

Arthur is shivering too, but not from the cold. Or the excitement.

He's sitting at the McBride kitchen-table, looking just a bit pink, as he watches his new little mate demolish a far-from-little, late-night snack. Jam, peanut butter, cream cheese, fish paste and chocolate spread, all in the one chunky sandwich. (Kirstie hasn't eaten like this for months. She wonders, between mouthfuls, what has given her back her appetite – it couldn't be having Princess here, could it?)

They hear the front door burst open and the singing begin. Arthur shivers even louder.

"*Away up in Clackan, with Dougal Mc…* "

It's that Mrs Ames again, doing a bad, tartan accent. They can hear Grandpa Brodie beside her, correcting her pronunciation. "It's Clachan, woman!" he tells her. "*Away up in Clachan, wi'*… Say 'CHHHH'."

It sounds like he's gargling with vinegar. And that they've been to the pub.

"I'll put the kettle on, Audrey and we'll have some tea," announces Grandpa Brodie.

He swings into the kitchen and sees Kirstie. Before he can say anything, she's explaining. "We're having a midnight feast. Don't tell my pa."

"Okay," says Grandpa Brodie. "Is her royal fartiness here too?"

When Kirstie nods, Grandpa Brodie bows humbly to the empty chair, then suggests that Kirstie finishes her 'Big Mac-Bride' sandwich quickly and takes herself up to bed.

"And tell your Princess to stay off the baked beans!"

Kirstie gets up. She's feeling pretty sleepy anyway, but when she turns round to beckon Arthur, he looks like he's been glued to his chair. In fact he looks like a statue, except that statues don't quiver and shake.

She can't stay here all night persuading him, not when Grandpa Brodie clearly wants her to call it a day. She just has to leave her new friend cowering in the kitchen. What is it with Princess and that funny Mrs Ames? she wonders.

So Kirstie doesn't notice, as she makes for her bed, that Arthur does finally get up from his chair a few seconds later, all the while scouring the cottage with his three green and very frightened eyes. He doesn't know exactly what he's frightened of, but he'll know it when he sees it.

In a couple of seconds, he sees it.

It isn't Mrs Ames. Although she does look rather disturbing and tartan, as she noses around the cosy living-room. It's what he sees next to Mrs Ames that has Arthur quivering like a jelly on a plate. A plate that's on a rickety train. In an earthquake.

He sees a dwarf.

Not just any old dwarf.

This one is jaundice-yellow and has red and black flaring eyes, rotten, slobbery, pointy teeth, a faceful of lumpy spots that no acne-cream could fix and a truly horrible smile. But – scariest of all – these *aren't* its most disturbing features. What is most concerning about the unlovely dwarf currently in the McBride living-room is that he is at least eight and a half feet tall.

Which is pretty tall for a dwarf these days.

The funny thing is that Arthur can see how this big, chubby (okay, really fat) dwarf could have been quite cute at one time. But with his crooked, yellow finger, and even yellower fingernail, pointing directly at Arthur – and his ugly grin widening – no-one could call him cute now.

"What's wrong, Arthur?" asks this astonishing creature, in a voice that is as deep as a mineshaft, yet rather calm and well-spoken. Like the wicked prince out of a dwarf royal family, which somehow makes him all the more scary. "Have you never seen an eight and a half foot dwarf before?"

Arthur, who is actually wearing a very girly nightshirt (thank you, Kirstie), just shakes his head. Because, actually, he hasn't.

"Are you another IF?" he asks, innocently. "Or are you just Scottish?"

The rather large dwarf roars at this, just as Grandpa Brodie returns to the living-room.

The curious thing is that while Arthur and the dwarf

are having this getting-to-know-you chat, Brodie and Mrs Ames are enjoying their own conversation. Totally unaware of the invisible, weird stuff going on right under their noses.

"While the kettle's boiling, Audrey, why don't you slip into something more comfortable?" suggests Brodie. "Like a saggy sofa."

But Mrs Ames is already yawning and telling Brodie to forget the tea. She should probably wend her way home, as her first guests are already arriving – or should she say 'retreating' – at Castle Peak. Arriving/retreating in great numbers, actually. Even larger than expected. Carloads of them. They seem a funny-looking bunch, a bit 'spaced-out', but at least they're smartly-dressed.

The tartan lady begins to make for the door.

"They call themselves the Whisperers," she reveals at the doorway, shaking her head in puzzlement. "Lord knows why."

But then, to Arthur's surprise, the oversized dwarf sidles over to the tartan lady, walking right through the furniture and even through Grandpa Brodie, and whispers softly into her ear.

Mrs Ames immediately nods, turns from the door and plonks herself back down in an easy chair. Really settling, as if she had no intention of leaving and is going to be here for at least the weekend.

"On second thoughts, Brodie, no rush," she laughs. "Bring on the tea!"

Arthur is totally bewildered.

He has never seen any of this sort of stuff before – certainly not on the faraway streets of Hackney, London.

So the fact that old Mrs Ames is taking whispered instructions from a big, weird-looking and not-at-all cuddly IF – and doesn't even seem to realise she is doing so – is pretty big news to him.

I've an awful feeling, Zack (he says, in his head, to his missing friend), that this is only going to get weirder.

32

'WE'LL CATCH UP WITH ZACK AND LILY.'

10.51pm: *Saturday February 16th. Lancashire, England. On the road.*

Zack could tell Arthur a few things about weird.

Right now he is watching a plastic ferret, on the dashboard of a huge lorry, frantically nod its head. But he doesn't think it's a Rogue. He's pretty sure this is simply a sign that Lily's lorry-driving isn't exactly the smoothest. Which is hardly surprising, considering she's fifteen, terrified and has never driven anything this enormous in her life.

None of this is helped by Zack asking if she can't go any faster.

"Oh, yeah right, I'll do a couple of wheelies, will I, Zack?" she replies. "No, I'll do that cool gear thingy I'm learning for my Formula One 'GCSE'!"

Zack looks at his Glimmer. It is flashing weaker than it ever has before. He shows it to Danny, who shakes his head, which Zack knows by now is not a good sign.

"If I don't find Arthur soon, Danny, it'll be too late!" says Zack. "We have got to get to Scotland, fast!"

Lily just sighs. Is she ever going to escape this madness? Trust her little brother to trip over the one guy in Britain even dorkier than he is. And, of course, she has already missed her Goth night.

"Two-four-six-eight, watch your green pal deteriorate!"

Holly shakes her head – did she really say that? Sometimes being a figment of someone else's imagination is really hard. So she tries to be a bit more helpful. "Zack, honey, with half the Rogue population of Great Britain on your tail," she says, "fading Arthur is the least of your worries."

This doesn't help Zack in the slightest but he tries to look on the bright side. "Maybe we've left all the bad guys behind us, Holly."

Danny and Holly just stare at him and Lily does too. She doesn't know what the bad guys are about, or why they're behaving the way they are, but they're out there. She's been around. She comes from a tough city. She knows some guys can be bad.

The lorry suddenly veers a bit too sharply into a slip-road and onto a busy motorway. The once dark, rural world is suddenly full of glaring headlights. They seem to be shooting straight into the lorry, which lurches violently. The others yelp as they bang against the sides.

"Don't blame me," says Lily, trying desperately to steer. "I don't usually do roads with an 'M' on them."

As the boys process this information, the events of the day start to hit her. Lily wishes she was back home with her permanently angry mum.

Zack just wishes he was back home with Arthur. Suddenly, from out of nowhere, he gets an awful flash – *perhaps Arthur has found someone new!*

No, he reassures himself. The guy would never find someone new. Not his Arthur.

33

'EVER HEAR OF ROGUE MAX?'

10.53pm: *Saturday February 16th. Cape Fury. Scotland. The McBride cottage.*

Someone very new is kindly explaining the situation to Zack's old friend.

"Up until now, my minuscule green chum," says the oversized dwarf, "you and I couldn't see each other at all. But I could *smell* you. Oh yes – I caught my first, nasty whiff of pure IF on the beach this afternoon." He nods towards Mrs Ames. "With her ladyship here."

So *that's* why I feel so scared, thinks Arthur, whenever Mrs Ames appears on the scene. But how come, he wonders, I can see this huge creature tonight, yet I couldn't earlier on? And how come the guy can see me, when just a few hours ago he could only sniff me?

Grandpa Brodie, of course, has no idea of the drama being played out right under his nose. All he's interested in is showing his special guest some famous Scottish hospitality. So he finds an unopened box of fine shortbread, a special and very sugary biscuit that has rotted Scottish teeth for generations.

He brings it back into the room with a flourish. This time he doesn't walk straight through Arthur, as Arthur is now on a far higher plane, swinging around way above Brodie's head. His small, whirling body is gripped tight in the dwarf's giant hands as his little, green legs flail helplessly in all directions.

"Sorry to leave you dangling," says Brodie.

This is to Audrey Ames, who isn't actually dangling at all. Not in the truly, dangly, legs-above-the-ground, sense of the word. Not in the dangly, Arthur sense.

"That's all right, Brodie," says Mrs Ames, then suddenly pauses. Because, as only Arthur can see, the big dwarf is whispering into her ear again, telling her exactly what to say. "But I'm worried about Kirstie," she says now.

Brodie looks surprised. "Kirstie? Aye she's a sad wee girl right enough, but… "

He doesn't finish, because the large dwarf is urging his human on again. "She's got an invisible friend!" is the message she passes on.

"Och, I know that, Audrey," says Brodie, adding "but that's a good thing, isn't it?"

"In her case, I wonder," says Mrs Ames, which is rather an odd thing for a stranger to say. Her next admission is even odder. "But, actually, Brodie, I had the sweetest little imaginary fellow when I was a 'wee lassie'. A tiny, yellow dwarf I called Mr Teensy-Weensy."

Mr Who??

Arthur tries to look at the far-from-tiny dwarf, which isn't that easy when you're being swung around a room by your legs at enormous speed and you think your stomach is going to come out of your mouth or somewhere even less pleasant.

"*Mr Teensy-Weensy?*" repeats Arthur, who thinks it's a really silly name.

The giant dwarf, formerly known as Mr Teensy-Weensy, shrugs. He's a little embarrassed.

"Audrey was very young when she dreamed me up," he explains. "But I'm not bitter, Arthur, that she finally tossed me aside, all those years ago, without a backward glance. Like a putrid sack of last week's rubbish!"

To be honest, thinks Arthur, you do sound a bit bitter, mate. He wonders when exactly the dwarf moved back into Mrs Ames' life. Was it when she was already a grown-up?

"So, why are you doing this?" asks Arthur, not unreasonably, as his head flies right through the living-room light-fitting. But the answer is not reassuring.

"Ever hear of Rogue Max?" asks Mr Teensy-Weensy.

Arthur just shakes his head. All these new names! *Who?*

"Well, Rogue Max knows all about you", continues Mr Teensy-Weensy, to Arthur's huge surprise. "Oh yes. Oh yes, indeed." He adds this last bit with relish. "He knows especially that your dear friend, Zack Farmer, isn't even *bothering* to leave Hackney and search for you. What do you say to that, Arthur?"

Arthur just stares at him.

His eyes are now directly in line with Mr Teensy-Weensy's, although his body is dangling at least five feet above the floor. How does this creature know about Zack? How does he know about any of it? Is there a sort of website for IFs that Arthur wasn't aware of? But he tries to remain defiant.

"I don't believe you," says Arthur, although sadly he does. Because he knows Zack.

"Oh, I think you do believe me, Arthur. Because you know Zack," the dwarf smiles. "Just think about it – why else would you have found yourself a new, little pal so quickly?"

While Arthur is thinking this through, Grandpa Brodie is of course still chatting to Audrey Ames. The real world goes on, even if it is not nearly as separate from the imaginary one as we would like to think.

"I had an invisible friend once," says Brodie, "but I kept forgetting what he looked like!" At this he roars with laughter and Mrs Ames graciously joins in.

Mr Teensy-Weensy isn't laughing. He sits down on an easy chair and pulls the quaking Arthur onto his enormous, dwarf lap.

"Rogue Max thinks it's time," he says.

Time for what? wonders Arthur. Probably not for a picnic or a ticket to the FA Cup Final. He hazards a guess. "Time to fade away?"

He knows that this is what IFs must eventually do and he's pretty sure it's what's going on with him right now. Look at his dwindling colour! And there's no getting away from it – he's hundreds of miles from Zack and the precious Glimmer he left behind him. He's quite certain that Zack has moved on by now. Maybe forgotten all about him. Perhaps he has even made a new, imaginary friend.

Ah well. That's life, he thinks. Yet, actually, he can't deny that he's just a tiny bit cross about it all.

Mr Teensy-Weensy's answer rocks him to his shaky, green core. "Fade away? Goodness no, Arthur," explains the dwarf, with a smile. "Time to go Rogue, like me."

34

'NO ZACK. NO GLIMMER. NO CHOICE!'

10.58pm: *Saturday February 16th. Cape Fury. Scotland. The McBride cottage.*

Arthur just stares at him.

Rogue? What's Rogue when it's at home?

He has absolutely no idea what Mr Teensy-Weensy is talking about. But he senses that it probably isn't good, so he tries once more to struggle out of the creature's powerful grip.

Anyone who has ever squeezed a balloon would know what Arthur looks like, as little green bits of him seep out in all directions from between Mr Teensy-Weensy's massive, yellow fingers.

"Oh, poor Arthur, you look so confused," laughs Mr Teensy-Weensy. "Allow me to clarify. No Zack. No Glimmer. No choice. Ha!"

That 'Ha!' was a laugh, but not one you'd be likely to hear any human make.

"You can *see* me, Arthur. And I can see you. Which I'm

afraid means that you're *practically* ours already." The giant dwarf sighs deeply. "It's just a nuisance about that horrid little girl 'adopting' you. Bit of an obstacle, that. Yet I'm an optimist. I'm convinced it could be simply a matter of days, even a matter of hours... "

Arthur is dumbstruck. He has no words left inside him. He also has absolutely no interest in the fact that right next to him, Grandpa Brodie is rolling up his trouser-legs, grabbing Mrs Ames' tartan shawl (which spins her neck around like a top) and playing a CD of Scottish bagpipe music really loud. It sounds to Arthur like a sheep being crushed in a blender.

"Have I told you my theory, Audrey, about a Scotsman's knees?" exclaims Grandpa Brodie, over the music. "I reckon that, thanks to our longstanding habit of wearing the kilt, our knees have evolved quite differently from your pasty, English variety... "

Brodie doesn't get any further, which is probably good news for Mrs Ames, because he's interrupted by Stuart, in his dressing-gown, shouting sleepily from the doorway.

"DO YOU KNOW WHAT TIME IT IS?" Calming down a bit, he adds "Sorry, Mrs Ames. I try to keep the house nice and calm, for Kirstie. AND FOR MY OWN SANITY!"

That calmness didn't last long.

Mrs Ames does understand, she has had children of her own, which is why she gets up immediately from her comfy chair. "I'm just going, Mr McBride," she says.

It is only Arthur who hears Mr Teensy-Weensy telling her to sit right down again.

"No, I'm staying, Mr McBride," she announces, re-planting her ample, tartan bottom firmly into the chair.

Stuart is quite put-out by this, but Mr Teensy-Weensy isn't letting Mrs Ames go. He hasn't finished with Arthur. Which makes Arthur understand that Rogues, just like IFs, really have to stay pretty close to their humans, in order to get done whatever fiendish stuff Rogues do. They can't just wander about all over the place, on their own.

"We *need* you, Arthur," says Mr Teensy-Weensy. "In fact we need both you *and* Zack Farmer very much indeed. You've come along at just the right time for us."

"How do you—?"

"I'm still talking, Arthur," says the dwarf, who is still talking. "Yes, we need you both. But we don't need you both in *exactly* the same place. Oh no – not just yet." And then he adds, mysteriously, "We're not quite ready for the castle."

Arthur stares at him – *castle?* But the dwarf still hasn't finished.

"So, you see, we do really have to keep your Zack Farmer from finding you. And, of course, from giving you your precious Glimmer back," he explains, like it's the most obvious thing in the world. "Oh no, my friend. Not before you've gone *completely* Rogue. Or that would so spoil everything."

Everything, thinks Arthur. What's everything? And what possible plan could they cook up that needs him, Zack *and* the Glimmer?

"You're probably thinking, what possible plan could we cook up that needs you, Zack *and* the Glimmer," says the dwarf, perceptively. "Well, actually... I'm not telling you. But it's a goodie, believe me." The huge dwarf smiles again, which isn't pleasant. "And while my dear friends south of here are on finding-and-capturing-Zack duty, my job here is to make sure you stay ever so close to me – *and far away from him*. You do see, don't you, Arthur? Until the time for your 'reunion' is absolutely right."

Arthur is so puzzled. He simply doesn't see at all. What time? Right for what? But even in his terror, he picks up on one thing his new enemy just let slip, that simply doesn't make sense.

"'*Keep Zack Farmer from finding me*?'" he repeats. "But I thought you said my Zack wasn't even looking for me."

Gotcha! Nice one, Arthur, thinks Arthur.

For a split second Mr Teensy-Weensy is thrown off-course. Arthur seizes the opportunity. He slips out of the Rogue's big, yellow grasp and scampers away.

But the huge Rogue isn't thrown for long and within seconds he is up and after the little green IF. Walls are no barrier to either of them, as they rush in and out of the kitchen, through the fireplace and right into the neighbour's lounge, where an elderly couple are watching Braveheart on DVD for the forty-seventh time. Then it's back into the McBride living-room once again.

By this time Mr Teensy-Weensy is seriously angry. "You can run, Arthur – but you just can't run terribly well."

He's right of course, because poor Arthur is tired and flagging.

It looks like it's all over – Mr Teensy-Weensy is about to catch him and this time Arthur knows he will be caught for good and he'll turn completely Rogue before Zack can get the Glimmer back to him. Mr Teensy-Weensy knows this too, which is why he's wearing that horrible, yellow smile of his.

So neither of them expects what happens next.

Arthur suddenly transforms, mid-flight, into a tiny, Scottish doll.

The sort they sell in souvenir shops all over this proud country. A miniature warrior, wearing the full tartan kilt and regalia, but with a lot more style than Mrs Ames – which is hardly difficult.

Mr Teensy-Weensy is caught off-stride and looks completely flummoxed. Where on earth has the stupid, little IF gone? Arthur is equally surprised, but he has the presence of mind to seize the moment and leap well away from the dwarf.

He doesn't simply leap anywhere. Not Arthur. He leaps straight into the arms of Kirstie, who has come quietly down the stairs and is standing right there in the doorway, with an armful of her favourite dolls from foreign countries. She has her eyes shut tight and is imagining hard.

Thank you *so* much, Cur-stee.

Of course, Kirstie has no idea who exactly is chasing her new friend, because humans can't see Rogues. But she had a pretty good idea, from the look on Arthur's face just now (and the fact he was running around like a maniac), that somebody or something rather unpleasant was on the chasing end.

That's why she has changed her Princess's looks for a while. But now she has to get rid of the unseen enemy.

"Who wants to see my dolly collection?" she says, cunningly. "Before it's taken away for crushing."

She decides to show them one at a time to Mrs Ames,

who she suspects might be a big part of all the trouble. "Now this wee one is a Beefeater. He's English and podgy like you, Mrs Ames. Ooh and you must hear about this one. It's a long, long story but—"

This is quite enough for Mrs Ames. She is out of her chair and at the door in a flash. Grandpa Brodie is starting to feel like it's bedtime too. Who wants to talk about wee dolls at almost midnight? So Mr Teensy-Weensy, who now has no idea what on earth Arthur looks like, is forced to follow his old, tartan friend to the door.

"You think you're so smart, Arthur," he announces into the air, "but you can't fight destiny."

Then he adds something which confuses Arthur even more. "We'll see you at the convocation."

The what?

35

'HE'LL FIND THEM, RUTHIE.'

11.05pm: *Saturday, February 17th. Edinburgh, Scotland. City Hotel lobby .*

Arthur is not the only one who is confused.

If I ever see my kids again, thinks Ruth Farmer, I'll kiss them and I'll cuddle them – and then I'll lock them up in their rooms forever.

But she has no idea if she'll ever get to do any of these things again. This is why she is sitting with Niomi, in a deserted hotel-lobby late at night, drinking muddy machine-coffee with Detective Inspector Duncan Silk of the Edinburgh Police.

The kindly policeman is looking more surprised than a detective-inspector is supposed to look. Aren't they meant to have heard everything, thinks Mum.

"*An imaginary friend!*" he says. Now he *has* heard everything. He's trying not to shake his head too obviously – he's trying really hard to be polite and to take all this information in.

"His name's Arthur," says Mum, quickly adding "I mean – it's what my son calls him." This is just in case the detective-inspector thought Mum and Arthur were on first-name terms.

"And you posted him," repeats the policeman.

"I know it sounds silly," says Mum, "when you say it like that."

"It'd sound silly in Latin," says Niomi, who really isn't adding much to the conversation. Although Mum is gripping her best-friend's hand like a vice, so she must be of some use.

"Can you remember *where* you posted him to?" asks the policeman. "Please don't tell me the North Pole, with Santa."

The stocky detective runs his hand through his bright-red hair. It really is the most fiery hair Mum has ever seen. True Scots hair, she supposes. But beneath it is a friendly, intelligent face, even if right now it wears a genuinely puzzled expression.

"*Here! Scotland!*" explains Mum. "A little village called Cape Fury." She shrugs her shoulders, a bit apologetically. "It was the remotest, most faraway place I knew – and I knew it because it's where I honeymooned." Even Niomi looks shocked. Then Mum adds, a touch guiltily. "I told Zack his dad was up there."

A tall, female detective-constable, in a tight, grey overcoat, is standing just a little way behind Silk. The young woman shakes her head – now she's heard everything too.

"*Cape Fury?*" says Silk. "You really weren't taking any chances were you?"

"But what were they doing in Manchester, Detective Inspector?" asks Mum.

"Call me Silk. No idea, Mrs Farmer. But fear not, we'll

catch up with Zack and Lily," he promises. "They'll be on camera somewhere, at a station or a bus stop. We can track Lily's mobile."

"She's not even answering it," says Mum. "Which isn't like her."

"That girl would text from her own coffin," adds Niomi, helpfully.

Silk asks Mum for photos of her kids, which she gives him on the promise that he'll return them. For the first time on this long night, Ruth Farmer begins to cry. "They're all I've got, Silk. The kids I mean, not the photos."

Silk gets up and nods as he walks off. It's a reassuring nod, he's a parent himself, he does understand.

"He'll find them, Ruthie," says Niomi kindly. "He'll probably even find Arthur." She laughs. "Hey, maybe I know Arthur. The men in my life always make themselves invisible!"

From the revolving door of the hotel, Silk looks back. This has to be the strangest story he has ever heard. *Posting an imaginary friend!*

The Tall Detective follows him out.

"If we do find this Arthur," she says, in a soft, Scottish accent, "he's going to be awfully hard to handcuff."

11.10pm: *Saturday, February 16th. Cape Fury. Highlands. Castle Peak.*

Mum and Arthur might not be quite so confused if they could hear what Rogue Max is saying, in the bleak Castle just a couple of hundred miles up the road from Edinburgh.

But they wouldn't be any less terrified.

"Great news!" says the voice. "Tomorrow our convocation of Rogues is about to get a brand-new, little IF recruit. Yes, my evil friends, we are going green!"

It waits for the inevitable cheer from the gathering – because this was actually rather witty. They all know that little, green Arthur is at his turning-point. Another IF gone bad.

Yes!

The first convocation of the most important Rogues in the world is now in session. All gathered together in one dark place, to plot even darker things to come. All rejoicing in this happy coincidence of events – an angry mother posting her child's IF *to the very same tiny town that they have chosen*. And even, most laughably, for the very same reason.

It's the remotest spot on the map.

And now – joy of joys – that same, over-imaginative child is actually *on his way here*, holding his best-friend's Glimmer in his unsuspecting hand.

How wonderfully unique. A combination almost too good to be true.

"Soon, my fellow Rogues," announces Rogue Max, "down in the deepest dungeons far beneath us, will be one very special, eleven-year old Hackney lad. With a *very* useful imagination. As our own dear Prime Minister would say – now for the future!"

Feet begin to stamp. Human feet. (Because of course the Rogues are not alone.) Thunderously yet somehow mechanically – as if a switch has been firmly pressed, a sinister engine started. Rocking the old structure to its medieval foundations.

It is the sound of triumph.

Sunday.

The day of reckoning.

Grow up, Zack Farmer!

36

'THAT LOOKED LIKE
THE PRIME MINISTER!'

7.45am: *SUNDAY, February 17th. On the border of England and Scotland.*

If you were to ask Zack Farmer right now what's the last thing he would want to hear, while his fifteen-year-old sister is driving a massive, borrowed truck down a road she has never been on before, using controls she can only just reach with her small feet and hands, he would probably say police-sirens.

"Oh no!"

The sound of law-enforcers approaching at great speed from behind.

But that's just what's filling their ears. And drivers always assume that police-sirens are intended just for them. (Especially if they *are* actually doing something wrong.)

Fortunately for Zack, Lily, Danny and Holly, they are utterly mistaken.

These particular sirens are simply to warn other road-users that a police motorcade is coming through and that someone really important needs to get to somewhere equally important. Without the inconvenience of far less really important road-users getting in their way.

Flanked by six motorcycle-outriders, the important black car passes the unimportant red lorry at great speed. But Danny thinks he has just managed to catch a glimpse of whoever is in the rear seat, because one of the darkened windows is slightly open.

"Hey!" says Danny, excitedly. But it comes out 'hgghh', because his mouth is still a bit full; they managed to find a load of chunky chocolate-bars in the driver's glove-compartment and Danny just managed to grab one before Lily could eat the lot. (Lucky it isn't the Sugar Police on our tail, thinks Zack.)

"*That looked like the Prime Minister!*" Danny cries. He has a sudden thought. "You don't think he's going where we're going?" He sees how totally ridiculous this is. "Nah. Why would anyone in their right mind go to Cape Fury?"

"I'm going to be sick," says Zack.

"The Prime Minister does that for me too," says Holly, misunderstanding. "Anyone see his rag-doll?"

But Lily is glancing across at her little brother. "You are *not* going to be sick, Zack. You say this every time we're driving."

Zack would love Lily to be right. Especially when he throws-up on her leg, into her handbag and all over Danny's guitar.

"Oh, YUCCHHH!!!" yells Lily.

So what they had feared the police would do, Zack

manages all by himself. Right on the border between England and Scotland, he brings the borrowed, red lorry to a standstill.

Fortunately, not far up ahead is a parking-area, beside a beautiful lake. (Or, if they are *already* in Scotland, a 'loch'.) Lily swerves off the motorway and parks the lorry, but it feels more like a crash-landing than a gentle docking.

Zack rushes out to find a huge litter-bin, in which to be sick all over again. Bye bye chocolate-bars.

His older sister is her usual, sympathetic self. "*I can't believe it!* You've spewed all over my brand-new phone! If we live till we get home, BIG if, you are so dead, Zack."

How do people like this ever turn into mums, Zack wonders. But he soon realises that this is the least of his worries.

37

'HOWSABOUT IMAGINING
ME BACK WITH ZACK?'

7.50am: *Sunday, February 17th. Cape Fury, Highlands. The cliff-tops.*

Kirstie usually loves the dawn.

It is when ordinary places can be at their least ordinary and beautiful places look even more beautiful.

So it is with Cape Fury this Sunday morning, as dawn rises with a promise and a glow. Even the sea sounds like it has decided to be just that bit gentler, as it glides and brushes against the rocks. Ushering in the day with a whisper rather than a boom.

But right now Kirstie McBride is scared out of her wits.

Not because of the dawn itself. Any other time she would probably consider this one a real stunner, even with that oddly disturbing redness she can see in the distance. She has a real eye for beauty, her mum's eye as people tell her. No, it is where she is going, this dawning Sunday morning, that scares her. The unearthly castle way up on a hill.

Castle Peak.

Fortunately, she's not going there on her own.

Unfortunately, the person she is going with is now just eighteen inches tall and seems only to be able to move by dancing in the traditional Highland manner, with his hands up in the air and his feet arched and pointy. Rather than walking with his usual cool and rolling Hackney-strut.

"Can you not go a wee bit faster, Princess?" she asks, turning back to him.

Arthur, still dressed in his tartan-doll outfit, tries to walk faster, but it always comes out like Highland dancing.

"Now I really am a flipping Scottish soldier," he moans, as he bounces, but of course this means nothing to Kirstie. "Oh my days! Can't you *re-imagine* me now please, Cur-stee?"

"Do you really want to be grabbed by that nasty, big dwarf you saw?" she says. He shakes his head vigorously. "And it was you who heard stuff about the castle, remember?"

She may only be eight, thinks Arthur, but she's not stupid. He tries again to make sense of what has been going on, but it isn't easy.

"All I know is old Mr Teensy-Weensy said summit about me 'n my Zack hookin' up at the Castle – but not just yet." He points up to Castle Peak. "So maybe *that's* where they're keeping him, way up there! Or it's where they will keep him, innit, when they catch him." He looks up at the confused girl. "I've *got* to see for myself what's going on up there, Cur-stee. For Zack's sake."

He tries to dance a bit faster towards Kirstie and falls flat on his face. This is just too much for him – and he's even lost his back eye! He throws her his most imploring look.

"For pity's sake babe, can't I at least walk properly?"

She stares at him really hard, closes her eyes and suddenly he's Arthur again. Or at least the fading version.

He struts around, untwisting his spindly, pale green legs and shaking his skinny arms in relief. His third eye is back and he can see the road behind him.

"Thanks, Curst," he says and then an idea occurs to him. A brilliant one that might just fix everything. "Hey Curst, you're good at imagining. *Howsabout you imagine me right back with my Zack?* Wherever he is. Howsabout that, eh?"

Kirstie stops in her tracks and gives him an odd look.

Actually it makes her rather sad that her Princess should still want to go back home to his old friend, but she can understand it. Well, sort of understand it. Even if she can't quite understand how he arrived here in the first place.

So – with a deep sigh – she begins to stare at Arthur in a different way.

But not for long.

Suddenly they hear the sound of engines. Cars are coming towards them, as if out of nowhere, their windows blackened. Bathed in a glow of the deepest red.

Instinctively, Kirstie and Arthur hurl themselves into a drainage ditch by the side of the road. To hide.

But Kirstie can't stop thinking about what her Princess just asked her to imagine.

38

'EVEN YOU BELIEVE OUR DAD EXISTS!'

7.55am: *Sunday February 17th. On the border of England and Scotland.*

Zack Farmer feels terrible and he knows it isn't just from the vomiting.

He feels guilty and angry and embarrassed and scared, and if there are any other rubbish emotions a person can have at a time like this, he's got these too. But if he had to pick just one, it would be anger – directed mostly at Zack Farmer.

I am such a baby! he tells himself – and not for the first time. No wonder people bully me. No wonder I've got no friends. No wonder I'm losing my Arthur. He turns to the older boy. "I'm so sorry, Danny. If those Rogues find us here, we're finished, aren't we?"

"Don't worry, pal," says Danny, comfortingly. "We've lost them now. Even *they're* not that clever." He puts a kindly arm around Zack. "And you're doing great. Really." The older boy looks at Lily, who is furiously shaking out her soggy, sicky phone. "This should be your job, L-Lily."

Right. *That's it,* thinks Lily!

Maybe it's because of her phone, maybe it's the stress of all the running and hiding and driving a truck and being exhausted and not knowing what on earth is going on or maybe it's just everything all muddled-up together, but Lily just loses it.

"Listen, Pavement Pete, I am driving a nicked lorry to somewhere that doesn't make any sense, to find someone who doesn't even exist, so that we can stop ourselves being chased by things that aren't there in the first place. Ooh and then we can save the whole world from overgrown, hacked-off toys! And my brother's just barfed on my phone." She kicks the litter-bin really hard. "*Like I'm d-doing my b-bit!*"

Zack tries to calm his angry sister down. "When we find Arthur, we'll find our dad. Oh man, Lily, even *you* believe our dad exists!"

"Yeah, he exists all right," says Lily, crossly. "But not where *you're* looking for him."

Zack just stares at her. What?

Lily can't stop herself now – and Danny isn't quick enough to stem the tide. "L-Lil…?"

"*Mum made up the address, Zack!*" blurts out Lily. "She knew Cape Fury was the farthest and most out of the way place in the country, because our dad dragged her up there on their honeymoon. But she doesn't have a clue where he is now. Know why? BECAUSE HE DOESN'T *WANT* US TO KNOW!"

Zack is unable to move. Or to speak.

It's as if whatever the Rogues have been trying to do,

Lily just did. She's stopped him dead in his tracks. He can feel the tears wanting to come, burning in his eyes, but he's not going to give her the satisfaction. Oh no. Not here. Not now.

So, finally, as dawn slowly rises, he just turns and wanders off. Away from the big, red lorry, away from the road, away from anything familiar. Danny and Holly stare after him, helplessly.

The homeless boy turns to glare at Lily.

"*What?*" she asks, defiantly. But she knows what.

"Feel b-better n-now?" asks Danny.

Lily yells at him, although he is standing right next to her. "STAY OUT OF THIS!" Turning away, she calls to her brother. "*Sorry* Zack… ZACK? Sorry, babe."

She moves towards Zack and tries to give him a hug, but a hug from Lily is the last thing he needs. Or, at least, the last thing he's going to accept. He stomps off towards the lake, away from everyone, not looking back.

Lily tries to follow, but Danny gently takes her arm. "He w-wants to be on his own," he tells her.

"*He's my brother!*" But something makes her pause. "How do you know?"

"Because," says Danny, quietly, "I'm on my own a l-lot."

Lily isn't going to let him win her sympathy that easily. She waves a finger somewhere into the thin-air beside him. "I thought you had 'Miss America'."

Holly knows who she's talking about, even if Lily is being sarcastic. The cheerleader looks at Danny. "*Sure!*" she agrees. "The special relationship."

Danny tries to backtrack, he doesn't want to hurt

his oldest friend. "Well… yeah, 'course I have. I couldn't imagine anyone better than Holly."

He throws Holly a reassuring smile. She gives a vaguely uneasy one back, as she turns away. "I'll wait for you in the truck, hon," she says. It's not like she needs a key to get in.

Danny can still see Zack, just standing by the lakeside. The water is hardly moving in the still, early morning air. A mother-duck and father-duck float slowly across it, with their sizeable family, making for a small, reedy island near the opposite shore.

Further along, looking almost as tranquil, are some weekend bikers having their enormous fried breakfasts. Large, bearded men and robust women, all with leather jackets, emblazoned with skulls and dragons and fire, zipped tight over their ample bellies. Their most prized possessions, the powerful motor-bikes, stand in a proud group beside them, like horses ready for the hunt. The bikers are laughing as they eat, enjoying the fresh air, the company of like-minded friends and the unhealthiest food known to man.

One of them sees Zack and waves a friendly mug of tea. Zack gives a half-wave back.

"Lily," says Danny, turning back to her. "I do know what it's like, you know, to l-lose a dad."

Lily isn't in the mood for sympathy, but she's finding it hard not to be a little curious. "Did he die, then?"

"No," says Danny, his long, thin face looking even longer, his almond eyes softer. "But he's doing his best." Lily looks confused. "Hospice. That's a hospital you don't get out of on your feet. His body's dying from alcohol — and probably still dying for it. Guess that's why I'm the only sober 'wino' in Manchester."

Lily shrugs. Okay, so Danny – son of a drunk and stepson of a brute – had a hard time. Well tough, join the club. But now, and she isn't totally sure why, she begins to tell him a story.

"My dad had this joke, when I was really little. He'd go out of the kitchen, then a few seconds later come right back in again, but this time with his hat and coat on, and say he was his twin-brother just arrived from Canada and had anyone seen my father? And, like a dork, I'd say, '*Yeah, he just went out!*' So then he'd leave and my dad would come straight back in, you know, without his hat 'n coat, and say, 'Anyone been asking for me?' And I'd get really excited and say, 'Yes! Your twin brother from Canada! You just missed him!!'

She stops and shakes her head, a few unwilling tears in her eyes. "*Kids'll believe anything!*" she says, a long-buried anger rising through her words.

Danny looks at her, as if suddenly some of the pieces that were floating loose are starting to click together, like a jigsaw of the heart. He can see now that Lily isn't someone who'll believe things too easily ever again. Or think much of the kids who do.

She notices him staring at her. The pure and gentle understanding in this strange, troubled boy's look makes her want to turn away, as much from herself as from Danny. She realises that for a few moments she has forgotten all about Zack. She turns back to the lake and calls.

"Zack – are you okay?"

Without looking round, he lifts up a hand to show that he is. Well, sort of.

Danny signals to Lily that he'll be in the lorry, then

catches Holly's eye. She's in the cab and has been staring at Danny and Lily as they talked together. Talked – unusually – without shouting.

Some distance away, at the lakeside, Zack watches the bikers as they laugh and chat over their breakfast. It makes him think about friends – the ones he has never had. Perhaps through his own choice or more likely because they found his imagination too full-on for their tastes. But he thinks especially of the one true pal he fears he has lost forever.

"How can someone I made up," he asks the water, as the first faint hints of sunlight glance over the rippling lake, "be more real than anyone else in the world?"

39

'HE IS COMING STRAIGHT TO US!'

Exactly 8.00am: *Sunday, February 17th. Cape Fury, Scotland. Castle Peak.*

The convocation has begun.

The huge, medieval room, its stone walls seeping like wounds that won't heal, is lit by so many candles that if Castle Peak had invested in smoke-alarms, the noise would deafen every seagull on its battlements. Not that there are so many seagulls sitting there these days. Perhaps they understand the evil that lurks within.

Yet curiously these candles don't even begin to steal away the sensation of darkness the room gives out. Darkness you can almost touch and smell, a clinging darkness of the soul. A chill breeze makes the flames flicker, casting dim light and shadow on all the humans gathered down below.

These men and women seem, from their bearing and their clothes, to be important people. People of standing, people who command respect. Which makes it all the

219

more surprising that their faces are immobile, their eyes blank and that all they do is nod. Almost as if each person has someone – or something – beside them.

Pulling the strings.

Rogue Max is about to reveal his plan. Even the candles stop flickering, out of respect.

"Convocation of Rogues," it announces. "Good fortune has brought us to this great moment." The inhuman voice fills the air. A blinding radiance of pure, pulsating, blood-red energy dominates the room and vibrates to each and every word. "Very soon we shall have the human-child, Zack Farmer, in our hands. A plan is in motion – he cannot escape."

Terrifying laughter resounds through the room. The laughter of a hundred. A thousand. Yet the human faces don't move. It isn't them doing the laughing.

"But for now, we wait," says Rogue Max. "We wait until Arthur completes his journey to the dark side. *Our* side."

"ROGUE ARTHUR!" comes the universal cry.

"Very soon," continues Rogue Max, "the precious, green Glimmer will be ours. Not Arthur's. Not Zack's. It will become totally our own!"

"OUR GLIMMER!" rejoices the crowd.

"Poor, simple Arthur may think he has escaped, in some foolish disguise. But he is coming straight to us. Rogue Max knows this."

The convocation nods. No-one escapes Rogue Max.

"Just imagine it," utters Rogue Max, with a rosy glow. "Rogue Arthur *whispering* in his old friend's ear. As we Rogues all do, when we re-unite with our humans. The fools who think they are now 'too grown-up' for us."

The Rogues nod again. They know all too well the arrogance of departing childhood.

"That secret voice," continues Rogue Max, "right inside Zack Farmer's head. A young head so full of stories and pictures, so full of – imagination." And here the voice pauses, because here is the magic part. The deliciously unique part. The part that gets even Rogue Max excited. "But an imagination now boosted a millionfold by the very Glimmer he holds in his hand. This Glimmer will be Zack Farmer's downfall!" The voices pauses, for effect. "*And that of every other child on this earth.*"

And now, bursting forth from the unknowing *humans* themselves, comes the summation of all Rogue dreams. "THE ULTIMATE WEAPON!" they all roar. Although, of course, they haven't the foggiest idea what they're all roaring about.

Rogue Max knows that standing alongside every very-important-human, in that cavernous chamber, is his or her very own and terrible Rogue. Unseen. Laughing as they have never laughed before.

"Welcome to Cape Fury," says Rogue Max. "Now for the future!"

40

'I THOUGHT I'D NEVER SEE YOU AGAIN.'

8.06am: *Sunday February 17th. On the border of England and Scotland.*

Zack knows that he should be going, but he can't stop staring at the lake.

He takes out the Glimmer, which he is relieved to see is still pulsing faintly. He talks into its fathomless depths, as if it is his old mate himself.

"Wish I was you, Arthur," he says. "You *never* get scared."

"Oh, I wouldn't say that, Mister Farmer," comes a voice.

Who was that?!

Where did the voice come from? A voice that feels more familiar than any other he knows. He spins round fast. And can't believe what his eyes tell him must be true.

Arthur!

Zack Farmer is lost for words. Which is pretty unusual for Zack Farmer. His dearest friend in the entire world is beaming at him from just a few short yards away. A huge smile on his familiar, green face.

Zack rushes towards Arthur, with a mixture of excitement and relief such as he has never known before. There are tears in his eyes as he and his old pal hug, high-five and wrestle like lion-cubs on the dusty ground. To Lily, watching from a distance, it looks like her mad little brother has got into a fight with himself – and is losing. She shakes her head and lights a cigarette.

"*Where've you been, Arthur?*" cries Zack. "I thought I'd never see you again!"

"It takes more than a good posting to see off your old mate Arthur," says his old mate Arthur, in that same croaky, blokey voice.

The long-lost IF leaps around, so full of joy and fun. He even goes to the lake and starts to walk on the water, which is an old trick but a good one. "I see you've still got me old Glimmer," he shouts in relief. "Only just in time, eh?"

"Why are you wearing nail-polish?" asks Zack, not unreasonably.

"Don't you recognise a *princess* when you sees one?" says Arthur. When Zack looks totally blank, Arthur adds, as if this explains things, "It's been a long couple of days, mate."

"You didn't get to my dad's house, did you?" asks Zack, still a tiny bit hopeful, despite what Lily just said, but Arthur shakes his head. Zack shrugs sadly then suddenly remembers, as the panic comes flooding back.

"Arthur, we're being chased by the Rogues! They're the ones who whisper in people's ears and make them do bad stuff! First they just wanted to stop me looking for you, but now they want to kidnap me!"

"Well, you know why that is?" says Arthur. "To make certain you don't ever give me the old Glimmer back. So's you can't ever make me whole again."

"Yes but… they'd go to all this trouble, just to make one IF fade away?"

"They *hate* us, Zack. IFs and kids, we're the enemy." He shakes his head. "But I know a way we can stop 'em forever. Just you and me, pal."

"How?" asks Zack, excited, but still a little scared.

Arthur just smiles reassuringly, like he always does and somehow Zack feels safe again. That's how it always works. "I'll tell you in Cape Fury," he says and slaps Zack's back. "Let's go sort them out, Zacky boy!"

Zack stops breathing, just for an instant. But then the smile returns.

"Yeah. The 'A' team!" he says. "Oh Arthur, I want you to meet my new crew – Danny and Holly. I'm afraid Lily hasn't changed."

The two reunited pals hop and skip towards Lily. Zack has an enormous beam on his face.

"You okay, Zack?" asks Lily, who hasn't seen her weird brother smile like this for a while.

"I am now, Lily," says Zack. "*Arthur's here!*"

Of course, Lily can't see anyone, but curiously she finds herself feeling a bit disappointed by the news. As if it has changed things in a way that isn't totally to her liking.

"Oh. Right," she says. "Well, I suppose we've got to… ought to be getting back to Hackney, then."

"Well, we've nothing to stay for now, have we?" says Zack.

But suddenly his huge smile vanishes, just as swiftly

as it came. His voice changes completely. It's louder and much more urgent, until he's shouting right into Lily's face.

"LILY. RUN FOR THE TRUCK. NOW!" Not surprisingly, she looks surprised. "DON'T ARGUE! *NOW!*"

Lily is too shocked to argue with this new, forceful Zack. So she runs. Zack is beside her, then ahead of her. He looks back and sees that Arthur has swivelled round and is signalling to the group of bikers. *Bikers?* They instantly nod to the IF, drop their breakfasts and leap onto their waiting bikes. Zack almost stops dead in surprise.

"What *is* it about the North!" yelps Lily, still running.

Luckily, Danny has seen their panic and is throwing open the heavy, truck door. Zack and Lily leap straight in. They can hear the bikers rev up their mighty engines, as Lily tries to start the ignition, her hands trembling from yet another northern threat.

Finally, after a lot of false starts, plenty of pumping and throttling and cursing, the lorry begins to jolt. It's not exactly movement, but it's something. Danny grabs the cigarette that's still between Lily's lips and hurls it out of the window. Then he looks to Zack for some sort of explanation.

"Arthur would *never* ever call me 'Zacky boy'," is what he explains.

Lily just shakes her head – the world has gone totally mad. But Danny and Holly don't think so. Nor does Zack, not when he looks out of the window, the Glimmer in his hand. Not when he watches his Arthur, with whom he was just laughing and wrestling moments ago, suddenly transform into a big, fat, mangy-tailed, spitting squirrel.

SQUIRREL?

A huge squirrel with evil, pointed teeth and red-and-black flaring eyes. Cute, he isn't.

"See!" says Zack. "Arthurs don't turn into squirrels. Only squirrels turn into squ—"

His voice is drowned out by an unearthly, unsquirrel-like booming from The Squirrel.

"Get him, men. Don't let Zack Farmer escape!"

The lorry careers clumsily onto the road, sending gravel flying. But the bikers are already on its tail, nodding to a terrible melody that only they can hear, but even they don't understand.

Squirrel jumps onto the man who, just a few minutes ago, was happily waving his tea-mug at Zack. A man who suddenly looks like the biggest, scariest, hairiest biker on earth. The Rogue begins to whisper in his unsuspecting ear – the man nods and jams his foot down. The throbbing bike almost leaps into the air like a stallion.

"They're going to force us off the road!" cries Zack. "Hurry, Lily."

"I'M DRIVING AS FAST AS I CAN!" yells Lily, who's doing really well, considering.

"You're doing r-really well," reassures Danny, who knows you have to build up a person's confidence when they're being chased by a horde of demented bikers. "Hey, don't panic, love," he continues encouragingly. "We're a serious truck. They're just a few f-fat guys on bikes." He looks in the wing-mirror. Oh. "Just a few fat guys on bikes – with c-crossbows!" he gulps. "THEY'RE GOING TO BLOW THE TYRES!"

Zack grips the Glimmer and looks in the rear-mirror. It's like watching a movie, the sort you really don't want to see if you're already in a pretty panicky mood. The sort that comes out of the screen and right at you.

Each one of the dozen bikers, who are all probably really nice guys, thinks Zack, with wives and jobs and kids and pit-bull terriers and allotments, is carrying – as his very secret passenger – a foaming, bloodthirsty, whispering Rogue.

Zack tells himself he mustn't even try to imagine how these invisible fiends looked way back in childhood, when they were the cutest, best friends to the junior bikers. ('Friends' to 'fiends'. He's into those words again!)

Think Zack, think. What's the plan? Just for a moment he wonders where the real Arthur is. *Not now, Zack.* No time!

Okay, he says to himself. They've got serious bikes and huge muscles and crossbows. But we've got a homeless boy, a fed-up Goth, an imaginary cheerleader and me – an eleven-year old wimp. AAArrrrggghhhhh!!! .

Think Zack, *think*. There must be something else. Something that changes the odds.

Got it!

"This lorry," he cries, "what's it carrying?"

Holly looks at him and then looks round into the body of the truck. "Just crates. You wanna lighten the load, is that it?"

It's a thought but not the one he's going with.

"No. Let's open them!" says Zack. "There could be, I dunno, heavy things we can throw at them. Tins of food. Bricks. Encyclopaedias!" He's getting carried away. "Danny?"

Danny shrugs. What have they got to lose?

He joins Zack as they crawl over the seats towards the back, trying not to kick a frantic Lily in the head. They can hear the throb of the bikes growing louder. The men must be just feet behind the lorry's huge rear-door. Out of the corner of his eye Zack can see, in the mirror, the bolt of a crossbow scrape at enormous speed over the road beside them, the friction throwing up bright sparks as it just misses a tyre.

Danny looks around and finds some of the driver's tools under a tarpaulin. A wrench, a jack, a hammer. Heavy. Metal. Perfect. They use them as best they can to smash and prise open the wooden crates, with no idea what they might find within. All they can do is hope.

Hope turns to 'Help!' as the two of them just stare in total amazement.

"*Toys?*" cries Zack. And then he has to say it again.

"TOYS!"

41

'READY FOR YOUR FIRST CHALLENGE, ZACK?'

8.20am: *Sunday, February 17th. The Scottish borders.*

"*TOYS???*"

That makes three times.

"Oh, brilliant!" says Danny, shaking his head. "The driver must have been selling them on the black market. He probably steals them at night from the Toy-dumpers. This is all illegal stuff."

Lily calls from the front. "So that's how many crimes we've committed so far?"

"Don't forget to add fashion-crimes to that list, Cruella," says Holly, but of course this is wasted on Lily.

Danny and Zack swiftly unpack the crates. They'll just have to make do with what's here. The soft toys are useless, it would be like giving the enemy a cuddle. Zack looks for anything that's the least bit mechanical, while Danny scrabbles for as many rubber balls, wooden-blocks and other potential hindrances as he can find.

229

Holly watches them with mounting anxiety. "Better hurry, guys. Any minute those loons out there are gonna get lucky with a crossbow in our wheel and send us flying. Just as soon as they find the right place to do it."

Lily is putting all her energies into manoeuvring the huge and powerful lorry. Part of her is really quite proud of herself. After all these years, she's actually good at something (although 'driving a stolen truck away from barmy bikers' is probably not a skill that's going to help her career prospects).

Zack and Danny hurriedly put their armoury together. Zack has discovered a hoard of fresh batteries and is fitting them into whatever toys can use them. Danny takes a look at the stockpile and shakes his head. How will this ever work?

No time for second thoughts. Not when the first one is the only one you've got.

Zack looks at Danny – okay? Danny nods solemnly. Together the boys grab hold of the lorry's huge rear-doors and throw them open, letting the ramp fall down as much as it can without scraping the ground.

The noise that hits them is deafening.

It is as if the inside of their heads has become a speedway track and motorcycles are trying to zoom out of their eyeballs. But the noise is a lullaby compared to what they are seeing. A platoon of armed, helmeted and totally-brainwashed bikers, all metal and leather and reflections, under the command of forces beyond their – or anyone's – control.

"Hi, guys," shouts Danny, with more confidence than he really has. "*Playtime!*"

The bikers at the front are aiming their crossbows directly at the lorry's huge rear-tyres.

"*Now!*" cries Zack.

They unleash toy hell.

Rolling whatever they've found that rolls, down the flapping ramp and onto the road. Flying whatever they think might fly, into the exhaust-fumed air. And just hurling or kicking the rest. As crossbow-bolts shoot in all directions.

"As my old dad used to say," laughs Danny, a bit tremulously, "just one for the road!"

The bikers are plunged into a world they never expected. A world of miniature helicopters, motorised pedal-cars, speeding skateboards, rolling marbles, floating soccer-balls, clattering building-blocks. And finally a few teddybears and a rocking-horse, just for variety. Danny and Zack are chucking everything they've got at them.

The results are better than they could ever have imagined.

Perhaps it is the sheer surprise that does it. Or maybe it's these little toy 'weapons' messing with the big bikes' finely-tuned mechanisms. Whatever the reasons, Danny and Zack are thrilled as they watch bewildered bikers skid, topple and slide all over the road and each other. Their heavy, leather clothing and their heavy, leathery tummies make sure they're not badly hurt, but they don't look like they're going to be dangerous again today.

Or, at least, most of them don't.

The most fearsome-looking biker of all is still on the road. He's avoiding every obstacle and each new toy from the toy-box. And the boys now see that he has an even scarier human riding on the pillion-seat behind him.

His wife! Both are nodding as they grip their crossbows, each one directed at a different tyre. Even beneath their gleaming helmets, Zack and Danny can see that the eyes of the nodding bikers are blank and lifeless.

As if this isn't enough, Zack – pointing his Glimmer – can make out the horribly grinning face of the Squirrel. He's standing between the two married bikers, frantically egging them on. It looks like they intend to leap, bike and all, onto the dangling ramp and right into the lorry.

"Come and get me, nut job!" shouts Zack, as if he needed to make them any more angry. Danny just stares at him.

Now the Squirrel does a trick the boys never believed was even possible. It's clearly for Danny's benefit and the shock of it makes him want instantly to throw up. The rodent Rogue makes himself visible!

"I CAN SEE HIM!" cries Danny, recoiling. "I can see a huge squirrel!" He can't quite believe it, yet he knows it's true. "Yucchh! He's horrible, Zack." He's yelling now. "The Rogue is *letting* me see him!"

"Special occasion, just for you, smelly boy," laughs the Squirrel, as a creeped-out Danny takes in his first-ever Rogue. He gives Danny an unfriendly wave, then turns his attention to Zack. The words he utters chill Zack to his marrow, wherever that is. "Zack Farmer," he smirks, "are you ready for your first challenge?"

Challenge, thinks Zack, what's he talking about? He soon finds out, when the Rogue starts to sniff.

"We know there's an IF in there with you," says the Squirrel, then pauses for effect. "*Destroy* it. Or my biker friends will destroy your sister!"

Zack can't believe what he's hearing. *His sister?*

All he can do is stare at the Rogue, his mouth opening nearly as wide as the lorry doors.

42

'TO THE DEVIL WITH ZACK!'

8.20am: *Sunday, February 17th. Cape Fury. A ditch near Castle Peak.*

While Zack and his gang drive headlong into a new danger-zone, Arthur and Kirstie are still in their muddy ditch.

They can't believe how many cars are passing them. Each one has its windows darkened and seems surrounded by an eerie, red light. What Princess Annathesia said is true, thinks Kirstie. There *is* something going on up there at Castle Peak.

She raises her small, mud-spattered head above the rim and looks up at the castle. It's still quite a long way off, but her eyes are good and she's almost certain that she can see people. Dark figures are moving about, high up on the jagged, uneven ramparts. And they all seem to be nodding, a bit like that funny old Mrs Ames. Maybe it's an English thing.

As the cars weave away, she lifts herself up and climbs back onto the road. She feels it's safe to talk to her friend again, who she knows is right behind her.

"My ma used to say, if ever you need an answer, ask the sea a question. Maybe the sea knows where Zack is, eh Princess?"

The reply is not what she is expecting from a friend. Nor is the voice in which it is said. In fact it sounds like nothing she has ever heard in her life.

It doesn't even sound human.

"TO THE DEVIL WITH ZACK!" says the voice.

She turns very slowly, scared of what she might see.

She's wise to be scared. What she sees is even more scary than she could have imagined. Arthur's face looks like someone painted a horrible sneer on it while he was sleeping, then forgot to rub it off. His eyes seem to have changed colour – she can see the darkest black flickering in there now. And some fiery red.

Suddenly she feels very, very frightened.

43

'HELP! I DON'T DO BRIDGES!'

8.30am: *Sunday, February 17th. The Scottish borders.*

Kirstie isn't the only one who's frightened this Sunday morning.

"What's going on?" asks Holly, who still can't see any Rogues but can tell from Danny's face that something is very far from okay. *"Danny?"*

But Danny is staring at Zack. "Mate," he says, "they must be testing you."

"Testing me?" asks Zack. "Testing me for what?" And *do I really want to know?*

"Danny," pleads Holly. "Speak to me." He looks at her. It's a look that makes her start to work things out, things she would rather not know. "They want you to do something to me, don't they?"

"No," says Danny. She looks relieved. "They want Zack to do it." The relief instantly vanishes, as the pieces slot together and fear surges once more.

Zack looks back towards Lily, who as usual hasn't a clue what's going down.

"Go on, Zack," says Holly, nobly. "Save your sister. Even if she is part zombie. Close your eyes and just imagine me – gone."

Zack looks appalled by this. He's not even sure how it would work. *Imagine an IF gone?* Who does that? But he's desperate too. He stares from a terrified Holly to the perpetually-confused Lily to an equally terrified Danny. Then back to the grinning Squirrel. He tries to ignore the roar in his brain, which isn't just from bikes and lorries. Zack feels a pain like he has never felt before.

Finally, he shakes his head. He has made his decision. *"No way!"* he cries, defiantly.

Danny stares at Zack in admiration. And the Squirrel laughs.

"Just as we thought," says the Rogue, then whispers into the big biker's ear. "You know the orders, my old friend. Grab him!"

The bike goes even faster. The truck puts on even more speed. Suddenly there's a shout from Lily. *"HELP! I don't do bridges."*

Zack and Danny turn to look out of the front window. Looming dangerously close is an old stone bridge built over a river. The sort of river in which a huge, red lorry could make a very nasty splash.

But that's only the start of their problems.

Driving toward them, on the opposite side of the road, is a small car. As it approaches, Zack thinks he can make out a little boy in the back seat. Then he notices – because the Glimmer is still locked in his sweaty hand – that the boy has an IF sitting right there beside him. It's a Smiley-Guy, who looks exactly like a small child's drawing.

Zack rushes to the front of the lorry, to take a better look and to support Lily, although he's not quite sure how. The lorry and the car are getting dangerously close. It looks like there's hardly room for the two vehicles on the tiny bridge, especially with the swervy way Lily tends to drive. She'll either crush the little car to pieces or she'll go into the river.

Or perhaps she'll do both.

"Lily, grip the wheel," says Zack, as calmly as he can. "Look straight ahead and remember to breathe. You're doing fine."

Strangely, as if she trusts his judgment, Lily does exactly what her eleven-year-old brother says. How did *that* happen? The lorry straightens but it's no use. The two vehicles still look like they're going to become one fiery, smashed-up ball of metal any second.

"Lily, scrape the wall!" yells Zack. "Our lorry can take it."

Our lorry?

Lily does as he says – again. She swerves to the left and sure enough hits the wall of the bridge. Not hard enough to crash, but enough to knock some old stones into the river and make the lorry's paintwork quite a bit less red. With millimetres to spare, the little car just scrapes safely by.

Zack can see that the young mum in the car looks almost sick with relief. Thankfully, her small son doesn't seem to have noticed a thing, but it's Smiley-Guy beside him who catches Zack's eye. He suddenly beams a big, silly, drawn-on smile at Zack. With the Glimmer in his hand, Zack smiles back. It makes him think of Arthur, the real Arthur, wherever he is.

Suddenly a tiny glow makes Zack look down. The Glimmer in his hand is pulsing just a little bit stronger, the green light has become a fraction brighter. Yet he is pretty certain that Arthur is nowhere nearby.

So why is the Glimmer glowing?

Zack can't think about this now. He parks the thought in the back of his mind and turns to the rear of the truck and the Squirrel. To his surprise he notices that the 'animal' is looking at the flashing Glimmer. In fact he's staring at it unblinkingly, droolingly, adoringly – like it's the only thing on this earth that could possibly matter. The glowing disc has drawn the Rogue's attention completely away from what he is meant to be doing, which is grabbing Zack.

Zack seizes the advantage.

Reaching down into one of the toy-crates, he picks up the first thing his trembling fingers touch. Ironically, it's a fluffy squirrel – what are the chances? The sort of cute little squirrel the Rogue itself probably was, in his little-biker's mind, so many years ago.

"Remember him?" cries Zack and throws it in front of the speeding bike.

The big biker jolts in shock, swerves wildly to avoid it, then bangs smack into the dry-stone wall. He and his adored wife and even more adored bike fly right over the old bridge and into the river below. Taking Rogue Squirrel with him.

But not before a final bolt is fired from the crossbow.

"You can't escape, Zack Farmer!" cries the Squirrel, as he sails angrily through the air. "Not from Rogue Max!" The Squirrel laughs. "And not even from your little friend, Arthur!"

As the soaking bikers climb out of the river behind them, shaken but safe, Danny slams the lorry doors shut.

"Did you see how he slobbered over that Glimmer, Zack?" says Danny. "*Did you see!*"

He turns to his young friend excitedly but is shocked to see the crossbow's final bolt. It has entered the lorry itself and pinned Zack, by his jacket, to its side-wall. Danny quickly rips out the bolt and pulls him free but a sudden, sharp yelp makes him realise that the weapon has pierced Zack's skin. He's bleeding – fortunately not too badly – yet Danny knows that it must really hurt.

"It's like they were testing out a new weapon," says Danny, trying to clean Zack's wound with his not-very-clean hands.

"What?" asks Zack, wincing as the pain really starts to hit. "You mean the crossbow?"

"No, Zack,"says Danny. "I mean *you.*" Zack just stares at him. "I think *you're* the weapon they want."

Huh?!!

Zack just shakes his head – it's all a bit much for him. I'm a schoolboy, he wants to yell, not a superhero! And now he's *really* aching from the pain. Great! He remembers an expression his mum would use. 'I need this like a hole in the head!' But she's usually talking about him and Arthur.

A new and much more powerful thought crashes over him, like a wave. Calling up those long-ago times in Hackney and making him need to shout out loud.

"*THEY'RE JUST BULLIES!*" He recalls the bigger boys, the skateboards, the filthy canal. Was it only Friday? "*And you can't let bullies get away with things!*"

Before he has time to develop this thought further,

another new one takes its place. That's what's happening these days, he thinks. Things are moving too fast.

"Danny," he puzzles, "what did that Squirrel mean – I 'can't escape' from Arthur?"

Danny shakes his head, he has no idea. He moves to comfort Lily, who is still trembling. Finding a clown-shaped candy-dispenser on the floor of the lorry, still full of tiny sweets, he pops some into her mouth.

"At least they didn't damage the truck," he reassures Zack. Because, from where they're standing, Zack and Danny can't possibly notice a small crossbow-bolt clinging, like a limpet, to one of the lorry's rear tyres.

44

'I AM NOT YOUR PRINCESS!'

8.35am: *Sunday, February 17th. Cape Fury. A ditch near Castle Peak.*

Kirstie can't stop staring.

"Princess?"

The awful, rasping voice responds and the words are one long spit of venom. "I am NOT your Princess, you sad little girl!"

Kirstie's lower lip begins to tremble. Her eyes fill up.

"Go on – cry! Boo-hoo!!" continues the voice. "An unhappy child is a joy forever."

Arthur glares at Kirstie. But then he spies the tears that are on their way and suddenly he can't bear her pain. "NO!" he calls to her, more softly. "Cur-stee! Please, don't cry babe, innit?"

It's like he is being ripped in two, somewhere deep inside himself. Instead of being good old Arthur, or even good old Princess, there are two totally separate creatures in here, each fighting for dominance. And he is just the battleground.

"Yes!" he cries out, pointing to the distant cars and to

the castle, as the Rogue in him comes surging to the fore again. "These are my people. I feel it. I *know* it."

But even now there is a part of him, smaller than he might wish but still there, that wants to fight off the emerging Rogue Arthur. A remnant of IF, trying desperately to cling on, despite his giving up the vital Glimmer and abandoning all hope of Zack ever finding him again. His whole body, that little, green bundle of imaginative energy, is shaking from the struggle. Violently, ferociously, mirroring the sea below in its fury.

"*No!* They can't make me one of them, Cur-stee!" he cries. "Oh my days!"

But then the rough voice erupts from inside him, as his nastier, crueller self takes over once again. "*Come with us to the dark side, Arthur. Join us in the castle. Soon we shall have power over Zack – forever!*"

It's like some alien force is boring right into his brain. And giving him a headache. He careers around the small, Highland road, his triple eyes flashing, his head spinning.

He turns to Kirstie and for a moment is strangely calm. "You've got to leave me, girl, innit? I know now where I should be. Go home, Cur-stee. Please – GO!"

Kirstie stares him straight in his newly-wicked eyes. "I've not leaving you, Princess. Not ever."

"Then you're a stupid, little girl. And it's no wonder your mummy wanted to get away from you!"

Kirstie gasps, stunned.

Even the sea-birds squawk in horror as Arthur turns and makes his way towards the castle, shouting the awful words once again over his shoulder.

"I CAN NEVER BE YOUR PRINCESS!"

45

'HOW CAN ANYONE LOSE AN IMAGINARY FRIEND?'

9.05am: *Sunday February 17th. Edinburgh, Scotland. Police Headquarters.*

"A LORRY?!"

The tall detective loves watching Detective-Inspector Duncan Silk work.

The man knows how to brief a team of detectives better than anyone. He stays cool, he stays calm, he stays up all hours until the job is done. But even Detective-Inspector Duncan Silk is stunned by the information he has just been given.

"*A lorry!*" he says again.

He notices that his team, both men and women, young and not so young, are hanging on his every word. They know about Zack and Lily. They are on the case.

"A guy in Lancashire," he explains, "wakes up to find his big, red lorry missing. Then a cab-driver, just north of the borders, says he saw a young woman – a *very* young woman – driving one."

A middle-aged, female detective interrupts her boss. "Young women do drive lorries, sir. We can even vote now." The tall detective laughs. Right on, sister!

Silk rolls down a huge map of Scotland. He sticks a pin in Cape Fury, which immediately covers the whole tiny village. He is just about to give each detective a job to do, in order to find Zack and Lily, when one fascinated young policeman asks the boss if *he'd* ever had an imaginary friend.

Silk is horrified. He holds up two big, ginger-haired fists and explains that when he was a wee boy, these were his only friends – and they weren't imaginary. Then he sends them all on their way.

An older man, who is Silk's closest pal in the force, stays behind. There's a smile on his face. "When a guy is lying," he says, "his eyes always look down to the left. Who was it told me that? Oh aye, it was you."

Silk looks around and closes the door. "If you tell anyone this, Sandy," he says to the older man, "you're history!" The older man just smiles. "When I was about six or seven," confesses Silk quietly, "there was this wee girl – a sort of junior private-eye, like I wanted to be."

Sandy laughs. "Your imaginary friend was Nancy Drew!"

"Not at all," says Silk. "She was a tough, Scottish cookie." He turns to the map. "I'll ask the Cape Fury police, which is probably one guy on his bike, to look out for a red lorry. It'll be the only traffic he'll see all day."

The tall detective strolls back in, her long hair swinging, and takes an interested look at the map.

46

'WE'RE GOING TO SORT OUT THIS MAX DUDE.'

10.02am: *Sunday, February 17th. The Highlands. The road to Cape Fury.*

The ferret on the dashboard is still nodding, as the miles that separate Zack from Cape Fury fly by beneath the lorry's massive wheels. It's almost as if the toy animal can appreciate the music that Danny strums on his battered, old guitar.

But suddenly, as the music plays, the ferret's head stops nodding and slowly turns towards Zack. Its glassy eyes begin to flare red and black, its small mouth opens to bare evil fangs, dripping with blood. In an instant, it rips itself away from the dashboard and leaps straight for Zack's throat.

"*Aaahhh!!!*" cries Zack. As he wakes up with a scream.

"*Aaahhh!!*" cries Lily, in shock. But she's also pretty tired, so at least Zack's nightmare did the job of keeping her awake. Which, Zack reckons, is rather useful when you're driving a lorry.

"Sorry, Lily," says Zack, "bad dream," and turns, with the Glimmer in his hand, to find Holly's long legs standing tall on the seat beside him.

He looks up to see that her head is poking right through the top of the lorry, which isn't an open-top. This is just another advantage of being imaginary (of which there are a lot, like not getting fat or being spared pimples that burst.) Holly is taking advantage of it to the hilt.

"Guys, this is *awesome!*" she shouts down to the humans below, the strong Highland wind blowing not a single strand of her long, blonde, imaginary hair out of place. She is totally overwhelmed by the grandeur surrounding them on the deserted mountain road. The view is staggering. "Danny, take a look!"

But Danny seems more interested in Lily than in the Highland scenery. He's actually playing a Goth tune she requested, rather than his usual folksy stuff, which she hates. Although he's playing it in a bit of a folksy way, which Lily thinks is a bit rubbish actually, but sweet of him to try.

"Yeah. I see it, Hol," says Danny, casually. "Very nice."

Holly does a double-somersault out of the top of the lorry, back through the front window and straight inside again. Which is another thing you can do if you're imaginary – and really cross.

She plonks herself right between Danny and Lily, but of course Lily doesn't see. Neither does Zack, because he's too busy staring at the framed photo of himself with Arthur. But now it's almost like a photo just of him, with his arm stretched out to the side, looking stupidly on his own. The way his mum and sister would always see it in his room. Arthur is hardly there at all.

This makes Zack's thoughts all the more urgent. "Danny, you remember The Squirrel talking about this bloke, Rogue Max?" Danny nods. "Who do you think he is?"

"Dunno, do I?" says Danny. Then he considers it. "But there has to be a head Rogue honcho, who does all the – you know – strategy. Like the England football-manager, only good."

"Well," says Zack, determinedly. "We're going to find Arthur, we're going to give him his Glimmer back, then we're going to sort out this Max dude once and for all."

Danny and Holly stare at him. Is this the frightened little kid they met just yesterday in a Manchester station? The boy who talks to imaginary friends because he doesn't have any of his own. The boy who gets bullied by his classmates and his teachers and his sister and constantly told off by his mum. The boy who thought his missing dad might be waiting for him in some far-off place, a place his mum just dredged up from the scrap-heap of her memory.

But Lily isn't so impressed. She goes into that deep, American voice they used to have on movie trailers, before the government decided kids shouldn't see movies, or even trailers.

"In a world where evil, imaginary creatures are trying to take over the planet, their only hope is a boy who can't sleep with the lights off – and a guy whose lights are on, but nobody's home."

Zack and Danny actually laugh at this, so Lily does too. But it's not her usual laugh, filled with sarcasm and disdain for the world. It's a tired yet rather warm laugh, an almost-friendly laugh.

Holly doesn't see the joke. All she sees is danger and

trouble. "I know I'm imaginary, Danny," she says. "But I'm telling you all right now. *GET REAL!*" Danny stares at her. "We can't *win* against them, hon. No way. Not against the Rogues." She sighs. "Let's just go back home." She stops for a second, as a thought hits her. "Even if we don't actually have one."

Danny turns to Zack. "Holly could be right, pal."

They hear the sound of engines behind them and notice a long line of cars just turning a bend in the road. Where did *they* come from? The first car approaches the lorry, then passes it. The others follow. The gang see that the windows of each car are darkened and that the glowering sky ahead has turned an ominous, unearthly red.

Curious.

Zack says something that forces the others to think hard. "Wouldn't you want Danny to do the same thing for you, Holly?" He is trying not to stare at that sky or those cars. "If you'd been posted miles away and were fading fast."

Danny and Holly look at each other. The wisdom of an eleven-year old boy has made them lost for words.

How did I do that, thinks a surprised Zack Farmer, for once in his life rather proud of himself.

47

'GONE GONE TO HELP ZACK ZACK.'

10.03am: *Sunday, February 17th. Cape Fury, Scotland. The McBride cottage.*

Zack Farmer would be doubly surprised if someone told him his name was just about to fly off some confused Scottish lips.

Stuart is the first to sound the alarm this Sunday morning. Actually, he's the first to complain about sleeping right through his alarm. *Ten o'clock?!* He blames Brodie for breaking up his sleep last night. Him and his Highland-flinging with that weird English woman in tartan.

"*KIRSTIE!*" he shouts.

Kirstie doesn't need an alarm with her dad around. But of course Kirstie isn't there. Her dad calls again – no response. He looks to Grandpa Brodie, who's staggering out of the bathroom, seeming a bit worse for wear himself after last night's 'fling'.

The older man stares blearily at his son-in-law then goes and shouts through Kirstie's door. "Darling. I've just remembered a new massacre story. This one's with axes."

No response. Grandpa Brodie looks puzzled, he usually gets a good reaction to this. But Stuart is already through the door and into the pretty little bedroom.

Empty.

"*Kirstie?*" he says, in confusion.

If Lily was there, she'd recognise the scene. Whatever your eyes are telling you, sometimes you just can't believe that a bedroom is deserted. Then Stuart spots the note. Before he has the chance to read it, Brodie is by his side and they're reading it together. Yet not quite together, so that the terrifying words seem to echo around the little room.

"'*Gone… gone to help Zack… Zack,*'" they read. "'*He's in trouble… trouble… Please please don't worry… worry. I'm with Princess Princess… Annath… Annath… Annath..?*'"

"Annathesia," says Stuart, in sad amazement. It reminds him of when his dear wife was having her operations. Of the anaesthetics they gave her to make her sleep. Kirstie must have overheard.

"She thinks it's a pretty word," says Brodie, gently. But Stuart is already moving on.

"Who on earth is Zack?" he wonders aloud.

Brodie admits that he has no idea, but explains that Princess 'you-know-who' is Kirstie's wee, imaginary pal. Stuart looks at him in astonishment, but there is anger in there too.

"WEE PAL! What wee pal? How come you knew all this and I didn't?" But Stuart's anger can't sustain. It certainly can't stop the tears coming to his eyes – tears not just of sadness, but of fear and love and guilt and all the emotions that have been held deep inside of him, because he didn't know how to cope if they all came flooding out.

"I can't handle this, Brodie," he wails. "Not now, not after…"

He doesn't need to finish. For the first time, he allows his father-in-law – tough, kindly and sometimes incredibly annoying Brodie Gemmell – to put an arm around his shoulders and pull him close to his old and wheezy Glasgow chest.

"Stuart son, it's okay. It'll be okay. Och, our Kirstie knows this area like the back of her hand."

Stuart looks at him. "She's eight years old. We live on a cliff. There's a raging sea!"

Oh aye, thinks Brodie, I'd forgotten that bit.

Stuart is off the bed and down the stairs in seconds. "She could have been gone hours, man!" he cries.

Brodie doesn't know what to say. "She's only got wee legs."

Probably not that.

Brodie turns back to the curious note and tries to winkle out its meaning. "'*Gone to help Zack*'?"

10.04am: *Sunday, February 17th. Cape Fury. On the shoreline.*

Stuart and Grandpa Brodie might not be quite so fearful, if they were standing just a few hundred yards further along, down on the sandy shore. Okay, maybe a mile.

Because Kirstie has already begun to walk back home – on her own.

Yet she can't stop herself from turning and looking

back towards the castle. She can still see the little figure of Arthur walking slowly in that direction, up the steep, bleak, grassless hill, his whole body shaking as he fights the demons within him.

It looks to her like he is losing the fight.

48

'FURY COMES!'

10.05am: *Sunday, February 17th. The Highlands. The road to Cape Fury.*

The slow-punctured tyre, the one sporting a crossbow-bolt, is losing its own fight.

Swerving wildly on the narrow coastal road, the big red lorry hurls its terrified passengers around like beads in a baby's rattle. A few yards further on there's a crunch, but Lily and her passengers are bouncing about so much they don't even sense that the lorry has just smacked into something on the roadside.

It's the sign that reads 'CAPE FURY WELCOMES CAREFUL DRIVERS'.

Good luck with that.

10.06am: *Sunday, February 17th. The Highlands. Cape Fury.*

Sitting in his tiny cottage, directly opposite the newly-demolished 'Welcome' sign, PC McKay would have heard the crunch, had it not been for three things.

Struan, Shena and Sam. His triplets.

They're all crying at once. McKay and his pretty wife Morag are happily but tiredly swapping them around, trying to comfort them. Which isn't easy, because there is rarely a time when the McKays don't have a large item of food in at least one of their hands.

So PC McKay doesn't notice the huge lorry rumbling by, with his village's lovely sign wrapped around its front bumper.

In fact, there are a lot of things that escape PC McKay's attention this very special weekend.

10.08am: *Sunday, February 17th. The Highlands. Cape Fury.*

Two minutes later Zack, Lily, Danny and Holly are forced to notice things.

Like the deflated rear-wheel that has finally brought them and the lorry to a shuddering halt. And the friendly 'Welcome' they've just crushed to pieces.

They're standing beside the lorry, on the main road going into Cape Fury, surrounded by mountain peaks and seagulls. There are a few isolated cottages on one side of the road, just below the mountains, but on the other side there are just the cliff-tops, with the sandy shore down below. And, of course, those tall, giant's-teeth rocks.

Danny looks at the crumpled metal. He can just about make out the words 'FURY' and 'COMES'. "Think this

could be a sign?" he says, wryly. But all Zack thinks is —
We're here!!

He takes out the Glimmer but the signal is so faint
now. Even if Arthur is close, Zack reckons his old mate is
clearly very sick. He starts to move the magical disc around,
to the left, to the right, and to his amazement it suddenly
begins to flash more strongly. He checks the direction and
spots a narrow track leading away from the road and down
towards the very edge of the tall cliffs.

"*Danny, down there!* Where those seagulls are. Forget the
lorry, the lorry is dead. Come on, hurry! NOW!"

The others just look at him, as he brandishes the
Glimmer excitedly. Lily is waving her phone around, trying
vainly to get a signal. She suspects that Zack's vomit didn't
exactly give it a boost.

"You are so bossy these days, Zack," she says, tapping
the sick instrument. "Good job Mum can't hear you."

Danny suddenly moans. She senses his almond eyes
aflame and turns to meet them. But no, they're not staring
at her, not this time. They're firmly locked onto her
smartphone.

"What?" she says, a bit perturbed by the look on his
face.

"*That's it!*" he cries.

"What's '*it*'?" says Lily.

Danny's words can hardly get out fast enough. "*That's
how they always know where we are!* Zack, it's the Glimmer. It's
like a transmitter. And it's your touch that's switching it
on!"

He lunges for the Glimmer, but Zack pulls his hand
away. Danny grabs the younger boy's arm, tight. Their

eyes connect, each boy flashing the fire of his own determination, the total belief that he alone is right.

"*I need it, Danny!*" declares Zack, giving no ground. "To find Arthur. We've got to get it to him, before the Rogues can get to me!"

Danny says nothing, he just maintains his hold on the smaller boy's arm. It feels like the deadlock will go on forever, but gradually Zack can sense the homeless boy's shaky grip weaken and the tension leave both of their bodies.

"Then there's no place to hide," says Danny, resignedly. Zack has won. For now.

An adult voice breaks into their world. The voice of an old Scotsman. "*Kirstie...? Darling...?*" Too exposed to run, they quickly slip behind the big, red lorry.

And wait.

49

'THEY'VE REACHED CAPE FURY!'

10.10am: *Sunday February 17th. Scotland. Somewhere beyond Edinburgh.*

"I can't just wait around, Niomi!" says Mum.

Ruth Farmer has been trying and trying to get through to Lily and she reckons she has probably left more messages on one voicemail than anyone in history. "I can't just do *nothing!*" she adds, for emphasis. Now she's in the front passenger-seat of Niomi's little car, as they make their way northwards from Edinburgh. On the move again.

"Ruth, you *are* doing something," says Niomi, reassuringly. "You're giving me a heart attack!"

Mum stops speed-dialling Lily's number and the phone immediately rings. It isn't Lily, which is bad, but it is Detective Inspector Silk, so it could be good.

Only it isn't.

Unless it's good news to discover that your fifteen-year-old daughter has been seen driving a rather large and very borrowed, red lorry across Scotland. When Niomi hears this, she nearly swerves off the road herself. And when Duncan Silk hears that Mum is actually driving up to Cape Fury to look for her kids, he is almost as shocked as Niomi was.

Fortunately he isn't in his car at the time. He's in his office with his older colleague and the tall detective. He tells Mum rather crossly that he would have preferred she remain in Edinburgh, at her Royal College of Nursing conference. And left the searching to the people who know best how to search.

As he slams the phone down, he realises that part of his irritation is because he just can't seem to get through to the police in Cape Fury. He needs to tell the one man up there to look out for a big, red lorry, but PC McKay doesn't seem to want to pick up his phone. If they even have phones up there, Silk mutters.

He decides to go for one of his 'thinking walks' around the corridor of the police headquarters. It's rectangular, which allows him to work out what he has to do, without finding himself somewhere that he doesn't want to be.

"I want every man we can spare, Sandy," Duncan Silk tells his older colleague as they walk together. "I want squad cars, I want helicopters, I want road blocks."

Sandy nods, as he usually does to his younger but more senior friend. But it's the tall detective who moves in closer to Silk on his stroll along the corridor. "I wouldn't, Detective Inspector, if I were you," she tells him gently. "We really don't want to scare them. The wee girl's driving a lorry."

"Aye. Perhaps we should be a bit more low-key," Silk says to the older man, who now looks a touch confused.

So Silk adds "I'm handling this myself, Sandy," as they turn a corner.

"I'll come up there with you," says the tall detective. And Silk just nods.

Walking towards him down the corridor are some senior policemen, clearly in rather a hurry. Silk and Sandy move apart to let them through, but the tall detective doesn't.

She just lets them walk straight through her.

Which they do, without missing a beat. Straight through and onwards, like she doesn't exist. Like she's just thin air. Which she is.

If the real detectives could see her, they'd see a strangely cruel smile appear on her face, a smile that reveals just a hint of unusually pointy teeth. And they'd notice her eyes begin to flash an unsettling red and black. They might even see her head rise up and turn round in all directions, like she's picking up a signal. A signal that tells her some important news, which makes her happy and makes her laugh.

"Zack Farmer has reached Cape Fury!" she announces.

To which Detective Inspector Duncan Silk, of the Edinburgh Police, just nods.

50

'PRINCESS IS REALLY ARTHUR!'

10.20am: *Sunday, February 17th. Cape Fury, Scotland. The cliff-tops.*

Zack knows that the old man will find them behind the lorry any minute. And will probably call the police. He also knows that there's absolutely nothing he can do about this.

The man would, of course, have seen lorries before – even red ones. But he probably hasn't seen many with a village's Welcome sign wrapped around its bumper. Or a cross-bow bolt sticking out.

Zack can't understand why the old man hasn't spotted the little line of feet peeping down below the other side of the lorry. But perhaps the man isn't looking downwards. Perhaps he is staring up at the sky, which has grown disturbingly red. What's that all about, Zack wonders – before a new voice breaks into his wonderings.

"*Brodie?*"

Zack sneaks a peek from behind the rock. He sees a very round policeman, steering his wobbly bike with one hand as he stuffs a baked trout into his mouth with the other.

"*McKay!*" cries the older man, "we've been trying to get through to you! Do you never answer your flaming phone?"

"I do when I hear it," protests the policeman. "Why were you ringing me on a Sunday?"

"We can't find Kirstie," explains the old man. "She wasn't in her room."

"Oh?" says the policeman, leaving this particular mouthful unchewed. "Where do you think she's gone?"

"If I knew that, I'd be there finding her!" grumbles Grandpa Brodie. "I know kids aren't allowed in the park these days, but do you think she might be having a sneaky swing?"

"Is she on her own then?" asks McKay.

"Aye… except for her Princess."

"New hamster, eh? Well, she can't have gone far. Would you like a wee bite of my fish?"

Conversation travels in the open air. Words fly in the breeze like butterflies and nestle in ears that are listening intensely. One word trips a switch with Zack, as he peeks out from behind the lorry. He whispers it to his friends.

"'*Princess*'! That's what the Squirrel said! When I thought he was Arthur!"

But Zack's excitement is making him talk too loud. Danny signals for him to turn down the volume.

"Sorry," Zack whispers, "It's *him*, Danny! Princess is really Arthur! My Arthur. He must be with this Kirstie, whoever she is." This suddenly hits him. "Why's he with her? WHERE IS HE? He could be fading! We're wasting time here."

"Okay, okay Zack," says Danny to his frantic friend. "Just don't use the Glimmer, okay?"

"If I don't, I won't find Arthur!"

"If you do, the Rogues'll find you!"

Zack looks stumped. It's what his mum would call 'a Catch-22 situation'. He has no idea what this means and he instantly wonders if he'll ever be with her again, so that she can tell him.

Looking around him along the cliffs, he's shocked to see, for the first time, the huge, grim castle on the hill. It seems to be glowing, as if it's fuelled by a flame that doesn't burn. Zack starts to shiver. Even from here, Castle Peak fills him with a dread that he can't quite understand.

51

'HE HAS NO IDEA OF HIS DREAM-POWER.'

10.25am: *Sunday February 17th. Cape Fury. Scotland. Castle Peak.*

When ancient gangs of labourers and masons and quarrymen built Castle Peak so many centuries ago, and set it squarely on a huge, bare hill looking out to sea, they probably never imagined that one day, beneath its imposing towers and turrets and parapets, below its now crumbling but still thick, stone fortifications, there would be a car-park for over two-hundred executive cars.

Nor would they have guessed that the stamping of hundreds of feet, resounding through the massive, flinty pile, wouldn't be in response to a call to repel the foreign invader.

It would be to celebrate the arrival in Cape Fury of one rather small, eleven-year old boy with spiky hair and a glowing, green disc in his pocket.

Arthur can see the humans stamping. He can feel the

dark power surge through him, as he gazes down into the huge, candlelit room from a narrow slit of a window, high up on the castle's sea-facing wall. A window once used for firing arrows, without getting one back in the face. He has climbed up there, not just out of curiosity but because something inside of him tells him that he has no choice.

This is his place.

As he stares all the way down, he can hardly believe his red and black eyes. The humans, all smartly-dressed and some of them in military uniform, are not stamping out of loyalty or pride or excitement. They're stamping because they are being told to stamp.

Out of respect for the voice, the light, the shimmering radiance.

Out of unquestioning obedience to Rogue Max.

"They're here! In Cape Fury!" booms the unearthly voice, not hiding its satisfaction. "This is unimaginably perfect. The innocent, young fools are playing right into our hands."

The humans stamp some more. A large, black crow settles on the window-ledge next to Arthur and nearly sends him toppling. Despite what is happening deep inside of him, his dividing loyalties, he is feeling very scared indeed. Especially as he is just beginning to make out, standing down there with their humans, the other Rogues.

His horrible yet wonderful new fellows.

"The human-child still has the Glimmer. But he has no idea of his—" Rogue Max pauses, as if searching for the perfect word, but of course he is never lost for words. *"Dream-power!"*

'Dream-power', wonders Arthur. What on earth is 'Dream-power'?

The robotic humans echo this. "Never in his wildest dreams," they intone. (Because they've been told to.) Then Rogue Max does something that tears the whole Convocation apart. He gives an order he has never given before. *"Rogues of the world. Reveal yourselves!"*

Suddenly, as the intense light of darkness flashes around the cold, black walls, every human in the room is confronted – for the first time in his adult life – *with his own childhood IF*, now gone scarily, terrifyingly Rogue. Slavering and raging, drooling and grimacing, roaring and spitting.

The humans' worst nightmares – brought wickedly to life.

Instantly these very-important-humans, every man and woman, pass out with shock onto the cold, ungiving floor.

THUD!!! (In fact, quite a few thuds.)

But then, as he gazes down on the prone humans and their smirking masters, Arthur's face changes. The shock becomes a smile – not a nice one. He listens with new-found enthusiasm as Rogue Max finally lays out the big plan.

"With Rogue Arthur pushing his buttons—"

What did he just say? Arthur gasps – he's had a name check! He's important! No, he's vital. *Rogue Arthur!* What crucial task is Rogue Max going to spell out for him and his old friend?

"Poor Zack Farmer will imagine just what we want him to imagine."

Imagine what we *want* him to imagine! How exciting is that, thinks Arthur. How powerful!

As Arthur watches the pulsating red light that is his

new master, a more familiar figure enters the great room. Someone he met only last night, but feels he knows really well. The giant, yellow dwarf, the enormous small-person himself.

Give it up for Mr Teensy-Weensy!

On his face the ugly creature wears a smile of great contentment. His eyes are closed and it almost looks like he is dreaming.

Arthur scans the room with his new eyes and sees the same expression on all the Rogue faces. Their scaly lids are coming down over red and black pupils. Gradually he feels his own eyes close. What he reckons must be the exact same dream that they're all enjoying suddenly appears in his own darkened mind, as if on a cinema screen. It's like the best horror movie, except the effect isn't scary – it's exhilarating.

There is a prison cell…

Small, dusty, bare. And in it is himself – Rogue Arthur. He's whispering into something. *It's Zack's ear!* But this Zack looks even smaller than he did in Hackney – and weak from hunger. The boy is nodding as he holds the green Glimmer in his shaking hand. The Glimmer glows so brightly now. It seems that Zack is summoning up his own mega-powerful imagination. But this time it's an imagination that is being controlled by Rogue-Arthur (and the powers that guide him.)

The picture changes. Where are they now?

It's a village street and it looks like somewhere in England. There's a small child, quite cute in that sickly way small kids can be, and the child has his own imaginary friend – a cuddly penguin. The two of them are laughing together and playing and singing. They both seem so happy and full of joy. But suddenly, like a balloon being burst, the little penguin is gone. Vanished forever. The child is quite alone and crying his heart out – while Zack and Arthur watch from behind a tree.

Arthur opens his eyes.

On every Rogue's face is a beaming smile. Satisfaction on a job well done. An IF has been 'imagined' away long before its time – a child has been made unhappy forever. Arthur can feel himself smiling too, as his eyes close once more.

This time it's a shopping mall. He doesn't recognise it, but he has a feeling that Zack does. There are IFs all over the shop, on the concourse, up the escalators, in the gallery. All singing and dancing. Zack is there too – he has the Glimmer in his hand, but now he's holding it like a weapon. Green beams are shooting out like lasers, zapping each happy IF in turn.

Within seconds all the IFs are on the ground, writhing and squirming. A few more seconds and their energy has gone, they're fading away. Finally – *nothing*. Disappeared! Children are screaming. Arthur can see himself, in the dream they're all sharing, standing right behind his old mate Zack.

Whispering. Controlling. Smirking. And destroying.

Now the dream is over. Arthur's eyes are open again, all Rogue eyes are open. All ears are listening, as Rogue Max concludes.

"Soon there will be no more IFs for children to love. No more little friends to *feed* their imagination. And imagination, without nurture or encouragement, can only wither and die like leaves on the cusp of winter. Before long–" He pauses. This has to be the biggie, "– *imagination will be totally dead.*"

Imagination will be totally dead, thinks Arthur. How good is that? How – imaginative!

"But we will be alive," exults Rogue Max. "To rule the world!

Now the Rogues are cheering and whooping, leaping and raising their lizard-like limbs in triumph. Elation is pouring off them in waves. But then Mr Teensy-Weensy, quite bravely in Arthur's opinion, sends a little storm-cloud to interrupt the celebrations.

"Just one tiny irritant, Rogue Max. Hardly worth mentioning." He shrugs, a touch embarrassed. "There's this sickly-sweet little girl——"

Before he can finish, every Rogue in the chamber goes 'Yucchh!!!'

"Yucchh, indeed," continues the large dwarf. "But the trouble is, she has been feeding our chum Arthur with love and stuff. With – and I hate to utter the word – *friendship.* Which, as you know, might well be slowing down his journey over to the dark side."

Now the Rogues do more than 'yucchh'. They stick gnarled fingers down their throats and pretend to vomit. Which isn't very pleasant but Arthur can see their point.

"So, perhaps," persists Mr Teensy-Weensy, "just to dot the 'i's, we should——"

But the overgrown dwarf doesn't get to finish what he'd like to do to the obstructive Kirstie, because suddenly all the Rogues begin to sniff. Anyone seeing them would think there was either a big outbreak of flu or some seriously smelly feet going on.

Mr Teensy-Weensy gazes slowly up towards the high window that looks out over the sea. And stares straight into the flickering, changing eyes of the Arthur they've just been talking about. Arthur's face becomes bathed in a fiery red glow.

Rogue Max has seen him too.

"Get him, Rogues!" comes the cry.

As if they're one single, multi-legged, many-faced creature, the Rogues move towards the wall. They begin to climb. Arthur cannot escape – although perhaps, by now, he doesn't even want to.

Just then the door to the great chamber opens and Mrs Ames walks in. But of course all she can see is a cavernous room, full of well-dressed, respectable humans. All of whom happen to be lying in unconscious heaps on her floor.

"So you won't be wanting any tea then?" she says, knowing that when you run a nice retreat, the secret is letting your guests do just what they feel like doing.

52

'MAYBE IT'S ALL A BAD DREAM.'

10.34am: *Sunday February 17th. Cape Fury, Scotland. The cliff-top.*

Back on the cliff-top, Zack is running. He's running as if his legs are propelling themselves. Running away from the lorry, but still hidden by it, towards the path that leads between the massive rocks, right to the very edge of the cliffs. And beyond.

Running to what could be his final destination.

He has no idea how important he has become in Cape Fury – which is probably just as well. "I'm remembering something!" he says to himself, working things out. "That guy Kenny – the one who gave us a lift from Manchester last night – what was it he said? *'I hear they've got quite a castle in Cape Fury.'* Why would he even mention this, unless…?"

Unless…

Lily tries to call him, in an urgent whisper, as she follows reluctantly in his wake. "Zack – *ZACK…!*" No use. She shakes her head. "Maybe," she says to herself, "this is all a bad dream."

"Or maybe you are," says Holly, quietly. And unheard.

10.36am: *Sunday February 17th. Cape Fury, Scotland. Castle Peak*

Arthur is also wondering what sort of dream he is in.

Every Rogue in the huge, vaulted hall is staring directly at him, through red-and-black flaring eyes. Pairs of eyes he is pretty sure now match his own. He would love to turn away from the glare, but he is encased in it. Wrapped in the lethal, blood-red embrace of Rogue Max.

To be honest, Arthur is feeling pretty Roguish himself. He can lick the drool now glistening on his reddish-green lips, sense pin-sharp points developing on his little teeth and – worst of all – hear very bad thoughts forming inside his rapidly-darkening brain.

But there's still a bit of the old Arthur left in him, as he tries to lighten the mood. "Hi, you old Rogues," he chirps, "am I glad to see you, innit!"

Mr Teensy-Weensy isn't so sure. "Are you really, Arthur?"

"Too right, Mr T-W. I've seen the light and come over to the dark." His small eyes begin to fire, his skinny body snarls. He can't help himself. The Rogues, who are all watching him, start to cheer.

"So pleased to hear it," says the giant dwarf. "But hey, just to 'seal the deal' as they say, we'd like you to help us with a little something."

"Name it and it's yours, Teensy," responds Arthur.

"We want you to help us incarcerate Zack."

"Not a problem," Arthur assures him. "What's 'incarcerate'?"

"Just – you know – imprison. Hurl into a dungeon. That sort of thing." Arthur nods, but the dwarf hasn't finished. "Oh and we'd also like you to obliterate the little girl. If you'd be so kind."

There's a pause.

No-one says a word, while Arthur thinks about this. He has a pretty good idea what 'obliterate' means – it means bad news for Kirstie McBride. The Rogues are watching his face intensely.

"Now you're talking," says Arthur, as a little black tongue, like a viper's, shoots out of his grinning mouth.

53

'OH MY DAYS!'

10.45am: *Sunday February 17th. Cape Fury, Scotland. The shoreline.*

If Kirstie had heard what her Princess just said about her, she would probably be moving a good deal faster along the beach that leads away from Castle Peak. And she wouldn't have enough breath left in her terrified body to talk to herself the way she's doing.

"You are NOT going to leave me, Princess," she mutters. "Not you too. I won't let you."

But then she sees him. A small, determined figure, moving rapidly towards her, with two other slightly taller ones not far behind. Being a polite sort of person, in a village that welcomes visitors (there used to be a sign!), she can't let these strangers pass without saying hello.

"Hello," says Kirstie.

Danny smiles back politely, but Zack has other things on his mind. "I have never seen so much sand in my life!" he exclaims, a Hackney lad to the core. "*Oh my days!*"

What did he just say?

Kirstie stops, but Zack has already gone well past her. Something clicks in her brain. She turns and shouts.

"*ZACK?*"

Zack freezes. How on earth did the girl know his name? "Might be," he says, turning back to her. "Who are you?"

"Kirstie McBride."

"*Kirstie?*"

That's the name the old man was calling out – the one who told the fat policeman about a Princess! "WHERE'S ARTHUR?" he yells, although by now Zack is right there next to her. "Is he with you?"

Kirstie shakes her head, sadly. "I'm forever losing things."

The energy seems to leave Zack's body as tears of total desolation form in his eyes. "He can't have just faded away," he sighs. "Not Arthur. Not after all this."

The girl shakes her head again. "No. He hasn't done that, Zack. He hasn't faded."

For a moment Zack looks relieved, but something in her face makes him realise that relief is not what he should be feeling. Danny has got there too. The pieces are falling horribly into place.

"*That's what they wanted all along!*" cries Danny. "They needed Arthur to go Rogue – so they had to keep you apart. He must have felt you weren't ever coming for him."

Zack looks so sorrowful, as he thinks of the boy he once was. A small boy, full of fear, always running in the wrong direction, who might well have been expected to just stay home – instead of searching for his dearest friend.

Poor Arthur.

Danny grabs hold of him. "Zack, now that they've turned him Rogue, it's *you* he'll be coming for."

Zack has already worked this out. But he just pats the Glimmer in his pocket. "Then I'll need to be able to see him, won't I?"

"You might see him, honey," says Holly. "But you won't be able to stop him."

Zack has nothing to say to this, because he knows deep in his bones that they're right. He wishes now that he hadn't used up all of his sick on Lily's new phone.

54

'THE BOX!'

11.00am: *Sunday, February 17th. Cape Fury. The village playground.*

The sign at the entrance to the children's playground reads ADULTS ONLY.

But the adults of Cape Fury don't play there, because they don't want to upset their children, even if the Government does.

So it's rather unusual, on a wintry Sunday morning, to see an elderly man standing in the centre of an old, wooden roundabout, while another younger but far chubbier man, in the uniform of a policeman, pushes him slowly round and around.

"Is this the best you can do!" comes a voice.

It's Stuart, who has just entered the playground and sees the two men revolving.

"I'd do better," says PC McKay, "if your father-in-law wasn't so heavy."

"I meant in looking for my daughter!" responds Stuart, crossly.

"It helps us think, Stuart," says Brodie. "We've run out of ideas where she could be."

"I've asked my Morag to get all the folk in the village searching," says the policeman. "Did Kirstie ever mention this 'Zack' before?"

Stuart steps onto the roundabout. To his surprise he finds that it is actually quite calming, even if it does make more work for poor PC McKay. But Brodie just sighs sadly.

"I can't recall her mentioning a 'Zack'," he says, "but maybe that's just me and my memory. Perhaps I should have done more sudoku and less Scotch."

But all of a sudden he smacks his head, as if he wants to punish himself. Something has just occurred to him. Something he should have remembered before. "Oh, wait!" he cries. Then he cries 'ow,' because he smacked his head too hard.

His excitement gets to McKay who, without realising it, has begun to spin the roundabout even faster.

"You mind the way she kept going all Eastenders on us?" continues Brodie. Stuart nods vaguely, but can't see the relevance. Brodie is really racking his brains now. "*Hackney!* That was it!"

"Hackney?" repeats Stuart, puzzled. "Hackney in London? When did she talk about Hackney, for pity's sake?"

Brodie doesn't know whether to be angry or sad, as he stares at his son-in-law. "*All the time*, man! Did you not hear her? Were you not listening?"

Stuart looks a bit guilty, but he has to move on. "Okay, this 'Hackney-Zack'," says Stuart. "Maybe he could be the key. I'm not saying yes, but—"

He doesn't get any further.

Brodie suddenly leaps off the roundabout, but it's still moving, so he has to break into a run in order to stop himself from falling on his face. Yet somehow this only makes what he has to say more impressive, as he's now shouting it from a distance. "*THE BOX!*" he cries. In capitals *and* italics.

Then he falls over, as the dizziness gets to him. The other men stare at him and shout back. "What *BOX*?" Then: "Have you broken anything?"

Brodie hasn't. He picks himself up and rushes back to them, his face growing red from excitement. (And, of course, from all the whirling and running. He's not a young man.)

"Her weird talk," he explains, "it all started yesterday morning – when the postman delivered that empty, white box!" McKay has no idea what Brodie is talking about, but Stuart does and is listening intently. "There was another name she kept saying too," continues Brodie. "Andrew? No. Angus?" Finally, after every 'A' name under the sun, except for Archimedes, he latches onto it. "*Arthur!*"

Before Stuart can say anything, Brodie is off and running again. "I'm on a roll. Come on, Stuart."

Stuart is confused, but he knows better than to stop Brodie when he's like this. "McKay," he tells the baffled policeman, "you keep on looking, you hear me? You *and* the rest of the village. Search every nook and cranny in Cape Fury. I want my wee girl home!"

The desperation on the man's face makes McKay want to weep, as he thinks of his triplets safe in their nice, warm house and probably screaming their chubby, wee heads off.

The men are so busy and anxious, they don't see the little yellow car parked just outside the playground. So, of course, they don't notice Mrs Ames sitting there, all on her own, just watching them and nodding. And if they don't see her, they certainly don't hear her talking, as if to herself.

"New orders," she repeats, nodding even faster. "'*Stop the McBride dad and the Farmer mum from* ever *meeting up – at all costs!*' Uh-huh. O-kay. Will do."

Mrs Ames knows how to obey an order. Especially as she thinks the mission to stop the parents of Kirstie and Zack from joining forces – which Mr Teensy-Weensy and his Rogue pals clearly don't want at all – is coming straight out of her own brilliant, blue-rinsed head.

As IF!

She gets out of the car and calls to Brodie. "Yoo hoo, Brodie dear? You look troubled. Is there anything I can do?"

55

'IS THERE A GROWN-UP
WHO'D BELIEVE YOU?'

11.30am: *Sunday February 17th. Cape Fury. The path up to the cliff-top.*

If Zack had been there in that playground, with his Glimmer, he'd have been able to see exactly who or what was lurking beside the tartan woman. He would have warned Grandpa and Stuart about the giant, yellow dwarf. (Not that they – or anyone – would have believed him!)

But right now, as he clambers back up the steep cliff-path, he can't see anything aside from squawking gulls and a sky that is growing redder than any sky he has seen. He turns to look at the strange, little girl walking beside him. He's not an expert on little girls, but he doesn't think he has ever noticed such sadness clouding so sweet a face.

"I can't believe Arthur would turn Rogue," he says, which is obviously not something to give the girl her smile back.

He also can't believe how fast she is walking, on such tiny, thin legs. She's like a mountain goat. He guesses her

281

small frame must be more used to the terrain and the crisp air round here than him with his Hackney street-shuffle and polluted city lungs.

Danny is straggling too. Zack can hear his poor, homeless friend panting, like he's just run the London marathon in a suit of armour. I wish I could make Danny fit and well, he thinks — if the damage to his body, from years on the streets, isn't already too far gone. I bet Mum would know what to do about that.

He hears his sister sigh. But with Lily, it's more of a what-am-I-doing-here-when-there's-not-a-clothes-shop-in-sight sort of sigh. Mixed-in with sheer exhaustion from all that driving and an underlying terror that she really doesn't want to face right now.

"Pal, you've *got* to believe it about Arthur," says Danny, trying to catch his breath. "And now he's coming after you. Whether you can see him or not, he's your old IF. You're going to be in his power."

Zack looks like he is about to cry. I can't let Kirstie or any of them see this, he tells himself. So he coughs bravely into the Highland air and strides up to the top of the cliff.

Then he stops dead, his head poking just above the crest.

He had expected the cliff-top to be deserted, like the rest of the Highlands. But just a few yards away, on the main Cape Fury High Street and in every little side-road and alleyway, he can see people *searching* for something. Or for someone.

Lots of people.

Men and women, all very smartly-dressed, peering behind rocks and bins, beneath the odd car, around every tree. They must be the people of Cape Fury, thinks Zack, on the look-out for a missing, eight-year old girl. Perhaps they've just come out of church.

But Kirstie corrects him, before he can even speak. "They're not from round here," she says, chillingly. "I know everyone who lives in Cape Fury."

Zack looks more closely and notices that each of the searchers' heads is gently bobbing up and down.

Nodding.

"Then they must be from the castle!" he says, working things out. "It's not you they're looking for, Kirstie," he adds, without total accuracy. "It's me. They need to capture me – because of Arthur and the Glimmer."

He hears a huge, exasperated sigh from behind him. *"AAAAARRGGHH!!"* moans Lily. "That is IT!"

He turns to see that his big sister's face is a picture of utter frustration. "Reality-check, Zack!" she moans. "Whatever's going on round here has *nothing* to do with little, invisible, green men! OKAY? You're nearly twelve – this isn't infant-school! My mobile's still not dried out, thanks to you, but if this dump has a phone-box, we're calling Mum. Now!"

"L-Lily," says Danny.

"I'm talking to my brother!" she snarls. "Zack, it's over. Only you could have an imaginary friend who hates you!"

Kirstie gives a shocked little gasp. Right now she is so glad she doesn't have an older sister, especially one who's that daft she doesn't believe in imaginary friends. But it appears that this curious, older girl, with the blackly-painted nails and weirdly white face (Lily has found time, even with all this, to re-do her make-up) is now talking to her.

"Kirstie," says Lily, firmly but not unkindly, "you're going home too. Okay? Your mummy will be worried." Lily has no idea why the little girl suddenly has tears in her eyes.

"Lily's right, love," says Danny. "For once. You've got a home to go to – you're a lucky girl."

Kirstie doesn't totally get this. Everyone has a home to go to, haven't they? But she plonks herself firmly down on a rock just below the cliff-top's rim. Her face seems set, like one of the carvings under Cape Fury's old church roof.

"I'm NOT going," she insists. "No way, innit?"

Danny sighs. He's not used to little kids, but he knows you have to reason with them, get them on your side. He can see Zack peering up and watching the watchers intently. It can't be long before these odd, nodding 'zombies' spot them.

"O-kay," says Danny, thinking hard. "Kirstie lass, this is a bit of a long shot, but is there a grown-up somewhere – anywhere – who'd believe you, if you told them about all this? I know it's not very likely—"

"*There's my Grandpa Brodie!*" says Kirstie excitedly, much to Danny's surprise. "I think *he's* got an imaginary friend too!"

Danny and Zack exchange a look. Of course, they both know that her Grandpa Brodie has no such friend and won't believe any such thing – what adult would? That's part of the problem. That's why Arthur was posted and why Danny was rejected by his own family and chased by the Children's Army. That's why they're all on their own up here. But at least it will get the girl safely home.

"Then here's your mission," says Danny. "Go tell this 'Grandpa Brodie' what you know. But keep out of sight of this lot. *Go!*"

Kirstie is already scooting along the edge of the cliff, just below spotting range. "I know all the back ways. Bye Zack."

Lily is impressed. "Well done, Danny." Their eyes meet – he turns away, a bit embarrassed by her praise. "Come on, Zack. We're going to the village to make that phone-call. Show's over. Prepare to be grounded forever."

Danny gently touches her arm. This time she doesn't shrug him off. "Lily," he says, softly, "I may be wrong, but somewhere inside of you, I think you do b-believe. Really. Just a l-little bit."

She glares at him – *what?!!!*

Yet he and Zack glimpse just that tiny shadow of doubt, as it glances over her face. But then her little brother says something that throws even Lily Farmer.

"Know what – you're right, Lily," sighs Zack. "Truth is, I'm frightened now. Really frightened. I just want to get as far away from Cape Fury as possible."

To Lily's surprise, the brave and determined look that has become such a feature on her brother's face is rapidly falling away. Once again he seems his old, scared self. Little Spider-nerd, the friendless wimp who runs from everyone and stupidly jumps into canals. Even Danny is shocked by this. But Lily just smiles in relief. Finally!

"Can I hold your hand please, Lily?" asks Zack, quietly.

Lily is so touched by this gentle request, she doesn't have time to think that holding her brother's clammy, little hand is probably the last thing she would ever wish to do. By the time she does, Zack has already slammed his palm hard into hers. And pressed it tight. Their eyes meet. A tiny, green glow escapes.

And Lily screams.

56

'CAPe FURY HeRe WE COME!'

11.32am: *February 17th. Edinburgh, Scotland. A heliport.*

A police-car powers through the narrow, Edinburgh streets.

Sandy, the older detective, is driving. He enjoys the speed, weaving in and out of traffic, catching the beam of blue light as it flashes on the roof above his head. But what he really wants to be doing is taking a trip inside the helicopter – the one he knows is waiting just a few minutes away. He loves helicopters, has done since he was a kid. He knows there's a chopper waiting because he booked it for his boss, who is insisting that he travels alone.

Of course Sandy has no idea that Detective Inspector Duncan Silk will not be travelling alone. Because neither does Detective Inspector Duncan Silk.

"I wonder if our Zack Farmer has found that wee 'friend' he was looking for," says Sandy. He smiles at the nonsensical notion, wishing that he had an imaginary helicopter-friend.

Silk, sitting beside him, isn't smiling. But were anyone to see the tall detective, who is also in the car, they'd notice she has a far-from-pleasant grin on her face.

"Zack hasn't found his Arthur yet," she says, unheard. "But I'm guessing he won't like it very much when he does." She laughs long and hard at this.

Within minutes they're at the heliport.

The police helicopter is there, gleaming in the rare, mid-February sun. The blades are already whirring, the engine running.

The car stops just beyond reach of the blades. Silk rushes out and makes for the helicopter, ducking down to avoid being sliced in half. The tall detective doesn't care – the blades go straight through her, like a butcher's knife through a stick of salami, as she joins him in his seat. The pilot nods gruffly to Silk.

"Oh, one thing, Duncan," says the tall detective, as she settles down beside Silk. "Do you have that nice weapon I asked you to bring? You know, the one that makes grown men weep." Silk nods – he has it. He has no idea why he should have to use it. But he'll find out.

The helicopter takes off. The older detective waves it a sad goodbye.

"*Cape Fury, here we come!*" whoops the tall detective. "I just can't wait to meet you, Zack Farmer!"

57

'NOW DO YOU BELIEVE ME?'

11.33am: *Sunday February 17th. Cape Fury. The path up to the cliff-top.*

Lily is staring at her very first, real-life, honest-to-goodness IF.

She's a very tall and pretty American cheerleader. A cheerleader who poses in typical, cheerleader style. Lily's mouth has never been so open in her life – or her eyes so wide.

"Hi, Lily," says Holly, giving a twirl.

But the searchers have heard Lily's scream. They are alert and looking around. Now they're nodding big-time and moving towards the cliff-top. The older boy swiftly grabs the others and they scurry as fast as they can, to find cover behind a huge, craggy rock. But Lily can't shut up about this new revelation. And who could blame her?

"*Who ARE you?*" she asks this apparition in red, white and blue.

"Same gal I've been all along," says Holly, "but you were

289

just too dumb to believe it." She strikes another vivid pose. "Drop dead gorgeous, right?" Lily just nods. If anyone ever asks her for a definition of gobsmacked, here it is.

"See, Lily!" whispers Zack. "Now do you believe me?"

The searchers are getting close. Zack is sure he can hear sniffing, as they pick up the scent of an IF nearby. (Or at least their Rogues do and they're simply passing the message on.)

"I believe you," nods Lily. "Sorry, babe." Then she adds, rather politely for her, " Er – hi. Holly."

Zack smiles as his sister reaches out for Danny and gently touches his arm. "I'm really sorry, Danny. You know, for all that 'nutter' stuff. I really wanted to believe, honest. But something inside of me wouldn't let me." Her voice becomes unusually gentle. "But now I don't feel so – you know – alone any more."

They stare at each other, with a small smile on each of their faces. Lily's features seem to have suddenly relaxed. Zack had never realised what a sweet face his sister has, because of that expression of superiority she always wore, along with the hard, Goth look. Which he can see now might not have been the real Lily at all.

"Too late for sorry, sugar," interrupts Holly. "*'Two-Four-Six-Eight…* '"

"Oh, get over yourself!" says Lily, suddenly Lily again. "And who dresses like that for Scotland?"

Zack can see that this could get ugly, so he drops the Glimmer back into his pocket. Holly vanishes.

"That girl so creeps me out," shudders Lily, then grabs her brother. "Okay Zack, the world is even weirder than I thought. Now let's get out of here and go home."

Zack turns away from her and looks up at the sky. In the distance he can see the huge Castle on the hill, which is now completely bathed in a scorching red glow. "This is bigger than just me and Arthur now, Lily," he says. "A whole world bigger." Which sounds pretty good and noble to Zack, but all Lily can do is sigh loudly once again.

They're so involved in their thoughts that they don't hear PC McKay until he's virtually on top of them, standing there on the other side of the gigantic rock. He is about to walk right round it and discover them – which, naturally, will bring all the dangerous searchers running.

Game over.

Then the policeman's phone rings.

As he moves round the rock one way, the gang edge around it the other way, trying to stay out of sight of both him and the searchers. It isn't easy, but at least they can hear exactly where PC McKay is now, because he has to shout really loudly over the terrible phone-line.

"McKAY!" he yells. "Oh hello, Brodie… No, nothing yet on Kirstie… Sorry, you're fading… Brodie…? Och! *Helloooooohhh…?*"

And now the podgy policeman says something, or rather shouts something, which seems to strike a chord with Zack. It touches something deep inside his tired, confused brain. Unfortunately, he's not sure what it means.

"I sometimes say to my Morag," yells the entire Cape Fury police force into his phone, "that we should move the whole village up to flaming Castle Peak! AT LEAST THAT WAY WE'D HAVE SOME CONTACT WITH THE WIDER WORLD."

There's something here, thinks Zack. Something he's

missing. *Come on, Zack – what is it?* No. Nothing. Perhaps it'll come to me, he thinks. Or perhaps it won't. At least I know now that there can be no turning back.

As the big policeman continues to shout about Kirstie, Zack Farmer wonders – for a moment – if his mum has bothered to call the police about him.

58

'WHO CALLS THEIR CHILD UTH?'

11.40am: *Sunday February 17th. Cape Fury. Scotland. The McBride living-room.*

If Brodie and Stuart had known the Edinburgh police were on their way up here by helicopter, they would probably be delighted.

Because right now all they have to help them are Mrs Ames' strangely silent, nodding guests. They are scouring the whole of Cape Fury for one small, eight-year-old girl. (But not in order to restore her to her anxious family – so they really wouldn't be much help at all.)

Mrs Ames is far more interested in what's going on in the McBride living-room. Two grown-men with their heads practically inside a ripped-open and utterly empty, big white box.

"Who sends anybody an empty box?" she asks.

Brodie examines the bottom of it again, where Kirstie has scrawled 'Princess Annathesia' in thick, black magic-marker. "No idea," he replies, then looks even closer.

"*Hang on!* See! There, just beneath Kirstie's writing. There's wee bits of the old label still stuck on."

Stuart grabs the box out of Brodie's hands, which is a bit rude but the man is desperate. He puts on his glasses and tries to decipher it. "It must be the old address, the one the box was first sent to. You know, before somebody used the other side to send it to us."

He looks even closer, as if willing the old address to still be there, but somebody has clearly scraped it away. "No. Totally gone." He looks closer. "Oh, wait a moment, hang on… "

He points something out to Brodie and Mrs Ames. There's some very small printing right at the top of the torn-off address label, the sort of printing that companies and big organisations use, when they have to send off a lot of letters and parcels and want people to know where they came from, without having to write it afresh each time.

"'L OLLEG F NUR.'"

Stuart tries to puzzle it out, squinting through his glasses. "L OLLEG?" It means nothing to him, what's a Lolleg? But then, suddenly, it sort of does. "Could OLLEG be 'College'? Maybe. F – NUR? College – F… College of… Nur–Sing! *Royal College of Nursing!* There *is* a Royal College of Nursing, isn't there?" He ploughs on, excitedly. "Oh and here, see, there's something smaller typed under it… UTH FARM. What's a farm got to do with nursing?"

The three people look puzzled. Even the big fish in the glass case, on the wall above the fireplace, looks puzzled. Then Brodie remembers something, so he grabs the box and turns it over.

"See the address they sent it to? *'Stuart Farmer. The High Street. Cape Fury.* 'So maybe the person who sent it is a Farmer too. Uth Farmer. Could be a relative." Brodie looks puzzled. "Who would call their child Uth?"

"Not Uth," says Stuart. "*Ruth*! This Royal College of Nursing must have sent a Ruth Farmer something in a box and she's just used the box to send – well, to send emptiness – to someone called Stuart Farmer in Cape Fury. Her brother, maybe? But, of course, there's no such guy here, is there, so it came to 'Stuart *the* farmer' by mistake."

They don't look any the wiser. The whole thing sounds totally bonkers – why would anyone send absolutely nothing to their own brother, in a big, white box? But Mrs Ames – her secret mission in mind – seems determined to steer them onto a different track.

"I think you chaps are barking up the 'wrang' tree, as they say up here." The men look at her, because they don't say any such thing. "Little, wee Kirstie will probably trot through that door any minute and all this silly talk of boxes and nurses…"

"*Hackney!*" says Brodie, interrupting her. "Sorry Audrey, but I did say Kirstie kept blethering on about Hackney. Maybe that's where this Uth – I mean Ruth – is from."

Stuart just stands there, looking thoughtful. Hackney? In London? It seems like such a long-shot, but to be honest, what else do they have? "I'll get onto the Royal College of whatsits. See if they know who Ruth Farmer of Hackney is." He rushes over to the computer. "And maybe *she'll* know who on earth Zack is!"

Mrs Ames smiles. It's all rather exciting watching these

grown men rush around, but she does hope that the sweet, little girl is alright. The poor family seem to have had enough troubles recently, without all this.

But as she looks up, the smile freezes on her cosy face.

There, towering above Grandpa Brodie in the small sitting-room, is what looks like – yet surely can't be—

A huge, yellow dwarf!

And he's grinning horribly, through teeth in need of a good dentist. Has she become drunk all of a sudden – without going to all the bother of actually drinking? If it wasn't such a ridiculous idea, she would think he was a grotesquely blown-up version of the cute, little imaginary friend she had as a child. Now what was his name again – *Mr Teensy-Weensy*, that was it! But how can this possibly be – is she going insane?

Can tartan affect your brain?

It doesn't make her feel any easier when the creature actually speaks, in that smooth but quite horribly deep voice. Like it's coming right up from the centre of the earth, way beneath his huge dwarf-boots.

"Hello Audrey, haven't I grown?" says Mr Teensy-Weensy, with a ghastly smile.

Mrs Ames looks around, but as she watches the men hovering over the computer, she realises that only she can see and hear him (although she dearly wishes she couldn't!).

"I've got a little job for you," he says.

Glancing up into the dwarf's disturbing red-and-black eyes (which surely weren't ones she had imagined as a child), she sees them suddenly veer away from her towards the window. She follows his ugly gaze and notices a long stream of what look like her own curious visitors, from the retreat. But they're moving ever so oddly down the High Street, in a strange, unblinking, nodding line. It's as if they are prisoners or hypnotised – or both.

She looks back at the horrid, giant dwarf, who is happily waving to the passing throng, like they're his best mates. She wonders, with a shudder, what he can see that she can't.

"Audrey?" says Brodie. "Are you okay? You've gone ever so pale."

Mrs Ames just nods. She finds that her body won't let her do anything else.

59

'STOP THE SCOTSMAN!'

12.10pm: *Sunday, February 17th. Cape Fury. Highlands. The base of Castle Peak.*

"Zack Farmer, you have got to be flipping joking!" says Danny.

It's how Lily feels too. They're standing at the foot of the massive hill, staring way up at the bleak majesty of Castle Peak. The castle itself looks like a dreadful curse cut out of the rock, about to cast itself down upon anyone incurring its wrath.

"Okay, enough now, Zack," says Lily, who may have seen one imaginary friend, but that doesn't mean she's suddenly in love with them. Or with big hills, for that matter. "One word – 'WHY'?"

Zack thinks about this for a long second. Then he turns to her. "I'm tired of running, Lily," he says simply. It's the most heartfelt thing he has ever said in his life.

"So you've taken up climbing instead?" says his sister, who isn't in the heartfelt zone and doesn't like the look of this grim hill one bit.

"Ever hear the words 'Lions' Den?'" asks Danny. Zack just stares at him, because he never has. But he can work it out.

"Hold my hand, babe," says Lily.

Danny reaches out and takes her hand. Holly watches this and isn't too pleased. "I think she meant Zack – actually," she says, but nobody seems to be listening.

Zack, whose hand isn't being held by anybody, suddenly wonders what Mum would make of his being so far away from home. Or staring up at a creepy, mouldering castle by a tempestuous sea, inside which there are creatures not of this world, who intend to do him and the rest of humanity enormous harm. And that he might be the *only* person on this entire planet who can stop them.

At least this time she couldn't say, 'Oh, not again, Zack!'

12.30pm: *Sunday, February 17th. Cape Fury. Highlands. The McBride living-room.*

"Oh, not again!" says Stuart McBride, whose internet connection keeps failing. Does nothing ever work in this tinpot village?

Of course he has no idea that the appalling Mr Teensy-Weensy is currently just inches away from him, sitting on the ample, tartan lap of Mrs Audrey Ames. At least he's not heavy, thinks Audrey, although really this is the least of her worries.

Brodie smiles at Mrs Ames. It's a nice smile, kindly and affectionate, so he must wonder why she's returning it with bulging eyes, a floppy tongue and an extremely terrified sigh.

"The Royal College of Nursing has a big shindig going on in Edinburgh right now!" proclaims Stuart, jubilantly. His internet is clearly back on stream. "And guess who's speaking at a fringe-meeting there today?"

"Uth!" cries Brodie. "Uth Farmer."

"Ruth Farmer."

"I prefer Uth."

"Brodie, I want you to stay put," says Stuart. "In case Kirstie comes back. I'm off to find this Farmer woman." He looks a bit desperate. The whole idea does sound like rubbish. "It has to be worth a try, Brodie," he says, as he rushes off.

Mr Teensy-Weensy looks quite concerned at this turn of events, so he immediately shouts some orders into Mrs Ames' ear. "Do it now, Audrey!" he commands. "*STOP the Scotsman!*"

It's funny how a person can say something that they're sure is crystal-clear, but the other person still goes and takes it in a totally different way. This happens to Mr Teensy-Weensy now. It happens when Audrey Ames leaps up, grabs the first thing she sees – which unfortunately is that massive fish on the wall, the one in its glass case – and smashes it down on poor Grandpa Brodie's head.

He sinks like a stone.

For once, Mr Teensy-Weensy is almost lost for words. "Not *that* Scotsman, you human idiot!" he splutters, imaginary spittle going everywhere. "Stop the PARENT! *Remember?!*"

"Oh yes," says Mrs Ames, apologetically. "Silly me."

They hear the sound of an engine. The parent that needed stopping is driving off in search of that other parent, Ruth Farmer, unharmed. While the wrong person lies flat out on the carpet.

The huge dwarf sighs in frustration, which Mrs Ames can totally understand in the circumstances, but he tries to keep calm as he explains.

"You see, Audrey," he tells her, "we Rogues are only able do the sort of rotten, nasty stuff we do, because no sensible mum or dad believes in IFs any more. *They've totally grown out of them!* Like you, in fact – until possibly today. So they'd certainly never believe anyone who told them about naughty creatures like me. And all the damage we've been doing."

Mrs Ames nods in complete agreement, as the dwarf continues.

"But just think, Audrey dear, what if this were to change and grown-ups got just the slightest wind of the stuff we're up to? And the sort of important people we control! What if they started to *believe* their kids for once – and believe in IFs again? The days of the Rogues would be numbered!" He pauses and smiles his sickeningly confident smile once more. "But I'm afraid that just isn't going to happen."

The large Rogue is so busy explaining all this that he doesn't hear Kirstie coming in through the open back-door. (Nobody locks their doors in Cape Fury – it's that sort of place.) So he's totally unaware of her staring down in horror at poor Grandpa Brodie, lying flat on the floor. Nor does he see her looking up to find Mrs Ames standing completely on her own, still with her fishy weapon in her hands.

Fortunately for Kirstie the scream she really wants to let out gets stuck in her throat. Equally fortunately her little legs whisk her swiftly backwards into the kitchen and out of sight.

"Oh well, we'll just have to get rid of the parents later," says Mr Teensy-Weensy, rather casually. "And, of course, the little girl. But first, my dear Audrey, you're going to help me grab Zack Farmer. He's on his way up to the Castle now."

"The castle?" says Mrs Ames in surprise. "Why on earth is this Zack going to the castle?"

"Because he's brave," laughs the big dwarf. "And stupid. I do so love that combination."

"Well, we'll have to walk," says Mrs Ames, a bit shakily, as she looks down on Brodie. "I can never drive after I've hit a man with a fish."

She makes unsteadily for the door, accompanied by Mr Teensy-Weensy. Leaving poor Grandpa Brodie moaning on the floor.

60

'THEY'RE ONTO US, ZACK!'

12.40pm: *Sunday, February 17th. Cape Fury. Highlands. The McBride house.*

As soon as they've gone, Kirstie rushes straight back in.

To her relief Grandpa Brodie is making noises, even if they aren't exactly hymns of joy. *"Grandpa, are you okay?"* she cries. "Please, say something!"

Before he can say a thing, Kirstie announces that she's phoning the hospital.

"Forget the hospital, poppet. No time," says Grandpa Brodie. "You've got to help this Zack chap. I just heard the madwoman say he's on his way to the castle. Lord knows who she was chatting to, but it all sounds awfully nasty."

"Castle Peak?!" says Kirstie and she seems worried. She turns to go but then something else occurs to her. "Grandpa, the wee pal you're forever talking to, when you're on your own. What's his name?"

Grandpa Brodie gives a gentle smile. "He's called your Grandma. Now scoot."

Kirstie takes one last, concerned look at him then rushes off. Grandpa Brodie sighs and gazes up towards the heavens, his eyes a bit full and groggy. "Look after her, old girl," he says, and loses consciousness again.

12.50pm: *Sunday, February 17th. Cape Fury. Highlands. The road to Castle Peak.*

The searchers are still on the streets, urgently seeking a missing girl.

Yet Kirstie knows a few things these visitors don't. Things like back alleys, cut-throughs, bridleways, footpaths. Things like being small and nimble and nippy. And she has two more things they don't have.

Bicycle-wheels.

Soon she is pedalling her almost-new bicycle out of the village as fast as she can. It's the bicycle her ma told Stuart to buy, shortly before she died, yet it's one Kirstie has barely used. But now she's doing just fine – thanks Ma! – making sure, as she cycles speedily along, that no villager or scary, nodding stranger spots her. She knows the narrow cycle-path that goes right down into the lush valleys and through the shaded pinewoods, until it reaches the foothills of Castle Peak itself.

But she can't throw the image of poor Grandpa Brodie and his tartan attacker out of her head.

*****

Zack is striding alongside Danny and Lily, on the great hill, when they hear a rattling and a puffing behind them.

They spin round to see a red-faced Kirstie, peddling furiously uphill. They're as astonished to see her again as she is relieved to find them.

"How did you know we'd be *here*, Kirstie?" asks Zack, in amazement.

When she finally has her breath back, the red-faced eight year old blurts it all out. "My Grandpa Brodie heard Mrs Ames blethering about Zack and the castle. Just after she bashed his head in with a fish!"

Danny and Zack just stare at each other – *who's Mrs Ames?* What fish? But, to their surprise, it's Lily who puts an arm around Kirstie and hugs her close. Big-sister is surprising Zack quite a lot these days, but still probably not as much as he is surprising her.

"They're onto us, Zack!" says Danny. "I told you not to handle that Glimmer!"

"I didn't, Danny!" protests Zack. "It's safe in my back pocket. Deep down in my pocket. They haven't seen us or heard us talk, so there's no way they could have known for sure that we're on this hill right now!"

"No," says Danny, worriedly. "Yet somehow they do."

Zack sees his own puzzlement mirrored in Danny's dark, troubled face. But there's no time to talk, not now. "Come on *quickly*, you guys," he urges. "We've got to get to the top of this hill. We've got to save Arthur, before it's too late. T-E-A-M!"

He looks at Lily, who is on her mobile again. She shakes it and waves it around, trying desperately to pick up a signal. No joy. But she suddenly notices Zack staring intensely at her and the phone, deep in thought. She has no idea what's going on in her brother's mind these days, but at least she now realises that he has a mind, which is encouraging.

Zack turns away and increases his speed, up the bumpy path that winds round the grassless hill to the castle, way up on the high, flat peak. But he's so tired and it feels like he hasn't slept in years.

Danny looks around for Holly and has to smile. What on earth is she doing now? She's just standing there, a bit further up the hill, turning her head round and around at totally impossible angles. Not many cheerleaders can do that, he thinks to himself, almost proudly.

"Come on, old friend," he says, as he begins to overtake her. "What are you staring at?"

Holly hesitates. But then wraps a big smile round her perfect face.

"Just taking in the view, Danny. Just taking in the view."

61

'ROGUE MAX IS VERY HAPPY'

1.20pm: *Sunday, February 17th. The Highlands. A mountain road.*

Sometimes life can change in a heartbeat…

Stuart's heart – is beating like crazy.

As soon as he has left Cape Fury and can pick up a signal once again, he's making hands-free phone-calls from his car. First call – the conference centre in Edinburgh. But when he asks the receptionist there for a quick word with today's speaker, Ruth Farmer, he gets an 'earful'.

"*If you can find her!*" barks the receptionist. "The silly woman hasn't turned up! I've got a load of nurses sitting in a cold lecture-room, feeling even more murderous than usual."

Stuart is surprised. Why hasn't Ruth Farmer turned up for her own talk? Could it be something to do with this Zack? He desperately needs her mobile number, but he knows that people are wary of giving out this sort of information to strangers.

"I'm her identical twin brother!" he says. That was just

daft, Stuart. "I mean… we look a lot alike. Considering she's a woman and I'm – not."

Take a new tack, Stuart.

"Our mother has disappeared! We have the same mother – obviously. And I've lost my sister Ruth's number. I think my mum had it. And she's er missing. Did I just say that?"

This is getting stupider and stupider. But happily the receptionist is far too fed-up with Ruth Farmer to care, so she starts to give him her details anyway.

Unfortunately, as so often happens in the Highlands of Scotland, a mountain gets in the way. The line goes dead, right in the middle of the vital number.

Stuart shakes his head and groans in pure frustration. Where on earth is he going to go now? And where, in heaven's name, is the most important person in his life – the special little someone this business has started to make him really think about? Pretty late in the flaming day, Stuart, as Grandpa Brodie would doubtless tell him.

He hardly notices (and why should he?) the small car that is passing him in the other direction, on the narrow, mountain road. A car with two very concerned-looking women in it.

Yet, peculiarly, he does feel his own pounding heart suddenly take on a different rhythm, an extra skip, just for a brief second or two – at the exact moment that the two vehicles wiggle past each other.

What was all that about?

***

Ruth's heart feels it too. A connection.

But to what? Certainly not to the mountain landscape,

which may be beautiful but not today. Not when she has no idea where her most beautiful treasures, her children, could possibly be. Not when it reminds her of that honeymoon all those years ago. The trouble with being in mountains is that everything afterwards can go downhill.

She knows that her ex-husband is probably around somewhere. And that, for his own confused reasons, he needed to make a new life. Away from her, away from Lily and Zack, not caring about the damage this might do. Or simply not being able to cope with being a grown-up. But perhaps it takes two, she thinks. Perhaps something inside of her drove him away.

So why on earth did she send her precious boy, so full of unstoppable imagination, off on this wild goose chase (wild Arthur chase?) to find him? Did she drive her Zack away too?

"Ruth, calm down!" says Niomi, who can hear her friend's anxious breathing. And who, fortunately for everyone, is the one at the wheel.

"CALM DOWN?" yells Mum. "MY FIFTEEN-YEAR OLD DAUGHTER IS DRIVING HER LITTLE BROTHER, ON THESE TWISTY MOUNTAIN ROADS, IN A GREAT BIG, STOLEN LORRY!"

"Oh, yeah," says Niomi. "Kids, eh?"

They don't say another word for quite a while, just listening to the thrum of their own anxious bodies. Until a loud screech sends their heartbeats almost through the top of their heads. And it is Mum who causes it, with a single word.

"*STOP!*"

Niomi brings the car to an abrupt halt, right next to a

big, red lorry with a huge puncture and a crossbow-bolt in its wheel. They stare at the lorry.

"She parks well," says Niomi, who sometimes notices the oddest things.

They leap out of the car and Mum rushes off to inspect the vehicle, which has to be the one they've heard so much about from Silk. She isn't happy to see that awful scratch along the side. It looks like the truck smashed into a wall.

But Niomi is gazing around her, awestruck. North London is the furthest north she has ever been and this is a trip for her, even if it's not exactly a holiday. But as she looks about her, she notices something which is even more dramatic that a crashing sea or a beached, red lorry. It's a whole sky that is reddening in a way she has never seen a sky reddening before. But this, of course, could be because she has never been further north than North London.

They don't have many castles where Niomi lives either, but as she stares up at that big, ugly thing squatting right on the top of a huge and oddly lifeless hill, she's really rather glad. She is a nurse, so she has seen plenty of blood. Unfortunately, this is exactly what the current Cape Fury sky reminds her of.

But then she notices something else, something just as disturbing.

Long lines of smartly-dressed men and women are walking away from the town, in the direction of the ugly castle. The description she would give to them would be bloodless – as if all the colour and life have been drained out of them. All that these guys seem able to do is walk and nod, walk and nod, in a very peculiar way, like they've all got secret i-pods plugged in, each one playing the same funeral march in their ears.

Oh, hang on, who's this one?

Here's an older woman, dressed head-to-toe in tartan, walking briskly through the pale, robotic guys, right to the head of the line. She's nodding too but at least she's doing it with a bit of bad taste and gaudy colour. Go for it, girlfriend – get the noddies dancing.

"Niomi," says Mum, hurrying over. "The lorry is empty. Except for a battered, old guitar. But it's them. *Look what I found!*"

She shows Niomi the framed picture of Zack, smiling so happily, with his arm around absolutely nothing. Her heart doesn't know whether to pound with anxiety or leap with joy. Or both.

"Now what was the stupid address I wrote on that empty white box?"

***

PC McKay's heart is beating fine.

Which is miraculous, considering that his arteries are probably clogged-up from all the rubbish inside them. He's chewing a sticky-bun now, so he's feeling very mellow. And sticky.

It's only when the front door of Number 5, The High Street swings open, but there's nobody behind it doing the opening, that the chubby policeman grows slightly uneasy.

"Brodie?" he says, the bun stopping halfway towards his mouth.

The response is a groan and it's coming from the

floor. McKay looks down beyond his bun, right over his expansive stomach, and that's when his heartbeat goes into overdrive.

"*Brodie!* What are you doing down there man? The pub's not even open yet."

The policeman bends down (with difficulty) and notices the huge lump on his friend's head.

"It was that Englishwoman!" gasps Brodie. "The tartan one. She's a maniac!"

"Find me one who isn't," says McKay, who has never really cared for the English. "I'd best get you to a doctor." McKay begins to lift him up, but is halted mid-lift by a voice. It's an English voice.

"*Excuse me, officer…?* "

He turns to find Mum staring at him. She feels fortunate to have spotted a policeman so swiftly, in a village where she had wondered if any existed. Grandpa Brodie is also gazing up at this worried-looking newcomer, but it's clear that should PC McKay suddenly let him go, things could look down pretty swiftly.

As a trained-nurse, Mum can't quite ignore the fact that there's an elderly man here on the floor, with a huge, bleeding lump on his head, but she gives it her best shot. "*Have you seen a teenage English girl, in Goth make-up, with an eleven-year old-boy?*" she asks.

Unfortunately, in her anxiety, Mum grabs both the policeman's arms, which means he has to let poor Brodie drop to the floor again with a thud.

Owwww!!!

"Can't say that I have, madam," says McKay. "Mind you, with this sudden influx of visitors, who knows? They seem a strange lot if you ask me, very quiet and nodding all the time. In fact, I thought I vaguely recognised one or two of them from off the tel—"

Niomi interrupts. "Howsabout a little, green guy called Arthur?" Mum glares at Niomi, who shrugs.

But Brodie suddenly makes a sound that causes them to look down at him. He seems stunned – well, even more stunned than someone who has actually been stunned, by a fish in a glass case.

"Your name isn't Uth, is it?" he asks.

Mum stares at him in confusion, as he collapses again from the effort. But this time her nurse instinct kicks in and she bends down to support him. Her phone suddenly rings and she just as instinctively drops him again, with another big thud.

Owwww!!!

If I keep banging my head like this, thinks Brodie, they'll have to put *me* in a glass case soon.

"Hello…?" says Mum on her phone, listening to the unfamiliar voice. "Yes, I'm Ruth Farmer, who is this?… *Stuart?* "

She listens, but she can't figure this out at all.

Firstly, an old Scottish guy's eyes light up when he hears the name of her son's imaginary friend. Then the same man seems to know her own name – well, almost. Then another, younger-sounding Scotsman called Stuart, which is also her ex-husband's name, has somehow found her mobile number and now he's rambling on about Zack!

PC McKay is amazed too – her phone actually works in Cape Fury!

Niomi, however, is watching in fascination as yet

more silent nodders walk past the cottage, in an unearthly, robotic stream. "Has IKEA got a sale on?" she wonders out loud.

***

The tall detective's heart is nowhere to be found.

There may be three beings in the police helicopter, as it approaches Cape Fury, but only two of them have hearts that beat. The tall detective, in her tight, grey raincoat, doesn't even have a hint of one. But she finds it so heartening to be in control of those who do.

"That's the place," says the pilot, looking down on the rugged landscape that can still surprise him. But never more so than today. "I wonder where all those people are going."

Silk takes a look and sees the long line of mesmerised humanity, snaking its way back towards the castle. A chillingly imposing fortress bathed in a disturbing shade of red.

The tall detective, leaning casually and unnoticed on his shoulder, sees a lot more than the men. She sees her soul-mates down there (or they would be soul-mates, if they had souls!) She sees Rogues galore. Platoons of Rogues – battalions – regiments! All wending their way to certain victory, on this very special day of days. All sending signals up to her, through the red and black of their eyes.

But these aren't the only signals she is receiving. Reports are being beamed in her direction from one particular crooked path up to Castle Peak. These are the ones that matter most.

"Zack Farmer and his pals are doing *exactly* what we'd hoped," she announces, smirking in satisfaction. "Rogue Max is very happy."

She spins around to face the castle. "And on our left, gentlemen, you'll see Castle Peak, where I believe our very special, young guest is about to put on a very special show. Silk, I want us to circle around there."

Of course, the pilot can't hear her, but Detective Inspector Duncan Silk can. Yet the orders now whirling inside his brain, decisions he naturally assumes are his own, are confusing even to him.

What special young guest – what special show? And why aren't we landing?

The tall detective looks down once again, to the base of the hill, and laughs an unearthly, inhuman laugh. There, way down below, an old lady with horrible fashion sense is starting the long climb, nodding all the while to the gorgeously large, yellow Rogue strolling happily beside her.

Things are coming to a delicious head. The tall detective hopes nobody loses heart.

Ha!

62

'SEE WHAT A LITTLE IMAGINATION DOES FOR US?'

1.45pm: *Sunday, February 17th. Cape Fury. Scotland. Castle Peak.*

I've just remembered a book! thinks Zack.

It was one he discovered some time ago, hidden beneath floorboards, in a house that was being pulled down. A storybook that the child who once lived there had obviously been trying to save from the furnaces. Zack recalls how he would secretly read it to Arthur again and again.

Because Arthur's name was in it.

It told a story of medieval times, when noble warriors rode out from their great castles on what became known as the Arthurian quest. The reason being that it was inspired by that legendary ruler of Camelot, King Arthur. The knights were searching for the Holy Grail, whatever that was.

It occurs to Zack that another noble band are about

to enter an ancient castle, on their own Arthurian quest. But this time, hundreds of years on, it is a quest to find Arthur himself.

Unlike their predecessors, however, they are not warriors. They are an undersized, eleven-year old boy, his fifteen-year-old Goth sister, a homeless, mixed-race teenager from Manchester who sees invisible folk, a motherless eight-year old on a push-bike and an imaginary, American cheerleader.

Look at us, thinks Zack. *We don't stand a chance!*

But Zack Farmer is still leading – and Danny is still singing – as they take the final bend on the winding road up to the castle.

The sea, as slate-grey and cruel as the already darkening sky, crashes against rocks way down below, sending spray high into the air. There are no seagulls now. Perhaps because the strange, red light emanating from every window and crevice is putting them off. Or, perhaps, seagulls just have more sense. But Zack can spot large, dark crows, nesting all down the thick castle walls, almost camouflaged by time-blackened stone.

"'*He ain't heavy, he's my brother*'," sings Danny, the way people do when they want to show confidence, but are really trying to find it deep inside themselves.

"Do you know," says Lily, "you don't stutter when you're singing?"

"Like me to s-sing some more?"

"No."

He looks at her. She's smiling and it's a lovely smile, even if the tension just below the surface is all too clear. He laughs and Zack chuckles too. It will be a long time before they laugh again.

Suddenly they hear a loud boom, as if thunder could talk and was shouting in your ear.

"HELLO, ZACK!"

Zack turns sharply to see Mr Teensy-Weensy, who is now even bigger than before. (Although, of course, Zack has never seen him before, so he has nothing with which to compare him.) Zack looks down at his hands, they're shaking with fear. Yet they're not holding the Glimmer.

So how come I can see the Rogue? he wonders. But not for long.

He turns to the others, who look like they've been nailed to the craggy carpet of the hillside. *They can see the Rogue too!* The older ones hug Kirstie, as she begins to shiver uncontrollably.

Zack is starting to work it out – Rogues can reveal themselves at times of their own choosing, but they much prefer to function in the dark. If you looked like that, thinks Zack, wouldn't you?

Now Zack is stuttering too. But he's not going to sing. "Who – who are you?" he manages.

"I'm fine, thank you, Zack," says the mighty dwarf. "Hoo's yourself?" He laughs affably. "Wee Scottish joke."

Not a very good joke, thinks Zack (and you'd need to know that 'hoo?' is Scottish for 'how?', which he recalls from his dad) but the Rogue's laughter seems to act like a pump, making him bigger and bigger, fatter and fatter – until he dominates the entire landscape.

Until he *is* the landscape. They can hardly see anything else at all, either behind or around him. Just him.

"So sorry, am I dwarfing you?" he booms, as they recoil. He's full of them this afternoon.

If the Rogue could simply bend down and pick the gang up, they'd be history. But Zack has a feeling there's a far worse fate in store for him, a fate that has already been carefully planned. These guys always seem to be at least one step ahead.

"Are you – Rogue Max?" Zack ventures.

This makes the huge dwarf roar with a laughter that shakes the hillside. He bellows even louder. "HE ASKS IF I'M ROGUE MAX!"

"Who's he talking to?" asks Lily, in a voice that surprises her, because right now she didn't think she'd ever be able to talk again. It doesn't take long to have her question answered. The enormous dwarf swiftly shrinks down to his normal size – at about the same time as their horror mushrooms to totally giant size.

Revealed behind the dwarf, just peeping over the brow of the hill, are rank after rank of smirking, drooling, leering Rogues. Hundreds and hundreds of discarded and bitter IFs. Ugly with rage and hungry for vengeance.

Zack recognises some from before. Unfortunately. The rabid Squirrel and the nasty creatures on the motorbikes. Beside them the vicious Water-Sprite from the Manchester motorway, Pinocchio from the rusty digger, Tin Soldier and his evil Rogue pals from the pub. And of course the Prime Minister's very own rag-doll.

Which has to mean…

Zack can't hold the thought, there are too many spinning through his head. The red and black eyes of so many rejected childhood-friends pierce him to his soul. Jaded imps, twisted elves, former BFFs gone cruelly rotten. All radiating venom and fire.

But the worst is yet to come.

As the Rogue army marches brutally towards them, Zack and his friends can see that the creatures' feet (or hooves or claws) aren't touching the ground at all. *The twisted crew are all standing on the shoulders of the powerful men and women they control.* The generals, the politicians, world leaders and heads of industry, scientists and media chiefs. A United Nations of nodders. Well-placed, finely-tailored slaves.

And Zack now recognises, directly under the leering rag-doll, the Prime Minister himself.

All of the humans are moving forward on someone else's orders, masters of their own wills no longer.

"AM I ROGUE MAX?" repeats the dwarf, as he grows again. "Well, Zack, yes and no." He looks for confusion in the human-children's eyes and, to his satisfaction, finds it. *"We're ALL Rogue Max.* Or, as you kids might say, Rogue *to* the Max."

The Rogues increase their pace. Instinctively, our young gang back away.

They find themselves retreating to the stark castle that looms at their rear, as if this malign place is likely to protect them. But instead of pursuit, the Rogues again take them by surprise.

"What are they doing now?" asks Zack, running a hand through hair that feels like it is standing on end even more than usual.

As they watch, dumbstruck, the Rogues begin to lose their distinct, individual forms and start to blend into one enormous, pulsating field of pure red energy, pounding like a gigantic heart. Rogue Max!

But the awful light-show doesn't stop here. After a few, horrific seconds this demonic force finally resolves itself into a shape of unimaginable size. A shape that consumes the entire hill, the brooding sky, the Castle and the small, Arthurian band.

Kirstie screams. Zack puts an arm around her. Lily grabs Danny, as Holly gasps.

It's horrible. It's unearthly.

It's Zack.

His gigantic face is dominating the hillside, leering and spitting. Handsome no more. As the gang shudder uncontrollably, Mr Teensy-Weensy speaks through 'Zack's' enormous mouth.

"See what a little imagination does for us?" booms the voice. "There really is no escape, Zack Farmer, not this time. 'Game over' – isn't that the expression?"

Zack – the real Zack – retreats even further, but his eyes are unable to tear themselves away from the huge ones boring into his soul. Finally, the gang do the only thing they can. They turn on their heels and start to run through the heavy gates. Into the Castle itself.

"*Follow them!*" they hear the Rogue cry.

The massive Zack-face dissolves like melting wax, as the Rogues re-group into their original, terrible forms and follow them. Riding their powerless humans like horses.

I wish this was just one of my made-up stories, thinks Zack.

63

'WE MEET AGAIN, ZACKY BOY!'

2.01pm: *Sunday, February 17th. Cape Fury. The castle.*

The castle's huge courtyard is stark, dark and totally deserted.

At any other time Zack – who likes history – would find it fascinating. But not today. Today, burrowing through the fear and panic, is the itchy question he still wishes he could answer. *"How did they find us so fast?"* he cries, into the chill evening air.

A familiar voice beside them talks, but in a most unfamiliar way. "One of life's little mysteries," it rasps.

They all turn. Zack gasps – as he sees the red and black gleam in Holly's eyes.

"Holly?" shrieks Danny, the truth hitting him like a fist. "NO!"

The cheerleader is still cheering, but the joy has totally gone. "Let's hear it for Lily," she cries. "L-I-L-I. Or possibly – Y. The new gal in my Danny boy's life."

Lily looks at Danny and instinctively takes his hand,

which sort of proves Holly's point. "But you're beautiful," says Lily.

"Yes, but you're real," says the newest Rogue.

Zack watches Danny helplessly, as the older boy stares at his dear and only childhood friend. A lifetime buddy who is going unmistakably wicked before their eyes. But too soon another familiar voice interrupts them. The force of it causes loose stones to fall from the highest battlements and crows finally to fly in fear from their darkest places.

"OH, ZACK," booms Mr Teensy-Weensy, shaking his massive head.

They look around in shock to see that the once-empty courtyard is now heaving with Rogues. Through the open castle-gates they can see even more of them, blanketing the entire hillside. Some are even sitting on the roaring sea itself. Countless and beyond measure.

The forces of evil seem infinite.

As the gang stare in horror, they notice a tiny, green ball of light, way at the back, bouncing on the heads of Rogues and moving steadily closer. It is being tossed from one set of vicious-looking arms to another. Eventually it is caught by the giant dwarf in his huge hands and held out to Zack like an offering.

Before it even reaches him, Zack knows exactly what – or who – this is.

"*ARTHUR!*" he cries.

At last!

After what has seemed like years, Zack Farmer is reunited with his beloved IF. His Arthur. His best friend forever.

He can't stop himself – he rushes forward, overjoyed

and overwhelmed. Tears already clouding his eyes. Which makes what happens next all the more terrible.

"We meet again, Zacky boy," hisses Arthur.

Zack recoils in alarm, as the others watch helplessly. The giant dwarf just smiles.

"NO! No, it's not you, mate!" cries Zack. "Can't be. It's another Rogue trick – you're going to turn into a squirrel or a rat or something."

Arthur, to Zack's surprise, begins to sing. "*"There was a soldier… a Scottish soldier… Who left his son at home…!?"*

He can't sing any more, he's laughing too much.

Zack can feel the tears start to burn. The effort not to cry is forcing his mouth rigid. First Holly, now this – is there *no-one* he can trust?

"What do you want… Arthur?" he manages to ask this parody of his old best friend.

"We just want you to stay here with us, Zack," says Arthur quietly. "That's all, innit? In the nice, wee room that we have for you. With no nasty sunlight."

Zack understands exactly what Arthur wants. Sensing Danny's body grow taut beside him, he knows that Danny understands too. "No. I won't. Never!" cries Zack defiantly.

From his pocket he removes the Glimmer. But the Rogues just laugh – the time for using this 'gizmo' to save himself is long gone. From now on, as Zack knows, this powerful Glimmer will be turned on him.

"Then there's nothing more to say," rasps Arthur. He turns to the Rogues. "*Guys?*"

The Rogues continue to drive their mindless humans onwards. Which is scary enough for anyone, but it's the sounds coming out of their mouths – from both the

Rogues *and* their unwitting slaves – that make Zack and his friends feel sick down to their aching feet.

Worse than sounds. One name, repeated over and over again.

"Kirstie…! *Kirstie…!* KIRSTIE!!!

Zack looks at the little girl. Her sweet face is a mask of the purest terror. He peers up at Arthur, but his former friend has turned away. He is staring towards the cliffs and the raging sea far below.

"It's a long way down," says Arthur. "For a little girl."

64

'I THINK WE HAVE SOMETHING IN COMMON.'

2.23pm: *Sunday, February 17th. Cape Fury. Scotland. The McBride house.*

If Ruth Farmer had any idea that, just down the road, her children were involved in a life and death struggle to decide the fate of the entire world, she might not be attending to a total stranger who had been banged on the head with a fish.

Or perhaps – as a good nurse – she still would.

Niomi is supporting Brodie on the ground, while Mum checks that his vital parts are in working order. Fortunately they all seems to be, but the old gent keeps rambling on about some lunatic Englishwoman who dresses like a colour-blind Scot.

They hear the screech of a car. Which turns out to be a van, a white one, the driver's door already flying open.

"*What's up with Brodie?*" yells the big man, leaping out.

"Someone hit him with a fish," explains Niomi, which

doesn't make things a huge amount clearer. "But he'll be okay. Not sure I can say the same for the fish."

Stuart looks at the two women. Which one is Ruth Farmer? Only one way to find out. "Mrs Farmer?"

Mum looks up. Even with anxiety tightening her tired face, Stuart McBride can't help but notice what a lovely face it is.

"Mr McBride?" says Mum. Stuart nods. "I think we may have something in common."

Stuart nods again. "I'm afraid I don't understand any of this," he says, sadly. "I just hope my daughter is okay." He looks at Mum, then adds, "and, of course, your boy too."

The man looks so strong, yet at the same time so helpless, that Mum's heart goes out to him. Like herself, he's a parent on his own, simply trying to do the best for his child. And probably, again like her, finding that he always gets it wrong.

"Stuart…" she says, then stops. The name is so familiar to her. Yet, aside from the Scottish accent, this man seems a world away from the other one, the Stuart Farmer who was once such a big part of her life. *Focus, Ruth!* "Mr McBride… have you any idea where they could be?" she asks.

Stuart shakes his head, despairingly. "No. And 'Stuart' is fine."

Grandpa Brodie tries to raise himself up, but Niomi gently eases him back down. So he tries again, more forcefully. He desperately needs to speak, yet this unusually strong woman keeps stopping him. Finally, he manages to say what he must.

"*Castle Peak!*" he croaks, pointing into the distance, then passes out again.

Niomi just shakes her head – delirious! But Mum turns in the direction of that still-pointing finger. She sees the huge hill and so wishes she hadn't. Even from here it looks evil, its red glow like a warning sign. Niomi sees it too and, in her shock, drops poor Brodie on his head yet again.

Thud!!

Mum and Stuart are already rushing into the van.

"I'm sure your daughter is fine, Stuart," Niomi hears Mum tell the big farmer, a bit uncertainly. Niomi shakes her head and wonders whether she should follow in her own little car.

This is just so far from being a holiday.

65

'NOTHING'S GOING TO HAPPEN TO YOU, KIRSTIE.'

2.31pm: *Sunday February 17th. Cape Fury. Scotland. Castle Peak.*

"Kirstie! … *Kirstie!!* … KIRSTIE!!!

The Rogue chant continues as the threatening horde moves closer and closer.

"If you've any bright ideas, Zack," says Danny, "now would be a good time."

The Rogues and their humans are driving Zack, with his tiny group, back through the castle courtyard, towards the battlements. Danny looks sadly at Holly, fearing that she'll soon go completely Rogue and wishing they didn't have an enemy within their very heart.

Zack moves to stand in front of the terrified little girl. "YOU'RE NOT TAKING KIRSTIE!" he shouts at the Rogues, defiantly.

"Anything brighter than that?" murmurs Kirstie.

Arthur is smiling. To be honest, this new bravery

thing of Zack's has come as a bit of a surprise. He always thought that he, Arthur, was the daring one of the duo. But he's pretty sure it won't last.

"Okay then, Zack," he says reasonably, "you stay here and help us imagine away all the IFs around the world, and we'll leave your little friend alone." He laughs cruelly. "It won't be too bad down there," he says, pointing earthwards to where Zack can only assume the dungeons lurk. "You'll get fresh straw on a Thursday."

The Rogues proceed with scary deliberation towards him. Closer and closer.

Zack can only stare at them. Their fury seems unrelenting. What's worse is that he doesn't have an idea in his head. He thought he had a hint of something a couple of hours ago, but it must have been shunted aside by all the shocks he has just received to his system.

What was it? Something about… *Come on, Zack!* But all he can tell himself is – I'm eleven years old… I've had no sleep and not much to eat… been chased all over Britain… and I haven't even *begun* my homework. But this doesn't really help him much right now.

He just knows there was something else. Come on! *Come on, Zack!* Zack tries desperately to spool back over what's been going on these past hours, like the rewind on a DVD player, searching for a clue. An idea. A plan. Anything.

O-kay. There was this giant dwarf, Holly going Rogue, his own huge face, the massive rocks, the big red lorry, that nice old granddad, the rotten pub, the dodgy fairground, even the chubby policeman…

Hang on!

Yes!

I'm starting to get something.

What was it that big Scottish policeman was shouting on his phone? Something about moving the whole village up to the Castle? *'At least then we'd have some contact with the wider world!'* That's what he said. That's what struck a chord somewhere deep inside of me. But why?

Wait, he thinks. I'm having a flashback. A lorry on an ancient bridge. A little car with a kid, just scraping by. *A Smiley-Guy!* Why am I thinking about these things now? What's all this got to do with the mess I'm in? *Focus*, Zack!

And suddenly it comes to him. Yes! The pieces click together. *That's it!* (Or, at least, he really, really hopes it's it.)

Zack swiftly grabs Kirstie by her tiny wrist and runs with her towards the narrow, stone steps at the farthest end of the courtyard. They look hugely precarious – another of Zack's great words – worn down by centuries of warrior feet.

He's pulling her close to him, as they begin to climb. Higher and higher they go, away from the threatening courtyard, but Kirstie's breaths are starting to come fast, too fast and very shallow, a disturbing mix of fear and exhaustion.

As the steps narrow even further, Zack lifts the young girl up, with a strength he never knew he possessed, and carries her onwards. Up to the top they clamber and right round the craggy battlements, making for the other side of the castle – the side that looks out towards the sea.

I have to be up there, thinks Zack, even higher. As high up as I possibly can. But he's still not totally sure why.

Part of Kirstie wants to scream, to call for her daddy,

wherever he is. Especially when she sees, through a crack in the old castle wall, those jagged cliffs and crashing waves so far below. But part of her, a bigger part, trusts this serious stranger from far-off Hackney, who seems so much older and wiser than the eleven-year olds in her village. And a whole lot scruffier.

Zack can hear Arthur's mocking voice, stinging like salty sea-spray on an open wound. "Still running scared, Zacky boy!"

Zack tries to ignore it. "Nothing's going to happen to you, Kirstie," he reassures her. "You're with me now." Zack has no idea what this means and the words do seem a bit on the reckless side, but amazingly the little girl seems more becalmed.

There's no turning back now.

Without even noticing, Zack Farmer soon finds himself standing on the highest wall-walk of the tallest castle in the whole of the United Kingdom. He's relieved that Kirstie is too small to peer over the top of the battlement, but he can just see, through the gap-toothed stonework, the vicious rocks and the cruel waves that pound them. He wishes he couldn't. He hears the water smashing down below, with unrelenting fury.

If Zack Farmer has ever wanted to go to the toilet, it's now.

Then he hears something else. Something even more intimidating. (That word again!) The deafening sound of a helicopter, growing louder all the time. How on earth..?

Within what seems like seconds, the machine is almost close enough for him to touch. Not that he would. Not with the lethal blades whirring so near to his face. Not with a thick-set, red-headed man standing at the door, holding a particularly vicious-looking stun-gun. A weapon that could send him flying through the air in pain like he has never known.

Behind red-head, in the cabin of the Edinburgh Police chopper, Zack spots a tall woman in a tight, grey overcoat. Even before he catches her eyes, he knows from recent experience that she is not of the real world – which makes her ten times as dangerous. And she is making sure that he sees her.

He looks back to the man, who has to be a policeman. And, of course, the man is nodding, receiving whispered instructions from his own personal Rogue. Which Zack knows aren't going to be along the lines of 'go and make a nice cup of tea for them all.'

Somewhere beneath the whirring, he can hear footsteps. Grotesque, unearthly sounds erupting behind him like thunder.

The Rogues are approaching. Each one riding its human prey.

Stun-gun on one side. Rogue army on the other. The furious sea down below.

We're trapped, thinks Zack Farmer.

Game over?

66

'I'M AN OLD FOOL.'

2.45pm: *Sunday February 17th. Cape Fury. The road to the castle.*

The trouble with being a parent, thinks Ruth Farmer, is that you can't always see what your children want you to see. Or believe what they think you ought to believe. So most of the time you have absolutely no idea what they're talking about.

This is what's happening to her and Stuart, as they race like maniacs up the bumpy road towards the castle on the hill. (With Niomi following even more bumpily some way behind.)

All they know is what a possibly deluded old man has told them. (And what person wouldn't be a bit deluded, after being struck on the head by a fish?) They don't even know if they're driving in the right direction. That ugly red glow from the hill could be just a trick of the Highland sun.

Okay, there's that business about their kids possibly knowing the same imaginary friend. But right now they don't want to go there. Right now that is just too weird and spooky and – well – childish. (Mum is also a bit embarrassed that Zack still *has* an imaginary friend – he's nearly twelve, for pity's sake!) The only real connection is that empty white box and so far as Ruth Farmer is concerned, that box was one hundred per cent empty when it went in the post.

Wasn't it?

Yes, of course it was.

Ruth Farmer deals in practical things. Broken legs, raging fevers, dodgy hearts. She's not into anything 'mystical'.

So this is the spirit in which she takes out the photo of Zack, the one she found in the lorry. She just wonders if Stuart might like to see it, so that at least he knows the looks of the older boy who may have run away with his little daughter. It's an appealing look, a reassuring face. Not the sort of face that could be capable of anything troublesome.

She polishes the photo, removing any dust. Without disturbing his driving too much – these mountain roads can be a bit tricky, especially at the speed he's going – she shows it to Stuart. He glances at it and likes what he sees.

"Lovely boy," he says. "Handsome. And bright, I'll bet."

She likes the man even more for this. What mum wouldn't? Stuart wants to show her a photo of Kirstie, but his hands are on the wheel and the picture is in his wallet. So, instead, he hears himself saying "Kirstie looks so like her mother."

Where did that come from?

He shrugs in embarrassment – how on earth would this woman, this Ruth, know what his late wife looked like? Or care. But he glances at her and something in her eyes tells him that she does understand. Which in its own way is a bit spooky too – but not weird.

Not nearly as weird as what happens next.

"What's that on there?" asks Stuart.

"What's what on where?" says Ruth.

"On the photo. Next to your son. Next to Zack."

Ruth looks at the photo. It could, of course, simply be the way the low, late-winter sun is refracting through the window, but there seems to be just the faintest green glow under her young son's outstretched arm.

No. Just a trick of the light.

Surely.

2.50pm: *Sunday February 17th. Cape Fury. Highlands. The village.*

Grandpa Brodie is clinging precariously onto the podgy stomach of PC McKay. On a bicycle not built for two.

"I should've stopped Kirstie going!" moans Brodie, as they round a corner a bit too sharply. "I'm an old fool! And if you take corners like that, McKay, I'll be an old, dead fool."

McKay doesn't know what to say, so he hands him a bit of the Mars Bar he is munching.

"Sometimes food isn't the answer!" barks Grandpa Brodie. Which PC McKay thinks is a really stupid remark and clearly the result of a bad head-injury.

Brodie lifts his aching head towards blood-red Castle Peak and prays that things aren't as bad as they look up there.

They're not. They're worse.

67

'THERE WAS A SOLDIER...'

2.52pm: *Sunday February 17th. Cape Fury. The battlements of Castle Peak.*

"ZACK FARMER," shouts the policeman with the vicious-looking stun-gun. "Come over here, laddie. This isn't a toy. It's over, son."

The tall detective is behind him, enjoying the final round.

"I want to hear him scream, Duncan," she tells her unwitting puppet. "Make him scream, for me!"

I'm not waiting around to hear myself scream, thanks very much, thinks Zack. For you or for anyone. He picks up Kirstie, who is heavy with fear, and struggles along the ruined castle's wall-walk, where there's one more unusually tall and tapering tower, like a spike trying to burst the clouds.

The helicopter follows.

Into the ancient turret they go and up yet another narrow staircase, which this time winds like a corkscrew, right to the highest point. Which is tight, precarious and open to the moody skies. With barely any stone wall to protect them and a deathly drop way below, the chill wind yells around their heads and bodies, the dampness soaks them to the bone.

But somebody is already there, ahead of them.

Holly. Just staring at Zack, with her red and black eyes.

She's probably signalling too, thinks Zack, and sending out those powerful Rogue transmissions, but he'll have to deal with her later – if there is a later. The Rogues are down there, moving in for the kill. Arthur, his former friend, leads the pack.

He hears a worried voice. "*Zack…?*"

He looks down from the high tower to see Danny staring up at him from the wall-walk Zack just left. By his side is Lily, but the look on their faces is far from reassuring. It's a look that says there's little hope – and even less time. But Zack has no choice.

He has only one plan. A simple plan, a nonsensical plan.

He takes out the Glimmer and thrusts it high into the swirling air.

Danny looks totally baffled. But then he slowly starts to figure out what is in his younger friend's mind. "ARE YOU SURE THIS WILL WORK?" he cries, above the wind.

"NO!" admits Zack. "I'M IN YEAR SEVEN!"

Danny looks towards Lily, although she is hardly in a position to reassure him. She's rooted to the spot, eyes fixed firmly on the helicopter, which has moved round to meet them and is hovering noisily just feet away. The gust from the blades blows her jet-black Goth hair all around her strong but frightened face.

Below them, in the courtyard, the Rogues are gathering. Now the chopper begins to move away and up towards Zack on his tower. Standing at the rim of his open door, the red-headed policeman aims his stun-gun.

"What on earth is Zack doing?" Lily yells to Danny, above the noise.

"I think he's just calling a few friends," replies Danny, looking up. "Let's hope he gets a good reception."

Zack has begun to whirl around the tower, in the winter air, like a total madman. He brandishes the Glimmer in his hand, showing it to the glowering sky and the elements. Round and round he goes in that cramped, stony space. Faster and faster. Kirstie watches him, thinking that he is going to get very dizzy, very soon. She really hopes that it's worth it.

This is when Zack starts to sing.

"'There was a soldier…'"

His gang look at him like he has gone completely bonkers. So do the Rogues, actually.

But suddenly, as if he has flicked a hidden switch, electric-green signals flash from Zack's up-thrusted Glimmer, out into the glowering sky. East, west, north, south. Straight ahead – far afield – to the back of beyond and even beyonder. Reaching out to way, way in the distance.

Now all I can do is hope, Zack tells himself. As he closes his eyes tight.

No, not just hope.

Imagine.

68

'A SCOTTISH SOLDIER... '

Crunch time: *Sunday February 17th. Everywhere in the world.*

Zack can't see the little girl he first spied in the Manchester shopping-mall, the one with the ballet-dancing fairy IF. So he has no way of knowing whether, as the two pirouette together in the little girl's bedroom, a green glow suddenly bathes the imaginary friend's joyous face.

"*'A Scottish soldier'*," sings Zack, high up on his tower.

Nor can he know whether the vacuum-cleaner robot, belonging to the tough-looking Manchester lad, will pick up the green summons.

"*'There was none bolder...'*"

If he can't see these two English IFs, then he certainly can't know about the boy in the small, African township, skipping barefoot down the dusty road in the company of a yellow-and-black-striped elephant. It's only when the imaginary animal raises his trunk, to welcome the curious green light, that the boy himself knows that something special is going on.

"'With good, broad shoulder...'"

And so the signal goes out.

From the lofty tower of this Highland castle to an eleven-year-old boy selling nougat in a bustling Marrakech market. And on to a farmhouse on the American prairies, in which a ten-year-old girl in thick glasses, who wants to be an Army Ranger, has dreamed-up an imaginary Army Ranger girl pal wearing even thicker ones. To a devout, thirteen-year-old Chasidic boy outside a Jerusalem synagogue and then to a Japanese garden, where some girls are having a tea-ceremony with dolls from their toy-box and dolls from their mind.

Zack remembers so clearly what Danny said last starry night. '*Zack, lots of children have imaginary friends. Loads of them. Millions. All over the world. Not just little kids. Bigger kids too. Rich kids, poor kids, kids with snow on their boots, kids with the sun in their eyes. Happy kids, clever kids, lonely kids—*'

A lustrous green beacon is calling the vast community of IFs, all over the globe, telling them that there is big trouble out there. And that only *they* can help.

"He's fought in many a fray..."' sings Zack, with more faith than confidence, the icy wind piercing his lungs.

But will they help, these infinite forms of imaginative energy, called suddenly to action? Even more importantly, is it actually possible? Or is it just another fancy of Zack's wild but wrong-headed mind.

Could the IF of that young Canadian basketball-player in the wheelchair – a Martian in a wheelchair that's supersonic – really propel himself across the universe like a sound wave or an e-mail, reaching out to wherever the emerald-green call started?

Would the tiny, flamenco-dancing bull, who lives on the piano of the talented Spanish girl in Madrid, dance to a different tune if occasion demanded? Might those identical-twin IFs in outback Australia, who belong to two identical outback-twins, take that vital step to help their British cousins?

And finally, what about old Smiley-Guy – the one in that car on the ancient bridge – who made Zack's Glimmer suddenly light up as he scraped so narrowly by? The tiny moment that gave Zack such a big idea.

"'And fought and won'."

Zack hasn't a clue.

He turns back to the Rogues and finds himself staring right into the gigantic, bloodshot eyes of Mr Teensy-Weensy. The evil dwarf is now as tall as the tower itself. So Zack sings even louder. *"'Of battles glorious and deeds victorious…'"*

He brandishes the glowing green Glimmer right in front of Mr Teensy-Weensy's smirking, drooling gob. But the huge creature just shakes his head.

Oh Zack, Zack, Zack.

Zack looks down, way down, and sees Arthur, his old mate, doing the same.

Oh Zack, Zack, Zack.

Even a worried Kirstie is shaking her head, making Zack feel totally saddened and useless. All that effort and absolutely *nothing* is happening.

Oh Zack, Zack, Zack.

Well, not quite nothing.

"Zack, behind you!" cries Danny, his voice coming from somewhere nearby.

Zack turns to see that the chopper is nearly on top of him. The red-headed policeman is about to take the shot that will stun him, hurt him and end the story in dungeons and tragedy. The tall detective in the tight-fitting raincoat whispers final instructions into the man's upturned ear.

But she never gets to finish. Something suddenly soars up at her at enormous speed, knocking her off her feet and back into the chopper.

"Holly!" cries Zack, in relief.

"*All for one and one for all,*" cries the cheerleader, not quite turned bad. "*Pride can come before a fall!*"

The tall detective's talons dig into Holly's imaginary flesh. It's a fight to the finish.

"*Two-four-six-eight, who will I exterminate?*" yells the Rogue policewoman, giving as good as she gets. Not unlike Lily, thinks Zack, in this respect.

Danny has to get closer. Leaving Lily, he rushes up the twisty stairs of Zack's tall tower. But he can hardly bear to watch. His oldest friend is about to be destroyed before his eyes.

"*HOLLY!*" he cries. There's nothing else he can say, nothing else he can do. Holly just shakes her head.

"Save yourself, hon," she tells him. "It's too late for me."

The tall detective is still trying to give Silk his orders. Now Zack can hear Danny's anxious, troubled voice right there beside him. "Come on Zack, *hurry!*"

Danny's not totally sure what he's hurrying Zack to do. He's just feeling helpless and hopeless and Holly-less.

Zack holds up the Glimmer again. But this time he addresses the entire Rogue world. "Hey Rogue Max, what's the most powerful thing on the planet?"

The Rogues stop and look at each other. What's the kid talking about – who needs riddles? Zack just smiles to Danny while, in the swirling chopper by their heads, the two female Rogues continue their fight to the finish.

"As a very good mate of mine told me only yesterday," continues Zack, staring at the giant dwarf, "*the most powerful thing on the planet is a kid's imagination.*"

The Rogues down below just shrug. *A kid's imagination?* Yeah, okay, big deal. But Zack isn't done yet.

"SO – IMAGINE THIS!"

"Now, Silk!" yells the tall detective. "Fire now!"

Just as Silk is about to fire, Danny leaps in front of Zack.

Zap! The stun-gun flares. Danny collapses with a terrible scream, clutching his leg in agony.

"*Danny!*" screams Lily, watching from the battlement. To her amazement she realises that she is actually feeling this young, homeless man's pain. Not just in her heart but with her whole body. She can totally imagine the fire shooting up his leg and around his wiry frame and into his brain and is finding it almost too hard to bear.

What's that all about, she wonders, as she rushes over to the tower to join him.

"Bullseye," says the tall detective, kicking Holly aside. "I never liked him." But then she turns to the giant dwarf and says something that puzzles everyone. "It's going just as we planned, eh Teensy?"

And the giant dwarf just smiles.

Through his agony, Danny looks shocked. "Zack, what are they up to now?"

I have no idea, thinks Zack. He's still into telling them all to 'imagine this' and hoping something good will suddenly happen. So far nothing much has. In fact, less than nothing much. Yet something makes him turn around and look down the hill.

That's when he sees it.

What he was hoping would take place.

What he feared would probably not.

Down below, blanketing the hillside from the castle gatehouse to the very bottom, are IFs. Not just one or two IFs or even a dozen. He's looking at imaginary friends in their hundreds, thousands, maybe even tens of thousands.

From every village and town in the country, every country and continent and possibly planet in the universe. Everything a young person could and should and had dreamed up, in all the sizes and shapes and colours and sounds that a free and unfettered mind could think of. From fairy-tale characters to superheroes, from sea-monsters to extra-terrestrials to garden gnomes and that guy off the TV. From cuddly-toys to the almost-human.

And they're laughing.

They're cheering, they're jumping, they're playing. Their sheer, uninhibited joyfulness is already beginning to make the sky around them less red.

Now they're moving into the castle and towards the Rogues.

Zack looks at Danny, who manages to grin at him through his pain. Imagination has triumphed. Result! *We've done it,* exults Zack Farmer.

Haven't we?

***

Down at the bottom of the hill a white van hits the brakes.

Mum and Stuart look upwards. To their bewilderment they can make out a horde of smartly-dressed men and women, standing or shuffling or clambering towards Castle Peak. Like an executive slave-gang. All nodding their well-dressed heads.

"*Who on earth are they?*" asks Stuart.

Mum has no idea. But she doesn't like the look of them one bit.

69

'LET YOUR IMAGINATION RUN AWAY WITH YOU'

Smiling time. *Cape Fury. Highlands. Castle Peak.*

There's a whole lot of sniffing going on.

The Rogues can't see the newly-arrived IFs, but they know they're there.

"*Yucchh*, the stench of innocence," says Mr Teensy-Weensy, holding his huge, yellow nose in disgust. "There must be thousands of the grinning idiots!"

Even the tall detective, pinned down by Holly, is sniffing the air. But she's also smiling. Curiously, Mr Teensy-Weensy is also smiling. Arthur is smiling. Zack looks around – he can see The Rogues, and they seem just as thrilled.

Thrilled?

Why would anyone be thrilled, if they suddenly became aware of a massive army – an army of the brave and the good – ready to take them on in some sort of battle? Zack can't quite understand it, but he tries not to let it deter him.

"No need to sniff them, you big – dwarf!" he cries.

347

"Why not see them for yourself?"

Zack closes his eyes and grips the Glimmer tight. Summoning up that turbocharged imagination, the one everyone keeps telling him he has by the bucketful.

Gradually outlines appear – then colours. Then shapes.

History is being made.

For the first time ever, the world's imaginary friends become totally visible (and not just sniffable) to Mr Teensy-Weensy and all the other Rogues. Tens of thousands of them, in all their smiling, friendly innocence.

Zack fully expects the Rogues to recoil in total horror, repelled by the pure love and joy and fellowship that is being suddenly beamed upon them. Overwhelmed by the sheer force of goodness. But, to his huge surprise, they all grin and smirk in horrible pleasure, as if they have been given the biggest treat this side of Christmas and all their birthdays have come at once.

"So you're finally beginning to discover your power, Zack Farmer," smiles Mr Teensy-Weensy. "You really can, as the saying goes, let your imagination run away with you."

The dwarf turns to Arthur, his sidekick. "Arthur, my little friend, why don't you tell him?"

Tell me, thinks Zack. Tell me *what*, Arthur?

Zack doesn't have long to wait.

Mr Teensy-Weensy picks up Rogue Arthur and holds him high. Arthur's eyes flash with an evil red-and-black leer – even the back one is winking wickedly to his fellows.

"Okay, Zack," he says to his one-time friend, almost in a whisper. "Now imagine them all – *gone*."

And suddenly it becomes clear.

Brilliantly, horribly clear.

70

'DO YOU BELIEVE IN ARTHUR?'

Believing time: *Cape Fury. Highlands. Castle Peak.*

Of course!

This was their plan all along, thinks Zack. To encourage him to summon up every IF he could muster, all the imaginary friends in the world that he and his Glimmer could attract. So that they could all be exterminated in the one place, at a single stroke. Imagined clean away, each and every one of them.

By him. By oh-so-brave-and-clever Zack Farmer, manipulated by his very own little, green IF. By Arthur. In ways Zack could neither prevent nor control.

He feels sick to the depths of his stomach. No – beyond that, to his tired feet, rooted on the ground, unable to move. He looks at all the IFs, his innocent, smiling friends, and watches as sheer horror spreads like darkest night over their once-sunny faces.

They're looking back at him – the imaginary friends of the world. And they're terrified.

"We've played straight into their hands, Zack," groans Danny. Zack stares at him. *Is that it* – is that all his friend can say? He thought Danny had the wisdom of the streets – but maybe it doesn't work on hills. Danny struggles through his pain, trying to give Zack just a bit more ammunition.

"All you can do now is fight it."

Fight it? thinks Zack. How on earth can I fight all that negative energy? An energy he's already feeling in his body right now, surging like an electric current through his small frame, trying to dominate him. As Arthur – his new Rogue enemy – locks on.

He still can't believe it. *His* Arthur, his oldest and wisest friend, his buddy from those simple Hackney days, itching to make Zack Farmer the ultimate weapon for Rogue Max.

Zack shakes his head wildly, battling the forces that rage against him, as Arthur himself had done – without much success – not many hours before. His eyes meet Lily's. He wishes he could have been stronger for her too. He knows that once the Rogues kill imagination, they'll have the whole world in their power. His world, her world.

Kids would lose what it is that makes them kids – their spirit, their hope, their spark. If they think their IFs can just be destroyed in an instant, *why should they imagine any more?* And then what sort of grown-ups would they become?

But Lily is looking back at him in a way he has never seen her look before. Softer. Gentler. Yes! There's a connection here – finally – and a love he didn't know she felt for him, nor he for her.

She suddenly starts to hit her mobile phone.

Danny, who's still collapsed in pain, just gawps up at her. "Now you're phoning? *Now!*"

"Just putting you on hold, babe."

***

Down below, at the foot of the hill, Mum and Stuart know none of this and understand even less. What's that helicopter doing up there? Why hasn't Mum heard from Silk? *Where are their kids?*

But they make the decision together – almost without words – that they need to find out what's going on at the peak, in that weird castle. Stuart offers Mum his hand to help her mount the steep first step on the twisting pathway. She is just about to take it, when her mobile rings. She checks the screen.

"It's Lily!"

Frantically, she puts it on speaker. "Lily, where are you? Are you okay, darling? Where's Zack, is he…?"

"Mum, I'm fine," interrupts Lily, sounding more than a little shaky to Mum's sensitive ears. "Zack's fine. Well, for now." Ruth starts to talk. "Mum, just listen. Don't talk. *Please!*"

"Okay," says Mum, who has a thousand questions lying curled up on her tongue. "I'm just listening. But we're here – in Cape Fury. Is that a helicopter I can hear! Lily – are you up there?"

"Mum! *Enough!*" Lily pauses, then – "Do you believe in Arthur?"

What?

Mum looks at Stuart.

What?!

At the same time, but in a higher, redder place, Danny and Zack stare at Lily.

WHAT?!

Lily holds her mobile up towards Arthur, who still sits in the giant dwarf's hands, his wicked eyes glaring, his head shaking in disbelief.

"Do you really, *really* believe in him?" repeats Lily into the phone.

Lily hasn't a clue why this idea came to her, nor even if it's an idea at all. She only knows, from her own recent experience, that some things can change your life in ways you would never expect.

Mum can't believe what she's hearing. She certainly can't believe that it's Lily asking the question. Lily, who was even more sniffy than she was about the empty place at the table – the empty space in her little brother's head! She doesn't know what to say, so she keeps looking at Stuart, as if he's the one she has always turned to.

Stuart is equally bewildered, but Arthur is not his main concern. He shouts down the phone. "Where's Kirstie?"

"Who are you?" asks Lily, not surprisingly.

"Kirstie's dad. Hello, Lily. Now where's Kirstie?"

There's silence. Then a tiny, frightened voice answers. "I'm here, Daddy. I'm okay – I think. Well, I'd be better off not up a tall tower, with the sea down below and monsters all around me. But what about you? Do you really, really believe in Arthur – also known as Princess?"

Kirstie is looking at Lily, like she really, really hopes this is a good idea.

Mum and Stuart are both lost for words. They have absolutely no clue what is going on up there, but they realise that their kids are in danger. The children clearly don't want anything but a totally truthful answer. Not one of those 'yes, yes darling, of course I do' sort of responses. It feels almost like their young lives are depending on it.

"I believe that *they* believe in Arthur," says Niomi, who has walked up behind them and is a bit puffed and fed-up. "If that's any help." Which it isn't.

Stuart has an idea. "*The photo!*" he cries. "Look at the photo, Ruth!"

Mum stares at him then slowly takes the framed photo from her bag. They look at it together, their heads almost touching. Very slowly, a faint, greenish outline starts to appear just beneath Zack's outstretched arm.

"Arthur is green," she says quietly. "Zack always said he was bright green."

The parents look at each other, the usual disbelief turning into something quite new and different.

OMG! Everything that they ever thought was true has just been turned upside down.

Mum shouts into the phone, with a sincerity she doesn't have to fake now. "Yes Lily, I *believe* in Arthur. I really, really do."

Stuart grabs the phone. "Kirstie, I believe in Arthur too. And I believe in Princess Anaesthetica. Or whoever."

Up on Castle Peak all is deathly still.

The Rogues stop slavering; the terrified IFs try to contain their shuddering. Even Holly has her hand pressed tight over the tall detective's mouth to stop her giving out any more orders. But Mr Teensy-Weensy hasn't lost his look of quiet confidence. The only sound now is of the chopper blades whirring in the cold evening air.

The silence seems to last for hours.

It is finally broken by a song, a lilting melody, sung in a weak and croaky East London voice. A voice that isn't quite human.

"'There – was – a – soldier…'"

The song comes down the phone to the foot of the hill. Mum recognises it from old, but who on earth is that singing? Or rather – what?

Then she hears a young voice she knows so well. "… *'A Scottish soldier'.'"*

Zack's voice sounds strained, but it is starting to find its power. As he sings, he notices that Arthur, still in the giant dwarf's arms, is suddenly beginning to glow.

"'Who wandered far away…'" sings Arthur, with just a bit more confidence.

The eyes don't look quite so red now – or even quite so black. His pale skin is giving up its scaliness and developing a richer, emerald-green hue. His teeth are starting to lose their points. Soon Zack and his old friend are singing together. Not yet quite the way they used to, and they probably wouldn't win the Eurovision Song Contest (although they're nearly as bad as those who do.)

"'And soldiered far away'."

As all the other IFs join in (not very well, because clearly they don't know the words or the tune – and many don't even know the language), Arthur suddenly leaps out of Mr Teensy-Weensy's arms and right onto the parapet, next to Zack. Which gives Zack a glorious buzz, but is one giant step too far for the giant Rogue.

Mr Teensy-Weensy has had quite enough. No more Mr Nice-Dwarf. *"Get them, Rogues!"* roars the oversized Rogue. "Now that Zack Farmer has kindly let you see them, grind the IF vermin into dust. Every last one of them – Arthur included." He's getting into his stride now, relishing victory. "Then order your humans to march up there and destroy the children, with their bare, well-manicured hands. I mean DESTROY! I want no-one left alive to talk of this day. Not even the parents down below. *Kill them all.* Show no mercy!"

There's murder in his eyes, as they turn entirely black.

The snarling Rogues move forward on their human steeds. Vengeance is in the air. They whisper down into human ears and now, for the first time, the humans too begin to snarl and bare their teeth, docile no longer. Slavering like their masters, hungry for blood.

Things have suddenly become a thousand times scarier, thinks Zack. Talk about 'intimidating!'

What in the world have I done?

71

'WHAT IF?'

Showtime: *Cape Fury. Highlands. The highest tower of Castle Peak.*

Lily is clutching Kirstie's tiny hand. As Danny gazes painfully down.

"Look at all those IFs," he moans. "The poor guys will be mincemeat. Half of them can't stop smiling!" Without taking his eyes from the fray, he adds "I think it's all over for us too, pal. The humans are coming to get us. We're done for."

But Zack isn't listening. He seems to have gone into some sort of trance. "What if?" he murmurs.

Lily looks at him. "What if *what*, Zack?"

Zack is quiet for a moment. Thoughtful. Then: "What if imagination works both ways?"

They have absolutely no idea what he's talking about. Even Holly and the tall detective, still locked in furious battle on the chopper, stare at him. But Zack is looking down at all the IFs, his vast band of imaginary brothers and sisters. And suddenly he's smiling.

He raises his Glimmer high into the air, for all to see.

The imaginary friends, every one of the thousands and thousands of them, stare up at Zack and the Glimmer, as if they'd love to know what he's asking of them, but they really haven't a clue. All they know is that they're about to be exterminated any second by ugly Rogues, their energy snuffed out and switched off, and they will doubtless never see their loving human-kids again. Zack is sure he can see their tears glistening in the darkness, as winter night begins to fall.

But all it takes is one.

And this time the one is a grinning, blue chimpanzee in an American Football strip, who suddenly reaches right inside of himself and pulls out his Glimmer with a triumphant cry. As his fellows gasp, he thrusts it high in the air then lets it go.

His life-force. His energy. Ripped from within him.

But it doesn't fall.

It hovers above him, gleaming in the early Highland dusk.

There's a pause, almost as if the news is being relayed along lines and down ranks. Backwards. Forwards. Side to side. Then very slowly, one after another, each and every IF on that bleak hill finds his or her own Glimmer deep inside of themselves. And they send it, with love and with hope – as Arthur himself had once done – into the chill and darkening February air, high above their heads.

Soon a vast galaxy of gleaming Glimmers is lighting up the bleak, late-afternoon sky, arcing like the biggest, brightest, most multi-coloured rainbow anyone has ever seen. Beaming, glittering, hovering. But, most of all, transmitting every ounce of their positive energy right back into Zack's own Glimmer, still up there, in his outstretched hand, on that dark parapet. Until its incandescent green light glows with an extraordinary, almost blinding brilliance.

But this is only the beginning. The IFs now do something their enemies would never do.

They hold each other's hands.

And in that bright, shining moment they instantly become one overwhelmingly radiant source of pure, imaginative energy. The entire hill glows with their combined spirit of wonderment.

Their IF-ness.

The Rogues are blinking their red and black eyes, almost blinded by the light. But their fury hasn't dimmed. Mr Teensy-Weensy gives a condescending smile and shakes his head. "Oh, Zack," he mocks. "Zack, Zack. Zack. It's too late for special effects."

But Arthur can't believe his eyes. "They're sharing their power with you, Zack," he tells his friend, in awe. "Their imagination. It's yours for the taking, mate. Go for it. Run with it." He pauses, his small body trembling. "*Use it!*"

"Yeah, but Arthur," says Zack, turning to his old friend, for what he suddenly realises is probably the final time. "If your Glimmer goes…"

His old friend just nods. He understands. And he's telling Zack with his eyes – Forget about me. Just do it.

There's not much time. The grunting, 'programmed' humans are almost up the narrow steps and upon them, arms bared for action. These guys are real, not imaginary, thinks Zack. They're strong, they're under orders. Without even knowing why they're doing it, they could simply rip us all apart.

"Now that you've had your little light-show, which really is terribly pretty, can we please just get on with the business in hand?" booms the giant dwarf rather politely, from down below. "Which is your total destruction. If I'm not mistaken."

Zack isn't listening, not any more. He steps onto the outermost edge of the loftiest battlement of the tallest tower of the highest castle in the land. His feet teeter on the centuries-old, crumbling stones. The fierce ocean wind batters his slender frame and un-spikes his hair. One slip and he's history. The gang – and the IFs – stare at him with massive apprehension.

'*Zack…*' mutters Lily softly, scared that her very breath might send him toppling. Kirstie just closes her eyes.

But Zack isn't looking at Lily or at anyone. He is in his own head, his own world. His own mind. *I may have grown up a bit*, he thinks, as the piercing wind taunts him, *but I wonder if this is as far as I'm going to grow. Oh well…*

"Okay," he cries, "this one's for Arthur!"

He leaps off the stone parapet, over a hundred feet up, right into the pure evening air.

"*ZACK!*" yells Lily, in horror.

72

'IMAGINE THAT!'

High time: *Cape Fury. Highlands. Castle Peak.*

Danny and Kirstie can hardly bear to look.

The IFs gasp too. Tens of thousands of open mouths, terrified. Is Zack Farmer going to plummet like a stone to what has to be certain death, onto the cold flagstones below?

Looks a lot like it.

It's almost as if they're watching in slow-motion. The fall seems endless. Perhaps because every awful fraction of a second is being etched into their souls.

But hang on a moment. Perhaps Zack Farmer really *isn't* dropping like a stone. Perhaps he is sailing down, gently floating. Because their collective IF wills and spirits are reaching out to him, buoying him up.

Imagining him hover!

Just like I said, Zack tells himself joyfully, weightlessly. And with rather a lot of relief, actually. The IFs are holding him in place with their hearts and minds and imaginations, just as Zack is holding the brilliant Glimmer, engorged with an impossible light. He really is gliding calmly through the cold night air. But not without purpose.

He's heading directly for Mr Teensy-Weensy and the smirking Rogues.

The IFs hold their breath, or they would if they had any. But the giant dwarf just roars with laughter.

Not for long.

The moment Zack reaches Mr Teensy-Weensy, their eyes lock for a terrifying second that seems to last a year. There, in the big dwarf's evil face, Zack sees a shimmering, vibrating blood-red light. He knows with terrifying certainty that he is facing Rogue Max itself. The 'head honcho'. The combined energy of every Rogue around. But he has no idea whose power will prove the greater.

It feels like the entire world is holding its breath.

Silence.

Suddenly they hear a huge, agonised bellow, rumbling up as if from the earth itself. Followed immediately by a deafening bang, as the dreadful Rogue explodes with a bright, yellow flame, sending hundreds of bits of angry dwarf shooting off like a massive firework into the illuminated sky.

So long, Mr Teensy-Weensy!

The Rogue army look shocked and stunned. As indeed they would, being part of the very same malign energy. So, of course, it's their turn next, which isn't long in coming. They soon begin to melt and fragment, every last one of them, disintegrating with dreadful, inhuman cries.

Good riddance, Rogue Max!

An entire convocation of Rogues gone, never more to walk unnoticed. Never more to whisper into innocent ears or control unknowing thoughts. Destroyed by their own arrogance and a mammoth amount of imagination. The very imagination they were trying to kill.

Overwhelmed by the power of true and genuine friendship.

The last pair of crows decide there and then to leave Castle Peak for good. They've had more than enough. With a clatter of wings they fly off noisily above the carnage.

Zack, now landing safely at the foot of the castle, can only watch as the evil energy of the Rogue army dissolves into a huge, throbbing blood-redness. He stares in amazement as all that destructive power quivers and vibrates a final time, resolving itself into one last, desperate, bloody howl of anguish. Leaving a shock-wave spreading throughout Castle Peak that matches the sea in its fury.

"Imagine that," says Danny, watching from up above, with Kirstie in his arms and Lily supporting him.

Zack looks up at him and smiles in exhausted victory. This was a bit more than being chased through a Hackney market by two twits on skateboards. Phew!

"WE DID IT, DANNY!" he yells up into the sky. "All of us. We did it!"

Is that cheering he can hear?

Yes! The entire world-army of IFs is roaring in triumph, although if Zack were to walk through their ranks now, he might hear a lot of seriously odd-looking characters telling each other, in their various languages, 'Well, I never thought that would work, did you?' Or 'Please, sir, can I have my Glimmer back?'

But perhaps Zack is exulting too soon.

Not every last Rogue has gone.

The tall detective has shrugged off an exhausted Holly and is descending towards the courtyard with the police helicopter. Silk still holds the gun that can bring so much pain.

"Bring him down, Silk," she cries. "Hurt him!"

Obeying orders, Silk fires the stun-gun directly at Zack. There's no way he can escape. Well, actually there is. But this time it's not through anything he does. Fortunately for Zack, just as the weapon is fired, the tail-end of that huge Rogue shock-wave flips him like a surfer and sends him reeling away from the gun's trajectory.

He watches from the ground as this same ferocious wave hurtles onwards and sweeps up the tall detective in a cloud of red. Absorbing her into the explosion. Like the sea itself, you never know how it's going to catch you.

"*We'll be back!*" she vows, as she fragments with a piercing yell. "And you're first on our list, Zack Farmer!"

For a moment Zack can't breathe. That threat felt far too real. But the bad thought is almost immediately pushed aside by the word-music he hears from all around him. IFs, from every corner of the world, are thanking him and bidding him their own smiley goodbyes, as they make their way home again. Back to the humans who imagined them and love them. (And who can't quite imagine where on earth they've gone.)

"Thanks Zack… Merci… Gracias… Danke… Shukran… Ta… " That sort of thing.

Meanwhile very-important-looking men and women, in executive suits and military uniforms, are standing up, brushing themselves down, shaking their legs, arms and heads. As if awakening from a most unpleasant and highly uncomfortable dream.

Zack looks around him and suddenly stops. Isn't that the Prime Minister over there?

73

'ZACK, WHERE'S ARTHUR?'

Downtime: *Sunday February 17th. Cape Fury. Highlands. Castle Peak.*

Detective Inspector Duncan Silk is one of the first to be 'awakened' this incredible Sunday evening.

He runs a hand through his thick, red hair and realises that the hand has a gun in it. A nasty sort of stun-gun he didn't even know he owned. He quickly drops the weapon, as if he might stun himself with it any minute, then gazes around at the bleak castle on the hill and all the smartly-dressed people wandering around below.

People looking just as lost and aimless as he is. But a lot more important. "What the heck am I doing here?" he asks the universe.

He sees a young boy, who is walking very confidently back up the hill. "You're not Zack, by any chance?" he asks. Zack nods, because, by every chance, he is.

"Who are *you* – exactly?" asks Zack, not unreasonably, considering the man just tried to shoot him.

"Er… " thinks Silk, "I'm Silk. Yes. Detective Inspector

Duncan Silk, Edinburgh Police. Are you okay, pal – your mum's been worried? "

"I think so," says Zack. A thought hits him. "Hang on – where's..?

"Arthur?" says Silk. It's all coming back now.

"No – Lily! My sister. And Kirstie! Where—"

He turns and looks around, to see the others some yards away, staring at something on the ground. He rushes towards them and recognises, in sudden shock, the vivid red, white and blue.

It's Holly. And she seems to be fading fast.

Her voice, when she finally talks, sounds so different to that of the sparky cheerleader he first met in Manchester Piccadilly station. Was that only yesterday? "I'm sorry, Danny," she says. Every sound she makes seems to be such a huge effort.

"*Holly?*" is all Danny can say. He has never seen her like this and he can't bear it. He looks around, for the help he knows no-one can give.

"I *was* your best friend, wasn't I?" says Holly. Her eyes, no longer red-and-black, are just as Danny recalls them, beautiful and blue. But without the sparkle.

"Couldn't imagine a better one," says Danny. He's trying not to cry. "'*Two-four-six…* '"

"… e*ight*," murmurs Holly. "*Who do we appreciate?*"

She smiles too, but it's clearly painful. Summoning all her remaining strength, she turns to stare up at Lily, who is gripping Danny's hand. "You see that you look after him now, Lily."

"I promise, Holly," vows the new girl on the block. "Any tips?"

"Ditch the cigarettes. Lose the black. And a pom-pom skirt wouldn't hurt."

Holly smiles to herself. Her job is done. Her dearest friend seems to have found some happiness at last, after a childhood that wasn't exactly overflowing with it. And – perhaps just as important – a new buddy in Zack.

With this, she gently fades away.

Danny watches, shaking his head, then throws himself tearfully onto the empty patch of ground, where his best pal used to be. "Hol? Holly…? Ohhh!"

As Lily holds him and comforts him, Danny tells her tearfully that Holly was the only good thing in his life. Fortunately for him, he remembers to add, "Until today."

It's an evening of confused expectations. Lily notices that Zack has begun to look around anxiously. She asks him something he had never thought he would hear his older sister say, even if they both lived to be a thousand.

"Zack, where's Arthur?"

Zack just shakes his head. He knows that his old friend is no longer there. "The explosion would have taken him too, Lily. Without his Glimmer, he wouldn't have had a chance." He sighs and grabs a sad-looking Kirstie's hand. "He sacrificed himself – for us."

Lily's face softens, as he has never seen it soften before. What has *happened* to this girl? "Oh babe, I'm sorry. Really." She looks very thoughtful, as if she's beginning to work something out. Something quite important. "I suppose a big part of imagination is – like – just 'getting' how someone else can feel, right? I mean, y'know, *really* imagining it."

Zack nods. He couldn't have put it better. Well he

probably could, but he's still very glad she said it. And it looks like she hasn't finished.

"Hey, sorry too about our invisible dad," she continues. "The dork doesn't know what he's missing."

Zack shrugs. Funny, he's been too busy even to think about his dad. He imagines the guy is probably too busy ever to think about him. Some parents are just like that, he guesses, and he tells himself it's time he just accepted it. Even if it isn't the best state-of-affairs in the world.

Silk approaches, wearing a warm, friendly smile… "Guys, there are a few people down at the bottom of this hill just waiting to give you a good clip round the ear," says the policeman.

"No one's waiting to give *me* a good clip round the ear," says Danny, with a touch of regret. So Lily gives him a good clip round the ear, causing his already weakened knee to buckle. He gasps, then sees her worried face and smiles. Don't worry – he'll survive.

Zack reckons that at least things can't get any weirder. Until a bedraggled and very bewildered old lady, dressed hat-to-shoelace in tartan, appears at the brow of the hill. She's panting like an old Scottie dog after all her exertions.

"Can someone please tell me why I'm here?" asks Mrs Audrey Ames.

74

'YOU MUST HAVE
THE POWER NOW, ZACK'

Family Time: *Sunday February 17th. Cape Fury. The foot of Castle Peak.*

No sooner have the adults walked half-way up Castle Peak than Mum receives a call from Silk saying he'll meet them down at the bottom.

Niomi isn't best pleased. In fact her grumbling can be heard even over the rumble of the helicopter, as it makes its final descent to the base of the great hill.

They can't begin to fathom all the dazed-looking men and women, in their smart suits and military uniforms, wandering aimlessly past them as they make their way down. What was going on up there – a conference? Is someone planning a war? Some of them do look extraordinarily familiar and important.

But however important they are, they aren't as important as the people in the helicopter. It's a reunion like Silk has never seen before.

As soon as he slides open the heavy helicopter-door, Zack and Lily and Kirstie are grabbed and kissed and cuddled and hugged and squeezed, until there's hardly any breath left in their aching bodies. Everyone except Danny, who is being propped up by Silk, and who doesn't want to intrude on family reunions. It's not like his folks are going to be out there waiting to cuddle him. At least he hopes they're not.

Kirstie can't get used to how affectionate and huggy her father is being. This isn't like him at all – there are even tears in his eyes. She wonders for a moment if Grandpa Brodie has been sharing out his whisky.

"Daddy," she is saying, excitedly. "There was this great big, gigantic, yellow dwarf and he just exploded and everything!"

As for Mum, she's still in two minds. "I should be wringing both your necks, but right now I'm just too happy to see you."

Niomi, however, veers more towards the neck-wringing. "You couldn't just steal a Porsche or a Jaguar, could you?" she moans. "Oh no, it had to be a flaming great lorry!"

Zack explains very simply. "It was Dorothy's fault."

"Who's Dorothy?" asks Mum.

Lily gives her mother her very special, don't-you-know-anything look. "From the Wizard of Oz? Duh!" she says, like she actually saw the IF. Perhaps she now believes that she did. "She's totally black and white and lives up North somewhere with her little dog. Who's also black and white – obviously."

Mum isn't even going to go there. But she really wants

to show her children the new person she has become, so she smiles sweetly downwards into the crisp Highland air right beside Zack.

"Hello Arthur. I'm Zack's mum." She squats down and holds out her hand, ready to shake it.

"There's nothing there, Mum," says Zack.

Mum smiles lovingly at him. "It's okay, Zack. Really. I've used my imagination. I've moved on."

"So's Arthur," says Zack. "He used up his last bit of energy – for us. He's gone for good now."

"Oh."

Mum finally gets it. She turns to her son, who looks so very different from the grumpy and rather timid eleven year old to whom she said goodbye on Friday. He seems to have grown in every way. "Sweetheart. I'm so sorry," she says.

Lily looks sorry too, as she puts her arm around Danny, who has limped over to join them. Mum can hardly fail to notice this.

"Hello," says Mum. "And you are…?"

"Well, he isn't imaginary," chimes Niomi. "I can smell him from here. No one's getting into my car until they've been thoroughly disinfected." She looks at Detective Inspector Duncan Silk, who is smiling kindly, and adds "Except you, maybe."

Stuart stares at them all. The children so tired and stunned, the much-relieved adults reversed in everything they had always thought was true. He's holding a shivering yet contented Kirstie tight to his strong legs.

"Ruth," he says to Mum, which causes Lily and Zack to look at him. *Ruth?* "Can I suggest we all go back to my place? This lot are going to need a good Highland supper."

Zack and Lily – Kirstie too – are watching their parents' faces. What they notice are feelings that, even at this early stage, go a lot deeper than buttered scones and Aberdeen Angus burgers. What they don't feel is any fear of this at all.

Their thoughts are suddenly interrupted by a loud cry.

"That's her! That's the she-devil!"

Grandpa Brodie is yelling as he launches himself uneasily off PC McKay's sagging bicycle.

They look at him, so angry and dishevelled (with a nasty bump on his head), then turn to see where he's pointing. It's directly at Mrs Ames, who is struggling exhaustedly back down the hillside. Even her tartan appears to be wilting.

Brodie isn't going to let her get a word in, as he stomps over to her, still pointing his finger.

"She's the maddie who fish-bashed me!" He turns back to the local policeman, who is working his way through a catering-size bag of crisps. "McKay, put those away before you burst. And do your duty!"

Unfortunately, just as Grandpa Brodie says this, he notices the country's Prime Minister, dressed in a smart but dusty suit, walk a bit unsteadily past him. *Huh?* The man is on his mobile phone, talking very importantly.

"I want you to disband the Children's Army this minute," he is telling someone, probably back in London. "Then I want you to mothball the Toy-Crunchers, open all the parks and fairgrounds, crank up the cinemas and retrain the Sugar Police as traffic wardens… "

Brodie suddenly seems like he is about to buckle and

fold. He holds his head as if to keep it from falling off. "See, I'm *hallucinating!*" he says. "It was that bang on the head she gave me!"

Mrs Ames shakes her own head, totally confused about everything. "Oh Brodie, I have absolutely no explanation. Will you ever forgive me?"

Stuart suddenly starts to laugh, looking like he is proud owner of the best joke ever, one that he just can't wait to share. Kirstie and Grandpa Brodie both stare at him. "It's okay, Brodie," he grins. "Maybe the lady was just under the influence of a big, giant yellow dwarf, eh Kirstie?"

He rounds this off with a rich, joyful bellow, unheard in these parts for some while. Kirstie looks up at him – *how on earth did he know?* But Brodie is already hugging his laughing son-in-law, with tears in his eyes. "Och son, and I thought we'd lost you forever."

Kirstie smiles – she thinks she may well get a story from her dad tonight. Which will make a nice change from all those ones with axes and knives and Glasgow street-gangs.

Zack is looking around, at people reuniting and becoming close again. He sees real joy and happiness, but he can't quite seem to get there himself.

Not quite.

Closing Time: *Sunday February 17th. Cape Fury. The foot of Castle Peak.*

Suddenly Zack has a glimpse of the future in his mind.

Fairgrounds re-opening, kids reading storybooks, playing with toys. Sugar Policemen handing sweets to youngsters. Teenagers in the Children's Army growing their hair, throwing away their marching boots and going to the cinema, instead of chasing after scared, homeless boys.

Families learning to enjoy the simple but imaginative pleasures again. Together.

It sparks some sort of realisation inside him. He turns to his mother. "I'm sorry, Mum. For – you know – what I said about my dad. It had to be so hard for you all these years, being alone."

Mum shakes her head. "Thank you, love, but I wasn't alone, was I? I had you and Lily." She smiles the sort of soft smile he hasn't seen for far too long. She looks around her and takes a deep breath. "And who knows what the future has in store?"

He's just absorbing this, when he hears another voice. A small, piping Scottish voice, one he can't recall hearing before yet is somehow strangely familiar.

"And 'alone' is one thing you'll never be again, laddie."

Zack spins round. There, dressed in a pretty tartan skirt, looking all pink and curly and girly is – Arthur. Yet not Arthur.

"Princess!" screams Kirstie in delight.

"One hundred per cent Scotch. No farting," says the small IF, in a true, local accent. Her Royal Highlandness, Princess Annathesia of Cape Fury, gives a swift twirl and Zack can see the glint of a pink, disc-like shape deep inside of her.

Kirstie suddenly looks worried. She turns to Zack. "Is it okay, Zack?"

Zack looks at them both. The sweet, young girl.

The grinning wee IF. "She's *your* friend, Kirstie," he says, growing-up even more with every breath.

He feels a gentle punch on the shoulder. Danny, his new best-mate, is proud of him. But Zack is confused. "Danny, if Princess isn't *my* IF any more, how come I can still see him? Well, her.

"You could also ask, how come I can't?" says Danny.

Zack looks at him. The older boy is shaking his head. He didn't see what just went on with Princess, he picked it up from what the humans were saying.

"You must have the power now, Zack," says the older boy. "It's served its purpose with me."

Lily hugs Danny. "So, I don't have to share you with robots and teddies and spacemen?" she says.

Danny shakes his head. "What am I going to do with myself?" he moans, without the hint of a stutter. Perhaps because he's singing inside.

"Use your imagination," smiles Lily. Then she adds, "and I don't think you'll ever be without a home again."

Zack isn't listening. He's looking back at the great hill. He feels so much more fearless now, so much less 'intimidated'. So much more ready for whatever this strange and sometimes cruel, but never boring, world has to throw at him.

As he catches a final glint of red light, refusing quite to die on top of Castle Peak, he wonders if the world may well be calling on him again before long.

Meanwhile, he could murder a burger and chips.

He can just imagine it.

THE END (OF THE WEEKEND)

ACKNOWLEDGMENTS

My thanks to all the people, young and old, professional writers and avid readers, who have read this book and given me their invaluable input.

My thanks also to Carly Trisk-Grove and all her wonderful staff at the Café in the Park, The Aquadrome, Rickmansworth, and their 'Quiet Room', where the first words began and a lot of others followed. I can be more noisy now.

And to the most supportive person in my life these past 48 years. You know who you are.

ABOUT THE AUTHOR

PAUL A. MENDELSON is the BAFTA-nominated creator of several hit BBC family-comedy series, including 'May to December,' 'So Haunt Me' and the long-running 'My Hero', starring Ardal O'Hanlon as the hapless superhero Thermoman. He co-created 'Neighbors From Hell' for DreamWorks Animation and writes regularly for BBC Radio 4 Drama. He has several feature films in development.

Paul's first novel, *In the Matter of Isabel*, was published in 2017 by The Book Guild. Paul is married with two daughters, four grandchildren and 563 imaginary friends. He lives not very quietly in North London.